ELIZABETH A. DRYSDALE

For the seekers, the swipers, the hopeless romantics—

And for my sister Megan, whose dating stories were the spark that lit this book.

Chapter One

I try not to look up too eagerly as the classroom door swings open, the girl responsible for passing out the mail wheeling her little cart into the room. It's early, isn't it? I haven't had enough time yet to really build up my anxiety about whether there'll be a letter for me or not.

The flier for 'Family Weekend' has been slowly fading on the corkboard outside my dorm room for at least a week. Every time I glance at it, a knot tightens in my stomach. I wrote to my father about it, but I wasn't sure whether I should expect a response. Years of disappointment have taught me not to get my hopes up, yet sometimes, I can't help it.

The cart squeaks across the hardwood floor, passing between rows of polished wooden desks. My classmates take their letters with only mild interest.

My chest gets tight, each breath harder to find as the cart works its way closer. My father hasn't shown up to the last few Family Weekends, so I know better than to expect anything –but I still do. It's the same cruel cycle: convincing myself he's changed, that this time he'll show up, that he'll care—only to watch it all collapse like a house of cards.

The cart stops beside me. Its metal frame is dull and worn, like it's carried too many disappointments. I stop breathing altogether as the girl beside it hands me a letter, her face unreadable. My hands tremble as I try to open it— the adhesive clings stubbornly, and by the time I finally tear it open, the envelope is mangled.

My eyes skim the page. A familiar ache settles in my chest as I take in the string of hollow excuses, topped off with a half-hearted *Love you*. The words blur as hot tears sting behind my eyes, but I refuse to let them fall. Just a few more minutes. Then I can go. Just a few more minutes, and I'll be safe in my room, invisible and alone— where disappointment can't reach me.

It's moments like this that I miss Mom the most. I just know she would've come. She would've been like the other moms and made a big deal of it, bringing snacks and stories and love that didn't come with strings or silence. Her absence feels sharper in the wake of his, like an echo of everything I've lost and everything he'll never be.

If my father's taught me anything, it's how to bury my feelings so deep they don't make a sound.

I step into my dorm room and slam the door behind me. The Family Weekend flier I ripped from the corkboard crumples into a tight ball in my fist. My hands still shake as I cross the room, casting a bitter glare at Joan's side— bright, cozy, and annoyingly perfect. Her handmade quilt is neatly folded at the foot of her bed, and the wall above it is lined with photos of smiling relatives at holidays and birthdays.

In contrast, my corner feels more like a temporary shelter than a home. Despite spending most of my life at this school, my bed still wears the generic blanket it came with, and the corkboard above it holds nothing but a copy of my class schedule. No memories. No warmth.

The paper digs into my skin, leaving a shallow cut as I hurl it across the room. It knocks into one of Joan's framed photos—a birthday, from the looks of it—sending it tumbling to the floor with a dull thunk. I wince, guilt pricking at the edges of my anger. But I can't summon the energy to stop myself.

I'm mad—furious even—and Joan, with her cheerful pictures and normal family, suddenly becomes the nearest target. I know it's unfair, but the resentment burning in my chest doesn't care about fairness.

No. That's not right. I drag a hand over my face. Joan hasn't done anything wrong. She's not the reason my father keeps letting me down. My family's dysfunction belongs to them—and to me.

With a heavy sigh, I collapse onto my bed and fish my phone out of my pocket. I scroll through social media, liking random posts without looking at them too closely, doing my best not to think about anything at all.

The door clicks open, and Joan hesitates in the doorway, her gaze shifting from the fallen picture to the crumpled yellow flier. She wrinkles her nose as she walks to the side of my bed and peeks over my shoulder, catching me watching a silent ad for the latest dating app, Deannach Sióg. The longer the ad runs, the better I feel. Almost... happy... even after everything that's happened today.

Joan frowns, marring her pale complexion with a series of lines.

A hot blush stains my cheeks, but I refuse to turn it off. Many of the girls at school use the app, claiming the boys on it are cuter than any they could find in town. I'm not sure I trust it. — foreign apps always seemed to be full of bugs— I needed distractions, a way to forget. Looking at cute boys didn't seem like a terrible idea. There was something about the ad that felt... nice. I couldn't quite put my finger on it, but watching it made me feel good.

"You shouldn't get on that, Grace," Joan advised.

I prop myself up on an elbow, my irritation bubbling closer to the surface. "Oh, really?"

Joan hasn't been a terrible roommate, but she has a knack for meddling in my affairs. It isn't fair, but my patience has been tested beyond its limits today. She shrinks back into her pillows at the intensity of my gaze but doesn't back down.

"I'm just saying, I've heard terrible things about it. And the last thing you should be doing while all these girls are disappearing is trying to meet more strangers. Plus, I learned in my programming class that those apps ask for more personal information than they need and sell the rest on the internet."

She lies down, signaling the end of our conversation.

It's not like it's a big deal or anything. No one from our school has gone missing— just a few girls from towns nearby. Still, it's been enough to make the news a couple of times, and now some cities are throwing around curfews for anyone under 18. Like that's going to change anything.

Not that it matters to me. I already live by a curfew thanks to dorm rules.

Joan acts like I'm asking to disappear just because I

downloaded one stupid app. She worries too much. Like, seriously—this is how people meet now. It's not weird. It's not dangerous. It's just normal. And of course, she thinks she knows everything ever since she started those coding classes and learned how to use the word 'encryption' in a sentence.

I pull my scratchy blanket over my head and open the app. Making a profile is easy—stupidly easy, really. But I need the distraction. I'm not looking for anything serious, just something to take the edge off today.

Besides, if it makes me feel a little less awful, how bad can it be?

I fill out the generic criteria first. **Age: 17. Gender: female. Status: single.** What kind of question is that? How many people join dating apps when they have a boyfriend? I don't think I would. At least I wouldn't be honest about my status if I did.

The next page asks for a picture. I pick one from a trip away from school my father remembered (for once) to pick me up for. We went to the beach, not even one far away, just the local pier—*but* one of the selfies I took that day was fire. I'm backlit perfectly by the sun setting over the water, my blonde hair electrified in the light, freckles standing out against my pale skin, blue eyes sparkling as I stare at the camera with a half-smile. Perfect. What guy wouldn't want to talk to her?

The next stage of the profile is a questionnaire, one that the app guarantees will remain private. I'm not sure I trust them, Joan's warning lingering in the back of my mind, but I also remind myself that these questions could be used to generate matches for me. That's what the whole point of this is, I suppose. That's not what I'm here for, but the app doesn't need to know that.

I breeze through the basic questions at the top of the form, not wanting to dwell on them too long. It's not hard to come up with activities I like, what kind of guys I'd like to date, and what kind of student I consider myself. At the very least, it isn't hard to lie about the kinds of activities I think guys would like to see me interested in. Beach volley-ball? Is there really any girl who likes that? Whatever, down it goes.

The last couple of questions take me off guard. I debate whether to continue, my hand hesitating as I take a moment to breathe in the moist, heavy air inside the blanket. But I've already started this. I need to finish it. No matter how weird the questions are. I've kept these details hidden deep inside me for years, but now they seem to demand acknowledgment.

What is your blood type?

My blood type? Who really knows that? And in what world would that be necessary to know for dating? Are they making sure we can be blood donors to each other or something creepy like that? Very Addams family-ish. So, what do I say?

My blood is something I've been told *never* to talk about. not with doctors, not with friends— *no one*. The lesson was drilled into me so thoroughly that I still remember my mom crouching in front of me when I was four, her hands gently gripping my shoulders.

We were in the kitchen, and I'd scraped my knee outside. Nothing serious— just a little blood. I remember staring at it, curious as the afternoon sun hit the cut and made it look like the color shifted. My mom rushed in, eyes wide, and yanked a dish towel from the counter. she cleaned it up so fast, I barely had time to cry. Then she looked me in the eye and told me never to tell anyone what I'd seen.

I didn't understand what she was talking about then, and I've just assumed since that she must have been afraid of blood, but still, I promised her I would never tell and I haven't.

Now, sitting here with this stupid questionnaire, I can feel the tug-of-war inside me—part of me wanting to keep the secret, like I was taught, and the other part whispering, *it's harmless. Just write something down. It's not like it's real.*

So I do. I jot down **A+** and move on. It's the first blood type that comes to mind, and I doubt anyone will actually ask about it. Even if they do, it's not the truth anyway.

And that, somehow, makes me feel safer.

Do you consider yourself lonely? How close are you to your family?

Those questions touch on two completely different aspects of my life, and I let out a quiet, awkward laugh that comes out more like a cough. I can't explain why, but it's so much easier to write about my feelings than to speak them out loud.

Loneliness is part of the human experience, I type, pausing for a second. **Not something you can escape, no matter how much your life shifts around. It's just... there. Constant. But maybe this app can help with that, even a little.**

I stare at the blinking cursor, rereading what I wrote. It actually sounds kind of deep. Not desperate. Not sad. Just— true. Honest in a way I didn't mean for it to be. My skin prickles, like I've left the door open too wide without realizing it.

Now onto the harder part.

My mom died when I was four. I type the words

quickly, trying not to think too hard. **It's been just me and my father since then. He told me once I reminded him too much of her. I guess I believe him— she was beautiful in the few photos I've seen. Not that there were many for me to find. He packed them all away before I got old enough to ask questions.**

My throat tightens, and I blink fast as tears threaten to rise. I hate this. I don't want to feel this stuff—not right now, not ever if I can help it. I've spent years learning how to bury this part of me so deep it can't reach daylight.

Before I can second-guess myself, I hit *send*.

No rereads. No edits. Just gone. Out there now. I wince a little, suddenly unsure if I crossed into 'too depressing' territory. This feels like something you'd share on a tenth date—if that. Definitely not app-profile material.

But then again, the guys I'm hoping to match with? Let's be real—they're not getting past the surface. And that's exactly the way I want it.

The screen flashes white, then a little smiley face with a checkmark pops up. *Profile complete.*

Awesome.

I press a hand to my chest, trying to ignore the tight, fluttery feeling building there. It's probably nothing. Just nerves. Let's keep this moving.

The app loads into the main screen, and my photo appears in the top left corner. For a second, I just stare at it. I look... okay. Kind of cute, even. At least when I'm spiraling later, I'll have something to remind me that I'm not a total disaster. Hopefully.

The matches page loads next—pictures lined up on the left, short blurbs on the right. I start scrolling, curiosity outweighing caution.

My thumb hesitates over the screen, and I frown.

I don't remember writing a blurb for myself.

Did the app do that *for* me?

Weird. Also—creepy? If it can write bios based on answers to random questions, maybe it really *isn't* free. Honestly, if they're using some kind of AI to craft fake-deep summaries of my personality, they should be charging extra.

Still, I kind of want to know what mine says. Hopefully it makes me sound mysterious and cool—not like someone who just trauma-dumped in a digital journal and hit send.

The boy at the top of the list catches my attention just as I'm trying to shake off the weird knot of nerves in my chest.

His black hair defies gravity, sweeping over his temples like it's been styled by a breeze that knows exactly what it's doing. His green eyes glint with something that could be mischief—or just good lighting—and he's smirking at the camera like he knows secrets I'll never be told.

I know I should keep scrolling. A *smirk* in a profile pic? Come on. But he's... stunning. Not in a soft, angelic way, but in a sharp-edged, movie-trailer kind of way that makes your brain short-circuit a little.

A little spark of unease tightens in my stomach. Something about this feels... off. But I'm probably just overthinking it. Nerves. That's all.

His name appears beside his photo: *Galin.*

Unusual. But not *bad.* Definitely better than some of the names I've seen scratched into bathroom stalls or carved into picnic tables. His bio is short—*Likes staying up late and the occasional book.* Not exactly a Shakespearean sonnet, but okay. Boys aren't exactly known for their profile-writing skills.

Still, something about the app—it doesn't feel like any

normal interface. The way his photo seems a little too crisp, like it was lit for a photoshoot meant just for me. The way the screen pulses faintly, almost like it's breathing. Like it knows I'm hesitating.

I keep trying to talk myself into this, which is ridiculous. No one's making me do this. I could just close the app. Walk away.

But then Joan's voice echoes in my head—*you're too trusting, you're too impulsive, you never think things through.* And the idea of proving her right makes my skin crawl.

Backing out now, before I even go on a single date, feels like losing a game I haven't even played. And I hate losing.

I hover my thumb over the screen, still undecided.

Then, from nowhere, a thought sneaks in like a whisper through a crack in the door:

Maybe you will lose. Maybe you already have.

A chill ripples through me. I shove it away.

I'm just being paranoid. People use dating apps all the time. Nothing bad ever happens.

Right?

The rustling of paper tells me Joan's picked up the crumpled Family Weekend flier I left on the floor.

"Grace?"

I don't move. Not even a twitch.

Joan, of course, isn't the type to wait around for an invitation. She sits on the end of my bed, the mattress dipping beneath her. There's a pause while she watches me, fully wrapped in my blanket cocoon, face buried, trying to disappear.

"Come on," she says gently. "It's not that bad."

I roll over and pull the blanket tighter over my head, pressing it against my ears. I grind my teeth. She's always here when I least want her to be—and somehow always the only one who is. The joys of boarding school, I guess.

"It'll all be over soon," she adds, like that's supposed to be comforting.

Easy for her to say. Her dad didn't just ditch her for some twenty-something with a name that sounds like a cartoon character. Bambi? Tiffany? Something ridiculous and sparkly. At this point, I can't even pretend to be shocked. It's his signature move—bail right before family weekend, toss me a letter filled with empty apologies and some half-hearted plea for understanding. *Hope for my happiness,* he wrote. Right. Because his happiness has clearly been my top priority.

Honestly, maybe signing onto that stupid app was a mistake. If I hadn't gotten that letter, I never would've even considered it. And now here I am—hiding under a blanket with a phone full of secrets and a heart that's beating like it knows something I don't.

In a few days, the family weekend will come and go. I'll be stuck standing in the foyer of this creaky old school, watching everyone else fall into their parents' arms, pretending they've missed each other like crazy. It's all such a performance. We all know why we're here—because it's easier for them to send us away than to deal with us. But still, we smile. Still, we act like it's love.

All of us except me.

I've never even gotten the chance to fake it.

I breathe in the stale air trapped under my blanket, scrunching my nose at the taste of my own breath. This won't just pass. Not this time. I won't let it. I'm tired of pretending it doesn't matter. Tired of letting him get away with it.

But for now, hidden away where no one can see, I find new ways to push the hurt deeper.

"It's all right, Grace," Joan says softly. "Come out and let me help you."

And the thing is—she actually means it.

I grind my teeth, rolling to face the wall inside my blankets. Joan means well, but she's also the most *in-your-face* roommate I've ever had. Constant optimism and zero chill. I miss Beth. We'd roomed together for four years, and then one day her parents just showed up, packed her bags, and took her home to finish school. I haven't heard from her since.

I like to think it's because she's finally living the family life we used to dream about, too caught up in feeling safe to miss me. But sometimes, when I'm being honest with myself, I hope she's miserable. That she hates it, and that she thinks of me every day.

It's messy. I know. But feelings usually are.

The bed dips slightly as Joan moves closer.

"I know this feels terrible now," she says quietly. "But it'll work out."

I don't answer. I don't want her comfort, not when it feels like she doesn't understand the depth of what's been broken.

"And honestly..." her voice softens. "You can't be surprised. This isn't the first time he's done this."

I bite the inside of my cheek, hard. The taste of blood hits the back of my tongue. If I open my mouth, I might say something I can't take back.

Joan keeps going. "Just think, soon we'll graduate, and you'll never have to deal with another family weekend alone."

A hand touches my back. Gentle. Circles. Soothing,

probably. But it just makes my skin crawl. I shift away, but the hand stays put.

"Do you want to come with my family?" she asks. "I'm sure my mom won't mind. She was just asking about you."

Of course she does. Joan's parents are picture-perfect. Always showing up with fresh-baked muffins and perfectly wrapped care packages. I've seen her dad cheer louder than anyone at the fall talent show. Meanwhile, my father has managed to make it to *two* family weekends in my entire life. Two.

I've never understood why Joan even goes to boarding school. Her parents seem like the type who'd homeschool her just to keep her close. But maybe that's the secret. Maybe they send her away so they *can* keep loving her. Maybe they need the distance to stand each other. What a luxury.

"Besides," Joan says, too casual now, "you know this one won't last. Your dad's a chronic cheater. He'll just bounce to the next woman like he always does."

And that's it.

The words are true—but that doesn't mean she gets to say them. She doesn't get to pick through the ugliest parts of my life like they're public knowledge, like they don't still sting every time I think about them. Like they don't live just under my skin.

I throw the blankets off and sit up fast. Too fast.

"Get out." My voice is low and cold, the words clipped and crystal clear. "Get. Out. Now."

Joan blinks, stunned. "B-but Grace, this is my—"

"I swear," I cut her off, my voice shaking now, "If you don't leave right now, I can't promise I'll keep my hands to myself—and we both know I hit harder than I look like I can."

It's a threat I won't follow through on—we both know that—but the look on her face tells me it worked anyway. She stumbles backward, bumping into her bed frame, then makes a quick exit without another word. The door clicks softly behind her, because of course Joan would never slam it. That wouldn't be polite.

I sit there alone, breath hitching in my throat.

There was a moment—just a flicker of one—where I thought maybe I could trust her. Let Joan in, just a little. She was trying, in her own clumsy way. But I should've known better.

I *do* know better.

My shoulders tremble as my hands stay balled into fists, my pulse hammering in my ears. What was *that*? She was being nosy, sure, but it's not like I haven't heard it all before—whispers in the halls, knowing glances, the snide little comments about my dad's latest scandal. None of it is new. So why did I explode like that? Why now?

Joan didn't deserve that. Not really.

I throw myself back onto my bed and stare blankly at the ceiling, waiting for the world to stop spinning sideways. For my thoughts to stop being so loud. But instead of settling, everything just kind of dissolves—until all I can think about is the app.

I reach under my pillow, fingers closing around my phone like it's a lifeline. And instantly, I feel better. Not fixed, not really, but steadier somehow. Like the ache behind my eyes has been smoothed over with something warm. Comforting.

I tap open the app and it greets me with the same quiet hum of energy I felt before—nothing I can explain, just a gentle buzz in my fingertips that doesn't seem to come from the phone itself.

Only two pages of matches appear. I should feel annoyed, or at least mildly offended. Isn't my face cute enough for *more* than that? Did I answer the questionnaire wrong? Too honest? Not honest enough?

The doubts come in fast, rising like a tide. But just as quickly, they're swept away by a wave of calm so clean and sudden it steals my breath. It's like a warm blanket being tucked around my shoulders.

I tell myself I'm imagining it, that it's just a dopamine hit or whatever—but deep down, I *know* that's not all it is.

No matter how many faces I scroll past, I keep coming back to *him*.

The first one.

Galin.

Something about his picture won't let me look away. The dark swoop of his hair, the smirk that hovers somewhere between charming and dangerous, the gleam in his green eyes that makes it feel like he's already seen the deepest parts of me and hasn't run.

He's beautiful—not in a perfect, angelic way, but like something carved from shadow and confidence. Like he was made to draw you in before you realized you were too close to escape.

A soft gust pushes my curtain open, moonlight slipping through the glass and pooling on the floor. It's later than I thought. I should be exhausted—but I'm not. I should care about school tomorrow—but I don't. My chest is thrumming with this strange, restless energy that won't let me go.

I click on Galin's profile again, my thumb hovering like it has a mind of its own. Only two pictures. One is the smirking headshot. The other is... different. He's shirtless in a dimly lit room that looks more like a dream than a real place, shadows curling at the edges. The ink across his skin isn't just decorative—it *moves*, or it feels like it might. His tattoos twist and spiral up his chest, wrapping his wrists like cuffs.

Something in me stirs. A curious ache.

And then there's the button.

Bright red. Glowing slightly.

Message him.

It's like it's waiting for me.

I hesitate. Would it seem too eager to message him first? Should I wait for him to reach out? But what if he never does? What if I wait, and that feeling—the one that makes me feel okay again—just fades?

The button pulses once. It's bigger now. Almost like it's breathing.

I set the phone down, breathing hard. Shake out my hands. Try to get my thoughts back under control.

But it's like something's crawling under my skin, something that doesn't want me to stop. Not now. Not when I'm *this* close.

Laughter drifts in from the hallway, too bright and far away to touch me. It doesn't matter. None of it does. I'm not the kind of girl who chases boys. My father made sure of that. His one real compliment: *at least you're not like your mother.*

But I can't stop thinking about Galin.

And I know—*I just know*—if I want to feel good again, if I want that warm, buzzing calm to come back...

I have to message him.

Hands trembling, I pick the phone back up and press the glowing red **Connect** button. A quiet hum rushes through me—like the flutter of windchimes in a breeze or a warm breath against the back of my neck. I almost drop the phone.

A screen of prewritten messages pops up, each line in bold black letters that seem to pulse ever so slightly, like they're waiting. Some of the options are so forward I feel my face go hot. I cringe and pick the one that seems the safest.

Grace: Loved your pics

Immediately, I regret everything.

I cover my face with my free hand, body locked in place like a starfish on a too-small bed. *Loved your pics?* What am I, someone's mom trying to sound hip? He's going to read that and laugh—or worse, ignore me entirely. Someone like Galin probably has a dozen better options already lined up. Girls who know how to flirt. Girls who don't second-guess every word they type.

I squeeze my eyes shut. This isn't me. I'm not this insecure. This isn't about needing a guy or wanting someone to like me—it's about making a point. That's all. It's about proving I'm not the kind of girl who just gets tossed aside when it's convenient. If my father can leave me behind like I'm some footnote in his life, then I can do the same. I can show him that I know how to play cold, too.

Still, when I scroll through the other matches, none of them hold my attention. I try, really try, to convince myself that they're all the same. Just names and faces. Interchangeable. But the thought doesn't land. Not the way it should.

There's something about Galin that keeps pulling me back.

Like a string tied to my ribs, tugging, just a little, every time I try to look away. It's not obsession—not yet—but it's *something*, and it's growing fast. Too fast.

I roll onto my side and plug in my phone. Through a narrow split in the curtains, the night sky stares back at me, cool and indifferent. I try counting stars instead of sheep, but it's no good.

My mind keeps drifting to him.

His unread message status. His eyes in that second photo. The shape of the ink on his skin.

I blink hard, trying to push him out of my thoughts, but he won't leave. He doesn't *feel* like a crush. He feels like gravity. Like something I'm falling into, whether I want to or not.

A soft ding breaks the silence. A new message. My breath catches—but the sender's name isn't Galin's.

Disappointment crashes over me so hard I drop the phone onto the mattress like it's betrayed me. If it's not him, I don't care.

I curl my fingers into the blanket and try to slow my breathing, but I can't shake the pressure building in my chest. Like a tide rising inside me, pushing out everything else—thoughts, reason, sleep—until there's only *him*.

I don't know what's happening to me. I just know I need him to write back.

Because somehow, impossibly, I already know—

No one else will do.

Chapter Two

Galin: You up?

The message pops up on my phone, a sharp sliver of light splitting the dark. I bite my lip. It's 5 a.m. I'm awake—of course I'm awake—but I shouldn't be.

Across the room, Joan shifts in her bed, the mattress giving a little squeal. She'd be furious if she knew. She already warned me: "Grace, delete the app. It's weird." But after the night I've had—waiting, hoping—there's no way I'm ignoring Galin now.

The pressure in my chest loosens just from seeing his name. Maybe that's not healthy, but it's real.

Grace: Yep.

Blue dots flicker. My heart stutters.

Galin: Bit of a night owl, are you?

Grace: I guess that's what happens when your roommate snores like a dying lawnmower.

Sorry Joan. I can't seem too eager. He needs to think I'm cool, casual, unbothered—even though every part of me is buzzing.

Galin: How terrible. I adore the night. Though, it would be difficult to savor its mysteries with such a disruptive bedfellow.

Bedfellow. Who even talks like that? Still, there's something about the way he phrases things—like poetry made just for me. And the app... every time I open it, it's like stepping into warm water. Calming. Safe. Wanted.

Grace: So you're a night owl too?

Dots. Pause. Dots again.

Galin: I would not say that I am an owl, no.

Okay, what? Is he trying to be funny? Or cryptic? I almost toss my phone onto the mattress, but then—

Galin: But one does not need feathers to treasure the night. There are secrets only revealed to those who linger past the sun.

Grace: Like what?

I type it before I can overthink. A thrill runs through me. I know what he means. Maybe. Probably.

> Galin: Would you pledge your nights to me?
> I would teach you all the night has to offer,
> if you are willing to give them to me.

It's dramatic. Ridiculous. But, I do want someone to want me like that. And I'm tired of pretending I don't.

> Grace: Sure. Why not? I haven't been doing
> anything great with them anyway.

Too honest? Maybe. But if it scares him off, that's his problem.

> Galin: I can conjure a myriad of delights to
> enrapture your nights.

I can't answer. My limbs tingle. I jump from the bed, pacing like I've touched a live wire. I wave my arms, trying to burn it off without screaming. The rug mutes my steps, but Joan groans in her sleep. I freeze.

> Grace: So now that my nights are yours, are
> you going to share your thoughts with me?

> Galin: Not just yet. The pale peak of sunrise
> is already tearing us apart. I will see you in
> thirteen hours.

> Grace: You'll see me? Where are we
> meeting? I mean, I have school, but I could
> make something work...

But there are no dots. Nothing. Just silence.

I plug my phone in and pull the blanket up to my chin, watching as the sunrise bleeds across the dorm walls. I don't sleep.

"Bored Miss Elliot?"

I jerk, swallowing a yawn. "No, Mrs. Thompson."

"Then keep your mouth closed."

Joan lifts an eyebrow at me, but I just stare at my empty notebook spread across my desk. I can't focus. It's not the exhaustion—it's the anticipation. Galin. Thirteen hours. That's six-thirty tonight. It has to be.

When the final bell rings, I bolt. The hallway floods with girls in identical plaid skirts. I slide through them like a ghost.

"Grace! Grace, wait up!"

I sigh through my nose but stop walking so Joan can catch up.

"What's going on with you today?" she huffs as she gets close to me, and I start walking again. "Is this because of what I said yesterday?"

"You're entitled to your opinion."

"See, that's the attitude. I'm just trying to help you. That app is sketchy."

"So you said."

"Haven't you thought about all those missing girls at all?"

I purse my lips.

"I don't want you to be one of them."

"I won't be."

Joan brushes a few stray blonde hairs from her face. "I'm sure none of them thought they'd be the next ones to disappear either."

"I'm being careful."

"Fine. Do whatever you're going to do. It's not like I

could know anything about what I'm talking about." She throws her hands in the air and brushes past me.

It's not like I don't care about her opinion. She just doesn't understand what I'm going through. How could she? Joan has never had to worry about being so far away from her family, or even the social stigma that comes from being the scholarship kid. No, Perfect Joan's family can visit the school whenever they want and have more than enough money to send their only child to private school. With all of that going for her, she'd never understand what I'm going through. Why I need this.

Joan is amazing with technology. There've been a few rumors that she has a job waiting for her with Apple when she graduates. Just because she knows how to program doesn't mean she knows everything about this stupid dating app.

My feet are floating as I run up the wide marble stairs to our room, skipping dinner. How can I eat when my stomach is a bundle of nerves and hope?

With the door closed and locked behind me, I dig through my drawers. Flinging clothes across the room, I look for anything in my normal clothes that makes me look remotely attractive. A field of blue plaid skirts and white button-down shirts litter the floor. Running my fingers through my hair, I close my eyes and take a deep breath.

This is stupid. I know it is. He won't even see me, at least not all of me, not when our date will be through a phone screen. So why can't I let go of the idea of getting dressed up?

Squeezing myself into a pair of skinny jeans, I steal a slinky tank top from Joan's closet. My already tight chest feels like it's pressed in a vice. If Joan comes back, I'm dead. She's made it very clear that we don't borrow clothes. And by we, I mean me. I don't have anything she would be interested in. Lucky her. Still, I have to take this chance. I don't want to scare away the only guy who's ever been interested in me.

Swiping on red lipstick and spraying a fruity perfume in the air, I ignore the voice reminding me how dumb this is. He can't see me; he can't smell me. But somehow, getting ready makes it real.

The minutes tick by in an endless procession. Standing in the middle of the room, I shift from one foot to the other, hands clammy as I wipe them off on my jeans. I catch a view of myself in Joan's mirror and quickly glance away. My hair hangs in limp strands over my narrow shoulders, big eyes sunk in behind high cheekbones. I look every bit as unhinged as I feel.

My phone lies on the desk at the end of my bed, its screen dark. My ears strain to hear the telltale ping of a message coming in.

Footsteps pound through the hallway outside my door. Dinner must be over. Any minute now Joan will barge in and demand her clothes back, her face turning as red as a tomato. I pace through the room, trying to flush out the adrenaline pumping through my veins.

Ping. My heart leaps—but it's Joan. "Want me to bring you dinner?"

I resist the urge to throw my phone at the wall. It's not her fault. She doesn't know that I'm being stood up by the most beautiful boy I've ever seen. The same boy who made it impossible to sleep.

How stupid could I be? I should have known something like this would happen. And why do I care so much? What happened to wanting to date to mess with my father? Now I've reached a level of obsession I didn't even know I was capable of. The feelings aren't mine. There's no way they could be mine. If I were smart, I'd delete the app right now and forget this ever happened.

I reach for my phone to delete the app—but my hand freezes. That warmth returns. Like sinking into a favorite memory. I lower my hand.

I can't delete it. Not yet.

I yank the necklace from my throat and throw it on the bed. I'm starting on the rest of my outfit when the floor squeaks behind me. Glancing up at the locked door, I know it isn't Joan. There's no way someone else could have gotten in here with the door locked.

Silence presses on me, I can't even hear the movement on the other side of the door anymore. There's no way everyone disappeared so quickly.

Hands curled into fists; I rotate on stiff limbs. The back of my room is dark, shadows spreading through the space with reaching fingers.

The floor creaks.

I turn. Nothing.

Again. Creak.

"Probably a mouse," I whisper. But it sounded bigger.

I laugh to myself, uneasy. Turn toward the bed—

He's there.

A man. Standing beside my bed.

"Y-you…"

"In the flesh," Galin grins. "I told you I'd see you in thirteen hours."

My mind blanks. This isn't possible.

"Are you ready to go?" he asks, mouth twisting into the same smug smile from his profile picture.

I have to cough to clear my throat. "R-ready to go?"

"You promised me your nights. Did you forget?"

My frantic mind tries to remember our conversation. Did I say that? If I did, I didn't really mean it. Everything from the last thirteen hours blurs together; I don't remember writing anything. But even if I did, how could he think I was serious? Is he flirting with me now, and I'm missing it? My gaze drifts over the bed, and I catch sight of my discarded necklace. The pit in my stomach grows bigger. He's here. In my room. And I'm not even ready anymore.

"It is of no matter." He waves his hand through the air, the many rings on his fingers glinting in the light as he wipes away my disarray. "Let us go."

"Go where?"

He tilts his head. "Where your nights now belong."

I want to run. Scream. But the app's calm presses in again, thick and warm. I feel like I'm watching myself through a window.

"Let me grab my purse," I say, stalling.

"That will not be necessary."

He grabs my arm before I can reach the bag on the dresser. His fingers coil around my wrist, too firm—then tighter, until it hurts. I start to speak, but a sharp pop cracks through the air.

And then everything goes dark.

Darkness.

I can't see a thing. No light. No shapes. Just black. My eyes strain, but there's nothing to focus on. My wrist still throbs where Galin grabbed me, but there's no sign of him. Just this empty, suffocating void.

I feel the pressure building in my chest, sharp and unyielding. My breath comes in short, frantic bursts. I'm not panicking. Not yet. But the longer I stand here, the more it feels like the darkness is closing in.

I stretch my arms out in front of me, my fingers splayed wide, but there's nothing. Nothing to grab, nothing to ground me. It's like I've been dropped into the heart of a black hole.

"Galin?" My voice is thin and reedy in the heavy blanket of black. It doesn't even have the decency to echo in this obviously empty space. "Is anyone there?"

A deep chuckle rolls through the air, filling every inch of this suffocating space. I spin, my heart racing. The laugh didn't come from Galin. This... whatever it is, is toying with me. I clench my jaw, refusing to give it the satisfaction of hearing my fear.

I gather my thoughts. I can't let panic overtake me. There has to be something I can do. A plan. A way out.

I take a breath, slow and steady. The darkness presses on me, but I won't let it own me. If I can't see, I'll feel my way out. I start to move forward, one careful step at a time.

There's got to be a wall here. A surface I can use to guide myself out. I've got to keep moving. The air feels thick, like it's resisting my every step, but I'm not stopping.

The voice chuckles again, and the sound skitters over my skin like the crawl of something monstrous. It's letting me think I have a chance, making me believe I can escape. But I know better. I know what this is: a game, and I'm the prey.

But I'm not just going to sit here and wait for it to strike. I keep moving, my fists raised in front of me. I won't let it see me weak.

And then, I feel it—a light pressure, cold and sharp,

along my spine. I whip around, fists flying. But there's nothing. The air shifts, and I swing again, but the darkness laughs, its breath hot and rank, brushing my cheek.

"Is this fun for you?" I grind my teeth, refusing to flinch. "Come at me, or don't. I don't have time for your games."

The laugh lingers in the air, dark and mocking. The creature's patience is infinite, but I'm done waiting.

"You think you're clever, hiding in the dark?" I sneer. "If you want me, come out and get me."

The voice hisses, close now, its breath a soft rasp in my ear. "Silly girl, you think you're in control here? I could slit your throat and you wouldn't even know until the blood hit the floor."

"Big talk for something that has to hide to take on a girl."

I stand my ground, eyes darting around, waiting for the next move. I don't know what I'm up against, but I'm not going to make it easy for whatever it is.

"You're hiding. Why don't you just turn on the light, then?"

The voice chuckles again. "Who says there's no light? You think you understand this place?"

A pop cracks through the air, sharp and final.

"Enough of this," a voice commands, and the darkness writhes, unraveling in a way that makes the air feel alive. The shadows pull back, revealing a small table with a flickering candle.

Galin. He stands by the table, watching me like I'm some kind of puzzle he's trying to solve.

I shove down the panic threatening to rise in my chest. I'm not going to let him see me break. Not now. Not when I'm still trying to figure out how the hell I got here.

"What is this place?" I ask, my voice steady, despite everything.

Galin smiles, the same smile from his profile picture, but something darker lurks behind it now. "It doesn't matter where you are. You promised me your nights. That means you'll do as I ask. No matter where I take you."

I scowl, crossing my arms. "Flirting doesn't mean I agreed to this... whatever this is."

"You agreed. And in my world, that's a contract." His eyes narrow, waiting for me to argue.

"Verbal contracts aren't legally binding," I retort, my voice firm, even if I know I'm grasping at straws.

"They are in my world," he says, and there's something final in his tone that makes my stomach twist.

"In your world?" I can't help but laugh, a bitter sound that doesn't match the uncertainty bubbling in my chest. "We're both from the U.S. There's no difference in our laws. This is kidnapping, no matter how you slice it."

He watches me, silent. He's not even trying to argue anymore. He just lets me ramble, like it's all meaningless to him. And maybe it is.

"Your laws don't apply here," he says finally, with a sigh. "I don't expect you to understand yet. You will."

"Will you tell me where 'here' is?" I demand, my frustration growing.

"You wouldn't believe me," he replies.

"Why don't you let me decide that for myself?"

He grins, the smile both wicked and knowing. "Humans have never been very good at making decisions."

"Well, I'm not all humans. I'm just one," I say, my eyes narrowing. "What do you mean by 'humans'?"

I step back, taking in my surroundings. There's no way out. No door. No window. Just dirt walls closing in, and this man—this thing—who's somehow trapped me in here. I force my hands to stay steady as I run my fingers through my hair, looking for any sign of what's happened to me. No marks. No signs of being knocked out. Nothing.

"I think you already know the answer to that," Galin says softly, his voice almost a whisper. "As for where you are, it doesn't matter. There's nothing you can do."

I scan the walls again, my heart pounding. This can't be happening. It just can't.

"You are Under the Hill," he says, matter-of-factly.

I wait, but he doesn't say anything more. Like I should know what that means. I don't.

"What do you mean?" I ask, desperation creeping into my voice.

He smirks, clearly enjoying my confusion. "You'll figure it out."

"Yeah, I bet I will," I mutter under my breath. This is insane.

I bring my fists back up into a defensive stance, even though I have no idea what I'm supposed to do next. "I didn't promise you anything. I'm not going anywhere with you. So just show me the door and let me go."

He quirks an eyebrow, clearly amused. "You don't know what you're up against, do you? You realize," he says, his voice low as he steps closer, his every move graceful, predatory, "there's power in a name."

"What are you talking about?"

He touches my raised fist, and I flinch. "Knowing a person's true name gives you power over them here. Just as I have power over you."

"What's that supposed to mean?" My voice wavers, but I don't let him see it.

He leans against the wall, grinning. "You'll find out soon enough. Come. Let's stop pretending this is a game."

Before I can respond, he vanishes through the wall.

I reach out, my fingers brushing the earth as my heart pounds in my chest. There's no door. No way out. Just shadows and dirt. I feel a cold knot in my stomach. This is real. And I'm not getting out of here easily.

Galin's only been gone a few minutes when the shadow creature in the corner twitches, its body expanding until it consumes the entire wall. My stomach plummets as my body locks in place, fear rooting me to the spot.

"Hello again, girl child," it rumbles.

Its voice shatters the paralysis, and without hesitation, I squeeze my eyes shut and lunge toward the wall Galin disappeared through. A whip of black shoots across the floor and wraps itself around my ankle, but it's too late. Whatever wild magic resides in that wall grabs hold, yanking me through.

The dark tendril shrieks as it recoils, but I'm already flying through a haze of dark blues and purples. My body arcs horizontally, and before I know it, I'm plummeting through the void and crashing onto the cold floor.

Groaning, I push myself up and reach out. My hand lands on a shoe, and I follow it up a pair of sleek leather pants, then over a narrow chest swathed in black, and finally, I meet Galin's smirking face. Heat rushes to my cheeks as I scramble to my feet, desperately trying to regain some composure.

He doesn't give me time to brush myself off before

striding through a vine-covered archway. I follow closely, my eyes racing to take in my surroundings, but none of it makes sense. I've been transported to a place that feels both alien and captivating. It's as though the earth itself decided to reclaim a grand baroque mansion, its white walls gleaming under gilded accents while creeping ivy weaves through the cracks. It's like a wealthy hipster's dream... if they'd gone overboard with the green.

My sock-covered feet slide across the smooth tiles, leaving dust footprints in my wake as I trail after Galin, who moves with the ease of someone who's been here far too often.

"How did you do that?" I ask, my voice tight with frustration and curiosity.

"Do what?"

"How did you bring us here? How did we get from that room into this, this-"

"Palace?" he offers with a teasing grin.

"Exactly," I mutter.

He looks over at me, still grinning. "Consider the room we were in my receiving room; this is where the real entertainment begins."

"Entertainment?" I feel a flutter of anxiety settle into my stomach. Nothing good ever comes from that word around here. "But how did we get here?"

Galin gestures his long, tapered fingers around us. "'Here' is a relative term. And I think you already know the answer to your own question. Do you not?"

"I don't," I say, the confusion bubbling to the surface again.

"It doesn't have to make sense according to your rules. Welcome to the other side of the glamour."

Everything he says makes my head ache as I try to piece

it all together, yet the only real explanation gnaws at me, and I'm not sure I want to admit it.

"Will I ever get a clear answer out of you?" I ask, frustrated, as he halts before a pair of wooden double doors engraved with dancing fawns peeking through weeping willow branches.

"Answers mean so much more when you find them yourself."

"Great," I grumble under my breath, ignoring the way my heart skips at the mischievous smile tugging at his lips.

Galin throws open the doors, striding in with me scrambling to keep up, not wanting to get left behind. I peer around him and see a massive ballroom. Only half of the chandeliers are lit, casting long shadows across the floor, where bodies writhe like wind-up dolls with broken limbs, moving in time to a haunting tune played by a band on a raised platform. The musicians' hands are green, their instruments ancient-looking. The moment the doors slam open, the crowd falls silent.

"Galin," a woman's voice calls, smooth as silk. I hadn't noticed her before, sitting on a gold throne draped in flowers. She crosses one leg over the other, and I can't help but notice the slit in her black dress that opens as she leans back. Her long black hair falls in sheets behind her. "So good of you to join us."

Galin bows theatrically, the smirk never leaving his face. "You know I could never stay away from a beauty such as yours for long."

Her delicate brow twitches, but her posture remains icy, as though she hasn't heard him.

"Have you brought me a toy, then?"

I freeze as the eyes of the revelers all turn to me. My heart skips, and I instinctively step closer to Galin, my hands twisting nervously. *This is not good. What am I supposed to do now?*

"Not everything Under the Hill belongs to you, Tabitha," Galin replies smoothly. "I might like to keep this one around."

She laughs, the sound sharp like glass breaking. "You cannot be serious, Galin. I knew you would return when you needed more power. Why else would you have rounded up a human girl for me?"

"Again, I've made no mention of handing her over to you."

"Come closer," Tabitha purrs, her voice a dangerous drawl.

The crowd parts, and I stick close to Galin, trying not to be swallowed by the sea of strange, unsettling bodies. My mind races with options for escape, but none seem feasible. The only exit I can see is the door we came through, but there are too many creatures between me and it.

Galin doesn't seem phased by her, but my nerves are fraying with every step closer to Tabitha.

We descend the short flight of stairs, and I stiffen as a light-brown-skinned creature brushes against me, its hair a tangle of leaves, its eyes empty holes. I recoil, but it only leans back into the crowd. I keep my back straight and head high, trying to project some sense of confidence, though my stomach churns.

Tabitha leans forward, her dress falling open more as she reaches for Galin, her nails the color of dried blood curling around his arm.

"I've missed having you here," she murmurs, her gaze intense as it lingers on him.

"You know the reason for my absence," he replies, voice cold.

Her lips form a pout. "I do not see why such a little thing should come between us."

"I could say the same for you."

"I was hoping you had brought the little human as a peace offering; you don't have to provide a tithe."

My stomach drops at the words, and I stumble backward as my heart pounds harder. Cold sweat clings to my skin as I search for an escape—any escape. But the creatures around me grow closer, and the only exit is already crowded.

Galin rolls his shoulders, effectively dislodging her grip. "That would imply I am interested in peace."

"Do not be like that," Tabitha says as she rises in a fluid motion and runs her hand down his smooth cheek. "You do not need to fight with me."

"Was there anything else?" Galin's face is like stone as he backs away from her several steps, making it impossible for her to reach him without looking like she's chasing him down.

A slight frown mars Tabitha's face as she settles back into her throne. "Only this: do not expect that you will be able to continue hiding from me, Galin. Your presence at court is a requirement of your position. That means you will have to do whatever you must to maintain your power."

"And if I am not interested in power?"

Tabitha's smile turns cruel, revealing pointed canines. "Let us not pretend to be anything other than what we are, Galin. You could not contain your thirst for power if someone gave you a glass."

He picks lint off his shirt with a careless hand. "If that is it, then I should be off."

She drapes her arms across the armrest of the throne, red lips pulling up on one side. "You will be back, Galin."

"You have given me few other options."

He twists to leave, and I don't move out of his way quick enough, leaving us to walk side by side. Tabitha laughs, the sound moving over my skin with its sharp points. I grab at Galin's arm. Of all the threats in this room, he seems the safest.

"Better teach your pet some respect, Galin. If she proves to be too much, you know where to send her."

I glance back and immediately wish I hadn't as I see her perched on her throne like a spider in a web. I'm totally screwed.

With a rough hand, he shoves me behind him. I trip with the abrupt movement and fall to my knees, a hiss of pain brushing past my lips. Galin doesn't stop, even though I know he must know I've fallen. The creatures continue to give him a respectful, or perhaps fearful, distance, but they give me no such boundaries. His steps echo with excruciating slowness as my view of his legs is blocked by the impossibly thin and scabby hands reaching for me. They tangle in my hair, ripping away pieces of Joan's shirt. A strangled scream reverberates in my throat, but he doesn't stop walking.

A brown skinned creature steps in front of me, its eyes like deep forest moss as it peers down at me. With soft hands, it touches my face, tilting my head up to see me better.

"Do not be stingy," another creature says, flying towards me on wings like gossamer curtains. "If he left it here, we can all share it."

"Sharing is for the weak. I intend to consume it entirely," something behind me hisses.

"Galin!" I scream, my voice a raw, desperate plea. "Galin!"

From above the tree creature's shoulder, I spot him turning, annoyance flashing in his eyes. But right now, I'll take his annoyance if it means I get out of here alive.

"Away with you," Galin snaps, his voice low and dangerous. The creatures scatter at the command. He swings an arm, knocking a winged creature away with a sickening thud, a smear of red staining its face.

"Come," he orders, holding out his hand. I hesitate for only a moment before grabbing it, my fingers clutching onto him as if he were my lifeline.

He reaches a hand for me, and I grab it while choking back a sob. With impossible strength he pulls me to my feet, and I must run to keep up with him as he breezes through the room.

We reach the doors, and I glance back once towards the chaos that nearly consumed me. Tabitha sits on her throne, a gold goblet in her hand. She raises it towards me and takes a drink, red liquid dripping down her chin.

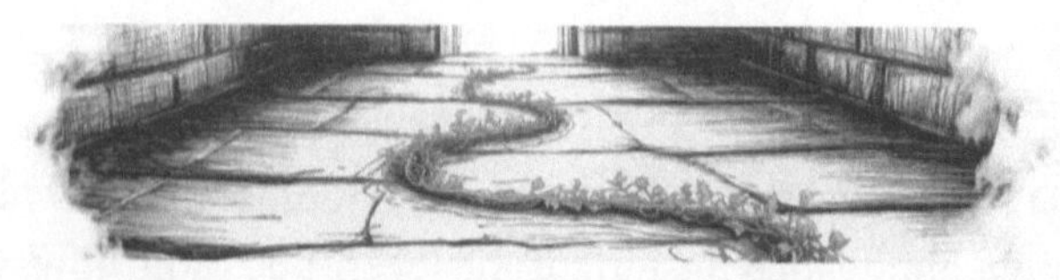

Chapter Three

Galin closes the door behind me, and I shut my eyes against the image I know I'll never forget. With only the thick wood separating me from the monsters inside, I know I should move, but my body won't listen. Galin steps in closer, his scent washing over me in thick waves of pine and earth.

"I have places to be," he says, his voice still cold from dealing with Tabitha. "Are you composed yet?"

Am I? How could I be? Everything here is a slap in the face of reality. I could have died in there. How is he expecting calm?

My silence must say enough. He sighs, and the next thing I know, I'm lifted off the ground, cradled against his chest. His arm supports my back, his other under my legs, and despite everything, the position calms me. I lean into his chest, breathing in that steady grounding scent. I should pull away—but I can't bring myself to.

He starts walking, carrying us farther from the door, each step easing some of the tension inside me. I shove the memory down, like I've done with others. I might never forget—but maybe someday it'll feel like a dream.

If not for Galin, it might be easier to believe that.

A door creaks open, and suddenly I'm tossed off him, landing in a pillowed heap. I blink up at a dark canopy, tiny points of light above like stars. Galin moves through the room, his expression unreadable. A clicking sound follows, then the soft roar of fire.

I roll to my side, realizing I'm on a bed as I take in the softly curving dark wood posts holding up the canopy of stars. And from the pine smell of it, not just any bed. Galin's bed. My body goes stiff, as if any movement will make this more awkward than it already is.

Galin sits on a wooden stool in front of a gilded fireplace at the foot of the bed. The wall behind him is the same cracked white as the hallway, but with fewer plants to give a magical look to the room. He runs a hand through his black hair, exposing ears that end in a point. My breath catches in my throat as I'm finally able to realize that he may not be as human as I thought. I'd suspected, but now I know.

As if sensing me, Galin turns, the easy smile back in place.

"Where are we?"

He rises, prowling towards me in a way that makes my stomach twist. "Obvious things don't usually require so many questions."

His hand trails along the side of the bed, and I resist the urge to flinch, to move. I won't give him the reaction he's probably hoping for. Not even when his hand continues along its course and rests against my thigh. I grind my jaw shut and try not to let my thoughts show on my face.

Maybe not convincing, but I try.

"So, you've brought me here—after tricking me into some ridiculous promise. What now?" My body is stock still as his pinky trails higher along my thigh. I can guess what he wants, but I'm not going to give it.

"Is this really so terrible Grace? Was it so awful promising me your nights?" His dark eyes turn black as he stares down at me. "I did not even make you stay at the party."

"That's what you call it?"

"Apologies if our celebrations didn't meet your expectations. I imagine private school parties must be very refined."

I scowl. "Private school doesn't mean I've never been to a party. And yours included... devouring guests. Not exactly my scene."

"He never would have actually *devoured* you. Maybe just a nibble. I am sure you would not have missed just the teeniest bit off your pinky toe."

"I'm sure I would've."

Galin leans back against the bedpost. "Do not sulk. We could enjoy each other's company."

"I doubt that."

"If you would rather not be with me, I can think of someone very interested in having you all to herself."

An unbidden shiver runs down my spine at the mention of Tabitha. I'd rather die than spend any more time with her than what I just did. There was a promise in her smile that I'd rather not be fulfilled. Comparatively, Galin is right. So far this hasn't been the worst way to spend an evening. Not the best by far, but definitely not the worst.

"Are you ever going to explain any of this?"

He runs his long fingers over his chin. "Perhaps I owe you something after you helped me out with Tabitha."

"That was helping?"

The words escape before I can stop them. I clap a hand to my mouth, but it does nothing for the words already hanging in the air. Galin quirks an eyebrow at me, saying nothing.

"She has been begging me to bring her a human for months. Walking in with one and refusing her? Delicious." He grins.

I ignore his use of 'one', like I'm not a person. I doubt saying anything about it would change his mind or give me any answers anyway.

"What exactly do you want to know?"

"Why am I here?"

Galin smiles. "Did I not already give you a reason for your presence?"

So, he's not really going to play fair. I didn't expect him to, but I'd hoped. I can't help it. If I figure out what's going on, then maybe I can find a way out. That's all I really care about, but somehow I don't think Galin will be very receptive to answering that kind of question.

"What are you?"

The question makes my skin prickle. After what happened in his 'receiving room' and the throne room, I'm not sure I want to know what dangers lurk under his fitted tunic.

"You mean, compared to what you are?"

"Are you trying to confuse me?"

Galin laughs, the sound stabbing through my growing headache.

"You are a human. Are you asking for the same label for me?"

"Yes."

I skip the sarcasm this time. I need to know.

"I am a fairy, of course."

"Of course?"

"My status should be obvious. I am a High Fairy—not some grubby creature clawing through dirt. Surely humans still know that much."

Forgive me for not recognizing something made up. Somehow, I don't think patronizing him will help me just now. I'm already stuck here with a gorgeous lunatic. And worse —my brain won't stop noticing how attractive he is.

"Let's pretend I don't know anything. What would you tell me about being a High Fairy?" I break eye contact, shifting to the far side of the bed. I need distance if I'm going to think clearly.

"Humans have grown ignorant, then."

My headache pulses harder. Conversations with him feel like walking in circles. What's his endgame?

"And if we have?"

"The most important thing to know: we're as dangerous as we are beautiful."

His smile gleams, firelight catching on elongated canines. It should scare me. And it does—a little. But after he saved me twice, I can't help but hesitate.

I glance down his body—flawless skin, lean frame. He probably thinks I'm ogling him. Maybe I am. But I'm also looking for signs of danger. Shouldn't he have claws? Barbs? Something obvious? Even venomous plants give warning signs.

His only weapon seems to be that infuriating, devastating smile.

I shake the thoughts loose. This is not the time to be admiring him. I'm being held hostage. I really am a mess.

"You have nothing to say?"

His voice breaks the silence. I'm done with games.

"When do I get to go home?"

His smile twitches, a flicker of something passing through his eyes. "When night passes."

So there's an end to this. If I can make it until morning, then I'll find a way out. Maybe even a way to get him arrested. Handsome or not, he deserves it.

"And what do you plan on doing with me until then?"

Galin shrugs. "I doubt I will be involved. You have plenty to do."

"Plenty to do?" My brows knit.

"You did not think I brought you here for amusement, did you? I have others for that. Using a human is beneath my status."

The grin he wears sharpens. Here it comes. The dark intentions of my kidnapper are about to be revealed. I'm not sure why I ever thought there'd be anything different on the agenda for tonight.

"Get up," he says, voice deep and commanding. My body moves before my brain catches up. "Follow me."

Galin opens the door and prowls through the hallway, leaving me to stumble after him. His smirk curls, revealing the tip of a fang. My stomach flips again—and I still can't tell if it's from fear or something far worse. The not knowing makes me hate myself a little more.

We walk through more white hallways tinged in gold and greed, so pristine it makes my skin crawl. I tuck my arms tighter to my sides, not out of fear, but so I don't stain whatever sick fantasy this place is meant to sell. Ahead is another pair of heavy double doors. Trees and sprites are carved into the gold, their figures weaving through branches like they're mid-dance, and as we get closer, they shimmer and shift with eerie life.

Galin rests his hand on the ornate handle, and my pulse spikes. This could be it. If this leads outside, I could be gone before he even realizes. My heart pounds hard enough to make my breath stutter. The open woods would be perfect. I'm fast. Faster than I look. If I time it right, I can disappear.

His dark eyes follow me as he opens the door and motions me ahead. I step forward, acting like I don't care, like I haven't already mapped out his weakness.

But it's pitch black beyond the doorway. Not night—complete absence. My shoulders sink. No wonder he let me go first. He knew I'd freeze.

Galin whispers something low, rhythmic, unfamiliar—and a red flame bursts to life in his palm. Its glow casts shadows along earthen walls, and the scent hits me next. Not soil this time. Something older, bitter. This place— it's still underground. Who would build something that expensive and beautiful underground? What's the point of all that gilded nonsense if no one ever sees it?

The thought strikes harder than expected, sorrow blooming sharp in my chest. I shake it off, but my eyes still sting. I don't care about this place. I really don't. But my body insists that I do. Pinching myself on the arm, the pain pulls me out of the fog of emotion and clears my head.

There. Better. No more misplaced emotion.

I rub the spot and keep moving. The silence stretches between us until it's broken by the sharp tang of animals. My nose twitches as Galin's small flame reveals the side of a wooden building.

I step closer, watching the flame curl in his hand

without consuming it. It should be impossible. I should be rationalizing, explaining, denying. But for once, I can't.

"How are you doing that?"

He gives me a look—patient and smug. "Magic."

"That's not an answer."

He smiles like it is. "Have you not paid any attention?"

He unlatches the door and light spills out, warm and blinding after the dark.The stable smell hits like a slap. I cover my nose, but it's too late.

"This is where you will spend the remainder of your time tonight. When day comes, you will be returned to your home."

A few horses are in the long row of stables. They shift in their stalls, flicking their tails at the flies that have inevitably found them, even underground. Everything has an air of neglect to it, despite the polished wood making up the stable and the bright warm lights filling the space. No one's been in here to clean in a long time.

"What exactly do you expect me to do?"

Galin's mouth quirks into a smirk. "Clean."

I stare at the closed door for a beat, then throw up my hands. "Seriously?"

I have no idea what I'm supposed to do. I've never even been in a stable before. The least he could have done was show me what his expectations were. That's assuming I'm going to follow along with what he told me to do. There's no reason for me to clean if he's not even here to make sure I do it.

What does he expect—gratitude? Instructions? Some kind of magical cleaning montage?

Please.

There's a low stool tucked in the corner, meant for someone who cares more than I do. I plop myself down, ignoring every mental whisper that reminds me of germs and all the unknown in this place. I've seen worse tonight than whatever bacteria are crawling around in here.

Leaning my head back against the wall, I let my eyes drift closed. If there are monsters out there, they can kill me while I nap just as well as they can when I'm alert. At least I won't have to smell this place while they do it.

And honestly? I'm tired of pretending there's anything I can do to stop it. My resistance will look the same either way.

Maybe when I wake up, this whole place will disappear. Just another fever dream, a hallucination I can forget. It's the only explanation that makes sense.

I cross my arms tight over my chest and let the dark take me. Sleep comes fast. The nightmare, for now, dissolves.

Chapter Four

"Are you coming to class today or are you planning to nap through it again?"

Joan's voice tears through the tail end of a dream— dark woods, flickering blue light, eyes like obsidian. I bolt upright and smack heads with her before I can stop myself.

"Ow!" she shrieks, staggering back and clutching her forehead like I hit her with a brick. "Was that necessary?"

I rub my own skull, wincing. "Sorry," I say, though I'm grinning. The weight on my chest eases when I see my dorm room—the too-firm mattress, the cluttered desk, the posters peeling off the walls. I'm back. Just a dream, a weird vivid, unnerving dream.

Joan scowls, grabs her messenger bag with an exaggerated huff, and storms out like she's the victim. Classic.

I waste no time ditching my pajamas, leaving them in a crumbled heap on the rug, and yank on my uniform—the plaid skirt and stiff white button-up never looked so reassuring, it's all so wonderfully average. I brush my hair, slap on some mascara, and sling my bag over my shoulder.

As I join the stream of girls heading to class, the normalcy is like oxygen. Even the rumble in my stomach from missing breakfast can't shake it. I don't even care. If skipping meals meant never going back to wherever my brain took me last night, I'd skip them forever. Well— maybe not *forever*. But for a while.

Sliding into my usual seat, I braid my hair and try to scrub Galin's face from my mind. But he lingers. Not just as a memory—more like a pulse. A whisper. I shake it off, but the whisper doesn't fade. It curls around me like the scent of something half-forgotten.

Ms. Greene starts the lesson, but I barely register her voice. My head aches, probably from lack of sleep, and Joan sitting beside me like a smug little gargoyle. I stifle a yawn behind my hand, but Ms. Greene misses nothing.

She walks over, heels tapping like warning bells. "Grace. Is everything all right?"

"Yes, ma'am." I shift in my seat, cheeks hot.

"Is there an issue with your bed?" she presses. "Or do you just find my class exceptionally dull?"

"No, ma'am."

Her lips purse. She's about to walk away when Joan raises her hand with calculated innocence.

"Yes, Joan?"

"I think I know why Grace is so tired," she says sweetly. "She was on that app again last night. The one we were specifically told to avoid? I told her it was a bad idea, but..."

I glare daggers at her, resisting the urge to throw my pencil at her smug little face.

Ms. Greene turns back to me. "Is this true?"

I scramble to remember last night before the dream took over. It's fuzzy. A blur. "I downloaded it, but I wasn't using it last night."

"Then what *were* you doing?"

"I...I don't remember."

Joan snorts loud enough for the whole room to hear. I want to sink into the floor.

Ms. Greene sighs, already tired of us. "Whatever's going on, I recommend shutting off your phone and getting a full night's sleep. Both of you."

As she stalks off, I turn away from Joan and open my notebook, trying to disappear. I doodle without thinking, letting my pencil move just to keep my hands busy.

When the bell rings, I blink down at the page—and freeze.

Galin.

His face, drawn in detail over and over. That half-smile. The arrogant tilt of his chin. The shadows under his eyes. It's him. Every sketch is him. But I didn't *mean* to draw him. I didn't even realize I was doing it.

I squeeze my eyes shut, inhale, exhale. Just a dream. A subconscious fluke. Totally normal.

I glance once more, just to confirm—

And the sketch *moves*.

His charcoal face turns to look straight at me. His eyes trail down my body and back up. He winks, and the smirk on his lips is sharper than I ever drew it. Too real.

I slam the notebook shut like it's a spider.

One... two... three...

I rush out of the classroom, heart pounding. My fingers itch to throw the notebook into the trash, but there are class notes in there. So instead, I shove it deep into my bag like that'll make it stop breathing.

Forget it. Just forget.

That's all I seem to be trying to do lately.

My phone pings.

Probably a meme from a class group chat. Or maybe Joan gloating. But when I glance at the screen, my stomach flips.

Galin: Thinking about me?

I let my phone slip back into my bag like it's radioactive.

Ignore him. That's how these guys work. You starve them of attention and they vanish. He's just a glitch. A leftover figment from the dream. That's *all* he is.

Another ping.

I don't look.

My jaw clenches. I'll delete the app the second I get back to my room. Joan was right about that much, even if she delivered it like a high priestess of smug.

But I'll *never* tell her she was right.

The rest of my classes blur past like fogged windows. I go through the motions but none of it lands. My notebooks are embarrassingly empty, and my stomach churns like I swallowed a stone instead of dinner. I barely noticed what they served in the cafeteria, which is so unlike me. Usually, I'm the first to defend the food—it's the only decent part of this place.

But today, everything feels off. Tilted. Unsteady.

My head pounds. Pressure builds behind my eyes every time I try to think about last night. I wish I had someone to talk to, but what would I even say? *Hi, I watched a drawing come to life and flirt with me.* That's a one-way ticket to a padded room. No thanks. I'll take the migraine and keep the hallucinations to myself.

Still... it *felt* real. The way his eyes moved. The way my stomach dropped when he looked at me.

I rub my temples harder. Joan's been avoiding me all day—thank goodness for small mercies. After throwing me under the bus in class, I'm not in the mood for her superiority complex. I don't even understand what her deal was. She's been uptight, but she's never gone out of her way to get me in trouble before. Was she really that bitter about the app?

Not that the app matters. Not really. Because none of it was real.

Right?

I duck out of the crowd heading toward tonight's movie in the gym. The thought of sitting in a room full of laughing girls makes my skin crawl. I need quiet. I need *away*.

In my room, I shut the door and lean against it, breathing like I've run a marathon. I thought being alone would help, but now that I am, I feel raw. Exposed. Like something's watching me. Like I brought something *back* with me.

I throw my bag onto the bed and follow it down. The thin blanket itches, but I don't care. I drag the half-deflated pillow over my head, count my breaths, and try not to think. In. out. In. *Forget.*

If I can just get some sleep— real, undisturbed, dreamless sleep— then maybe I'll wake up tomorrow and this will all feel like a bad joke. Just nerves. Sleep deprivation. Stress. Totally explainable.

I lie there until my breathing evens out and the silence thickens around me.

Then the floor creaks.

My limbs lock. Every instinct screams run, but I can't even lift my head.

There's a breath near my cheek— warm and real and far too close.

"You never responded to me earlier."

My eyes snap open.

Galin stands over me, shadowed in the low light. Too close. Too real. His presence is heat and smoke and pine, sharp at the edges, like something wild wearing a human shape. This isn't happening. I press my palms to my eyes, but when I lower them, he's still there.

"Are you ready to go?"

"Go where?" I croak.

"The same place as last night. Though I recall you were... less than productive in the stables."

"I never agreed to that," I snap, sitting up. "I said I'd *talk*, not work for you."

Galin tilts his head, his smile slow and amused. "That is not entirely true."

"But it's not entirely a lie either. So I'm not doing your dirty work."

He watches me for a beat, expression unreadable. If I were on my feet, I'd plant them wide and cross my arms. Power stance. But I'm not. I'm cornered in my own bed by something not quite human, and I hate how calm he looks.

I should've gone to someone. Reported him. Told anyone. But I was too desperate to believe it wasn't real. Past me was a real idiot.

He wags a long finger at me like I'm a disobedient child. "You are a slippery one. That's rare in your kind."

"Oh, so I don't fit in your tidy little 'humans are boring' box? Must be so disappointing for you."

His grin sharpens. "Surprising. Not disappointing."

The way he says it sends a chill down my spine. I hate the way my heart picks up. I hate how close he is, how *alive* he feels. I hate that part of me— some awful, curious, hungry part— *wants* to know what happens if I go with him again.

No. no.

"If you'd *move*, I'd like to get up."

He steps back with a mocking little bow. The scent of pine and smoke curls around me. He's always so *polite*— on the surface. Like a hunter letting the rabbit think it has a chance.

I swing my legs off the bed and scan the room. I need a weapon. A pencil. A shoe. Anything. My backpack lies nearby. Useless. But I grab it anyway, clutching the strap like it's a lifeline.

Galin watches, clearly amused.

"Are you ready?" he asks again.

"I'm not going with you."

He sighs like I'm a stubborn child refusing bedtime. "We have gone over this already. You do not have a choice."

"You saying that doesn't make it true."

"Belief isn't required," he says with a shrug. "Only compliance. Will you come, or must I take you?"

"I'll never go willingly."

His face doesn't change. "You have made your decision."

I swing the backpack at him. It barely leaves my hand before everything tilts sideways. The air turns cold, black smoke curling around my legs and wrists like ropes.

And then I'm gone.

My stomach lurches as we come to an abrupt stop. Galin stands across from me, openly mocking the seasick sway in my legs with a smug grin.

"Would you stop doing that?" I snap, though my voice still wobbles.

"You made your choice. We travel according to your willingness. There is nothing I can do about your decisions."

"And if I'd actually agreed to go with you?" I fold my arms. "Would you have chauffeured me in a pumpkin carriage instead?"

"Perhaps I would have shown you the way Under the Hill."

I arch a brow. "Right. Because honesty is your strong suit."

He shrugs. "It is your choice to doubt."

We're not in the creepy, soul-sucking chamber this time. Instead, I'm back in his room— if you can call it that. The fire crackling in the hearth casts soft flickers of light across the stone walls. The shadows still dance, but they seem indifferent to me here. Small blessings, I guess.

"So," I say, trying to keep my tone neutral. "What's your plan tonight?"

Galin sinks into a leather wingback chair like a man settling into power. "That depends entirely on you."

"You kidnapped me. Don't pretend this is a team effort."

"You have refused to complete the task I brought you here for. You have found power in our bargain, but offer me none in return. I am without recourse."

The way he says it makes something crawl down my spine. His words don't sound like a lie, but they don't feel like the full truth, either.

I inhale the warm scent of woodsmoke, but it doesn't

soothe me. It reminds me too much of him. Wild. Inviting. Dangerous.

"And what will you do now?"

"I already have plans." He brushes imaginary dust from his shirt sleeve.

"You have plans?" Doubt tinges my voice. "Let me guess. You're off to another secret meeting with shadow monsters?"

He smirks. "A party, actually."

I snort. "Of course. Because kidnappers deserve a social life."

Images of the room he brought me to yesterday flit through my mind. Cue the stress sweat.

"You are not here for my entertainment," he says, frowning like I've insulted him. "You are a solution."

"Charming," I mutter. "You really know how to make a girl feel valued."

"Regardless." He slaps his thighs with open palms. "I must go."

I try not to react, but the thought of him leaving me alone here— again— hits hard. This place is too quiet when he's gone. Too alive.

He watches me shift, picking up on my hesitation like blood in the water. "Would you like to accompany me?"

His body is stiff, as if expecting— or hoping— I'll say no.

I want to say no. I want to tell him to burn in whatever magical furnace he crawled out of. But being alone in this palace, surrounded by who-knows-what, isn't a better option.

I shake my head to ground myself. This isn't attraction. This is survival. He's the least monstrous thing I've met here— so far.

"I did not think it was a good idea for you to come with me anyway-"

"I didn't say I wouldn't go," I say, rubbing my arm. "I was shaking my head at the absurdity of all of this. You wouldn't understand."

Galin tilts his head. "Do I take that as a yes?"

"You asked," I say, forcing a smile. "Now you're stuck with me."

He looks like he wants to argue, but doesn't. Instead, he retreats into a wardrobe and pulls out a black shirt laced with delicate silver embroidery. He strips off the one he's wearing without a hint of self-consciousness.

I twist away, embarrassed by the heat rising to my cheeks. It's stupid. He's a supernatural creep with dubious morals. But that doesn't stop the rush of adrenaline, or how my eyes want to glance back.

He finishes dressing and walks toward me, all elegant menace. I glance down at my uniform, no longer painfully out of place.

"That uniform will not do," he says, eyeing me like I'm some failed art project.

"I'm sorry my kidnapping wardrobe didn't meet your standards." My words are confident, but I know my blush is still permanently staining my cheeks.

"You need something more appropriate."

"And I assume you have just the thing hanging in your magical closet?"

Without answering, he disappears into the wardrobe—literally disappears. One second he's there, the next he's just... not. My brain doesn't like it. Reality ripples.

He reemerges with a dress so pale a purple that it's almost grey, with silver threads woven through it in tiny stitches that make the dress appear to sparkle like stars. He comes toward me with a grin on his face. I take it from him and try to hide the shaking of my hands.

The dress is more delicate than it looks, and my hands stay open, afraid to actually hold it. The material feels almost weightless, as if I let it go, it will simply keep drifting towards heaven. And the smell... it's like it's come straight out of a flower shop.

I want to hate it, but it's beautiful. Unsettlingly beautiful.

"Put it on," he says.

I stare at the material helplessly. "There's no zipper. Or seams. What am I supposed to do?"

There's no way my body will fit through this as is. I'm pretty slender, but there's a few curves that need a little extra give.

"Do you require assistance?" he asks, stepping closer, his voice velvet and warning all at once.

"I'd prefer you vanish and let me figure it out," I mutter, but my hands won't stop trembling.

He doesn't move.

Fine. I strip, facing away, cheeks burning. I don't turn around, not even when I feel the whisper of the dress slip over my skin like mist. It fits perfectly. Of course it does.

When I finally turn, he's not looking at me. My confidence sags.

"Is it okay?" I ask against my better judgment.

"The dress is acceptable," he says. "Your hair, however..."

"Yeah, yeah. Next time I'll book a glam team."

But something about the way he said 'uniform' earlier sticks in my head. "How do you know it's a school uniform?"

"You attend boarding school, do you not?"

I narrow my eyes. I don't remember telling him that. Did I? And even if I did… not in the app. He shouldn't know that. Unless he's been watching me for longer than I thought.

"Shall we go then?" he asks, offering his arm.

I hesitate, then loop mine through his. The dress trails like starlight behind me. A shiver runs up my spine at the warmth of his arm against mine. Part of me wants to smile — just a little. The other part screams at me not to let my guard down. But even as my mind warns me, my heart skips, betraying me in the smallest, undeniable way.

He opens the door and leads me into the opulent hall-way. I scan for any sign of something. What though, I'm not exactly sure. A glitch in the matrix? A door with an exit sign over it? The idea of something like that here almost makes me want to laugh. Almost. If I weren't here against my will, then I think I could laugh. As it is, I'll keep looking for my escape no matter how nice things look.

Everything glitters— walls, chandeliers, floors. It should feel magical, but it doesn't. It feels like a trap with extra sparkle.

Trailing my hand along a vine-draped wall, I flinch when Galin whispers, "I would not touch that."

"Seriously? I can't touch *plants* now?"

"They're not all plants," he says with a grin. "Nearly everything here has teeth."

Perfect. A palace full of biting walls. I yank my hand back and keep it close.

The dress floats around me like mist, soft and enchant-ing. I hate how much I love it. I hate that it makes me feel beautiful, like I belong. I don't belong here. This isn't mine. None of it is real.

We turn a corner— and I'm face-to-face with the same

double doors from yesterday. Sweat prickles along my neck. This is where I could have easily died if Galin hadn't come back for me. What will I do if he leaves me behind or forgets me tonight? Is the party he's leading me to the same one we left behind last night? Is there just one big revel going on that he deigns to visit on occasion? That does seem like something that would fit with his personality.

"Galin," I whisper, but he doesn't hear me. Or maybe he does and doesn't care.

The side grin is etched into his face, dark eyes glazed over as he throws open the door and leads us inside.

Chapter Five

Music like a hundred reed flutes screeching at once fills the air— not like sound, but like pressure, like it's pushing into my skin and squeezing behind my eyes. Galin moves forward without pausing, like the dissonant wall of noise doesn't even register for him. Of course it doesn't.

If possible, the room is even darker than before. The creatures inside are more shadow than substance, slithering and shifting shapes that blur if I look too long. A low fog curls along the floor, licking at ankles, hiding where the dancers' feet meet the earth— or whatever this floor is made of.

Tabitha lounges on a throne at the far end of the room, set up high enough for her to enjoy watching the spectacle of her subjects as they writhe to the music. She watches the chaos with the bored delight of a queen at a gladiator match. Her dress tonight is the color of dried blood and black flowers weave through her perfect curls like they just grew there. She's immaculate. Terrifying.

And I hate how beautiful she is. She sits up there—

dark, dangerous, divine. She's the kind of woman you admire from afar but never try to become.

But there's something about her that reminds me of my mom... I push the thought down, my chest aching at just the thought of her. Of mom. She would've warned me not to touch anything. Not to trust anything. *Not to dance.*

Tabitha's eyes flick over me and Galin like we're dust motes in a sunbeam. Not worth attention. Good. My nerves are barely holding on by a thread.

I'm so focused on Tabitha that I don't notice Galin leave.

I spin around. "Galin?" The fog seems thicker now. "Seriously? You brought me here and just— vanished?"

He wouldn't leave me to die. Would he? I mean, I haven't exactly been cooperative, but... I must be useful. Or at least entertaining.

A hard shove hits my back, and I stumble forward, thrust into the mass of moving bodies.

Wings. Fangs. Skin painted in colors that glistens like poison flits before my gaze as I struggle to breathe. Hands with too many fingers. A blur of light and sound and movement surrounds me.

I can't breathe.

Something— someone— grabs my hand. A creature with skin like snow, not just in color but in temperature and texture. Not cold— just... soft. Untouched. He pulls me forward. I try to resist but my legs betray me. They begin to move, not my way, but *theirs*— like they've learned some ancient rhythm. The dress Galin gave me billows around my body like a comet's tail. I should be terrified. I should be fighting.

But I'm smiling. I'm spinning. Light pulses through me in time with the music— if it can even be called that.

There's no melody, no beat. Just *need*. Joy without reason. Motion without meaning.

I dance.

And I dance.

I dance with creatures that look like animals. Like moss. Like flame. Some have hands. Some don't. One of them has the face of a goat with the square pupils to match. Sometimes we don't touch— we just *writhe* near each other, synching to something older than breath.

And then I'm alone.

Spinning. Spinning. I don't even remember what it felt like to stand still. My feet aren't mine anymore. My mind is floating somewhere far behind my body, tethered only by the thinnest thread of self.

There's nothing before this. No school. No father. No Galin. Not even Mom.

No.

No. That's not right.

A face swims into view. Sweat beads across his forehead. Light brown curls twist around horns that curl like question marks behind his ears. His face is kind. Wild. Worrying. His upper half is that of a man in a fur coat, with the lower half like a goat, complete with hooves. A faun. Or something like it.

He waves a hand in front of my face. I barely react.

He grabs me.

And *pulls*.

I try to dance around him. Keep moving. But his grip is firm. And the more I resist, the harder he pulls. My steps become jerky, off-beat.

With one final yank, he tears me from the crowd.

The moment we break free, the spell snaps.

I collapse into myself, chest heaving. My sweat is cold. I

look down— and nearly gag. My shoes are shredded, like I just hiked the Appalachians. Ruined. I can't even imagine beginning to explain this to my father.

The faun watches me. He rubs one arm, like he's afraid I'll hit him.

"Thanks," I say, voice hoarse. "For getting me out of there."

He nods, still not meeting my eyes.

"I don't get it. What happened?"

Maybe that's a stupid question. He's looks at me like I'm crazy.

"Mortals cannot leave the dance of the Folk," he says gently. "Once they start, they will never stop."

"Wait. You mean... dance until I *die*?"

He winces like I said something rude. "Yes."

He looks at me with a pitying expression, like I'm a baby that doesn't know how dangerous the world around me is yet. My breath catches. He sounds so *sure*. And warm. His voice doesn't match his clawed fingers or hooved feet— it's deep and sweet, like honey and smoke.

"Many a human has joined the dance and never left it alive."

"How did you get me out then?"

He shrugs. "I do not now. You are... strange."

"That's the nicest thing anyone's said to me here," I say dryly.

He almost smiles.

The faun moves to leave, and panic claws up my throat. I shoot out a hand to stop him. We both hesitate, looking at where my hand rests on his furred arm. His eyes go wide, and I release him.

"Please— don't. Don't leave me alone," I whisper.

He freezes.

"You should not be seen with me," he says.

"Too late. I think we're past the point of subtlety."

He glances around, as if someone might be watching. Probably is.

"Please." I don't even recognize my voice. It's small. Raw. "I keep screwing things up. I don't know the rules here. I just… I don't want to die."

"You are like a baby," he says with a sigh.

"Worse," I say, lips twitching. "Even babies don't try to outdance death."

He tilts his head. "You are strange," he repeats. "But I will stay. For now."

"What's your name?"

He hesitates.

"You can just give me a nickname," I offer. "Something not magical. I promise I won't use it against you."

"Cillian," he says after a moment.

"Cillian," I repeat, the word strange in my mouth. "Is that your real name?"

He takes a step back, eyes so wide I can see the whites all around the pupil. "You cannot have my real name."

"Okay, okay! I'm kidding. Sort of." I hold up my hands. "I'll just call you that. No strings."

"Okay." He nods, not looking any more relaxed.

"So, is there anything else I should know? You know— besides the whole 'don't dance or you'll die' thing?"

He looks around, solemn. "Do not eat. Especially not the fruit."

"What fruit?" I ask, glancing around. There's nothing edible in sight. Just fog and teeth and shadows.

But he's already gone, melting into the crowd like smoke. My body twitches, wanting to follow him, but there's no way I'm going through that again. What will happen to me if I end up dancing and no one is there to pull me out? Will Galin eventually find me, or will he let me dance until I'm a broken pile of blood and bones? There's no way I'm going to get close enough to find out.

Looking around, I don't even know what food Cillian could be talking about. It's not like there's a buffet table set up for all the partygoers. All that's on the floor are the dancing creatures, no tables, no signs directing us to food. Just darkness and fog and bodies. Why bother to warn me about the food if it's not even an option? It'd be like me telling him to stay away from high heels.

The image of his little hooves trying to balance in heels makes me snort, a laugh slipping out of me before I can stop it.

"Having a good time?"

The voice behind me freezes the smile on my face. Galin.

Of course he's here. Of course he saw.

I swivel on stiff legs. He stands half in shadow, his eyes catching the light just enough to glint with amusement. He looks like the prince of a nightmare. Regal and impossible.

"You know the answer to that."

"I thought you wanted to come to the party," he says mock-injured.

"With you. *With.* You disappeared and I almost became a cautionary tale."

"I have kept an eye on you. You were never in any real danger."

"You let me get caught in a *fairy death rave*?"

He shrugs. "Some mortals enjoy it."

"Well, I'm not 'some mortals'."

"Clearly."

He doesn't look sorry. But his voice softens. "Are you ready to go home?"

The word hits hard. Home.

I nod, jaw clenched. My eyes sting. *Don't cry. Don't give him the satisfaction.*

He offers his arm. I take it.

His warmth grounds me. I cling a little tighter than I should.

We walk together, and I try not to see the strange creatures watching me. Judging. Laughing.

I keep my head down. I look broken. But I'm not.

Not yet.

I'm not broken.

Galin is silent beside me as he leads us back to his room. The hall are empty, but the ivy lining the walls shifts as we pass, curling inward like it wants to taste us. I shiver, remembering what he said about the vines. *Alive. Watching. Dangerous.*

My steps quicken. I don't let myself crumble the moment we step through his door, but it's close. The stone is warm, scented with pine and firewood and something darker— like rich soil or wet stone. It's stupid how safe it smells. Like the one camping trip I went on before Mom died, bundled in a too-big hoodie and eating burnt marshmallows by the fire.

I *hate* how badly I want to sit on the floor and breathe that in. Instead, I square my shoulders and lift my chin, trying to reassemble whatever scrap of dignity I've got left.

Judging by the amused flick of Galin's mouth, it's not working.

He settles into the chair by the fire with that same impossible grace, one knee crossed casually over the other, his sharp eyes glittering. He tilts his head at me like I'm a puzzle he half enjoys solving.

"Are you settled in your curiosity now?" he asks.

My eyes narrow. "What's that supposed to mean?"

"You have observed the parties. You've danced with the Folk. Participated.

Indulged. Are you satisfied?"

I cross my arms, too defensive, too raw. "I didn't follow you for curiosity."

His gaze doesn't move from mine. I can feel it. Hot, unrelenting, holding me in place.

"I went with you for safety," I blurt.

The second it leaves my mouth, I want to pull it back in. My stomach drops. Why did I say that? Why did I admit it?

His expression doesn't change much, but something shifts. The tilt of his body.

The intensity behind his eyes. He leans forward, elbows on his knees, the firelight catching the sharp lines of his cheekbones, making him almost seem alive with quiet heat.

"You associate me with safety?"

I don't answer. There's no good answer. Silence stretches between us like a thread pulled too tight.

"You're not the first," he says softly. "But you may be the first who actually means it."

I swallow, hard. He doesn't sound smug. He sounds... confused. Like he doesn't know what to do with the weight of my words.

"That is a very precarious instinct, little mortal," he

says, more to himself than to me. "Have I not warned you? I am every bit as dangerous as I am beautiful."

I roll my eyes before I can stop myself. "Maybe I don't find you very beautiful."

A weak defense. Because the truth is, his closeness unravels me, and I feel it all too keenly.

He stands slowly, his steps silent, predatory. I flinch but don't move as he stops in front of me. His hand lifts to my chin, fingers cool and deliberate as he tilts my face up to meet his gaze.

His voice drops low. "One wrong move, and I could leave you in a puddle of your own blood."

I stare up at him, throat dry. The moment holds, unbearably still, and beneath the edge of threat, something lingers—electric and almost tender.

He sighs, almost to himself. "Perhaps they added too much dust to the application."

"Huh?" The word squeaks out of me.

Galin releases my chin with a flick, like I'm something easily discarded. "Never you mind. Just watch yourself, little human."

The warmth in the room disappears. But for a heartbeat, the pull remains.

Everything blurs— his body, the firelight, the walls. Shadows spin like water down a drain, I'm falling, spiraling into darkness.

"Geez, what is with you lately?"

Joan's voice cuts through the quiet like a slap. I blink at her from my bed, squinting against the pale morning light.

She's halfway into her uniform already, smoothing her nylons up under her navy skirt like she hasn't said something biting.

"What's your problem now?" I mumble, my voice dry and sticky with sleep. I tug the blanket over my chest like it might shield me from her judgment.

Joan snorts. "As if you don't know." She slings her bag over her shoulder while slipping her feet into black kitten-heeled pumps. "Do you *ever* plan on spending a night in your bed again? You think I'm stupid? One of the night watch teachers is going to notice eventually, and I'm not taking the fall for you. I warned you about that app. I *told you* to delete it. You're spiraling, Grace."

"I'm not—"

"Save it. Straighten yourself out or I'll report you myself."

You mean like you tried to do yesterday?

I don't say it. It stays in my head where it belongs, swirling around in the cloud of sleep and dread. I'm glad for the delay in my brain-to-mouth connection. Exhaustion's good for something.

Joan gives me one last hard look, then turns on her heel. Her curls bounce mockingly as the door slams shut behind her.

I flop over, groaning into the pillow.

I *know* what I have to do. I just... don't want to.

Because this isn't a dream. I can't pretend anymore—not when the worn-out Converse peeking from beneath my blanket are still damp with dirt. Not when I still feel the lingering heat of Galin's touch under my skin. Not when I still wake up with his voice in my ears like a song I didn't ask to remember.

He says he's a High Fairy. He says I'm being taken to

another realm. And what's worse— I'm starting to believe him.

The thought alone is enough to make me nauseous.

No, I'll be keeping those little details to myself.

But real or not, he doesn't get to keep stealing me from my life. No one should be able to do that without consequences.

I stare at my phone for a long time before I pick it up, cradling it in my lap. I wrap the blanket tighter around me and let the seconds tick by. I'd wait longer, maybe forever, but I have class soon— and I'd rather die than let Joan hear this call.

With shaking fingers, I press 9-1-1.

The ring barely lasts a second.

"9-1-1, what's your emergency?"

My mouth goes dry. "I...I think I've been kidnapped."

Silence on the other end.

"Are you in immediate danger?"

"No. I mean— no, not right now."

"Do you know where you are?"

"Yes. My dorm. But it's not that simple."

"I need you to explain clearly, miss."

I clutch the phone tighter. "The last two nights, someone's been taking me. Kidnapping me. I wake up back here, but he takes me somewhere else. A... a different place."

There's a pause on the other end and I close my eyes and count breaths.

"You're saying you're abducted nightly and returned before morning?"

"Yes."

"Do you know who's doing this?"

"Yes. No. Kind of. His name is... Galin." I pause. "He thinks he's— he says he's not human."

A pause. A longer one this time.

"Have you been drinking or using any other substances?"

"No. I know how this sounds."

"Are you experiencing delusions or hallucinations?"

"No! I— I have proof. Sort of. My shoes. They're filthy. I come back with dirt, sometimes bruises. I'm *not* dreaming."

I'm not sure who I'm trying to convince.

"I can transfer you to your local police unit," the dispatcher says carefully. "But unless you have clear evidence of abduction or physical harm, they may not be able to help. These lines are prioritized for active emergencies— especially with the ongoing missing girls investigation."

That part hits like a gut punch.

Don't you see? I want to tell her. *I could be the next missing girl.*

"Would you like me to transfer you?" the dispatcher asks again, voice flat.

I glance around the room. My bed is made. No broken windows, no signs of a struggle. Nothing weird— except for the magic I'm not supposed to believe in and the Galin's voice still echoes in my spine.

Worn shoes won't convince anyone. But maybe, just maybe, if I bring something *back* next time...

"No. That's okay," I whisper.

I hang up before she can say anything else. The click sounds too loud in the stillness. My cheeks burn with shame. The call didn't go how I wanted. But it gave me something else: a direction. A plan.

No one believes me. So I'll get proof.

Whatever Galin is— whoever he is— I'll figure it out.

Before I lose myself to him completely.

Chapter Six

I spend all of class completely distracted. But honestly, what else is new?

Joan doesn't say a word to me, which is almost worse than her usual passive-aggressive lectures. Maybe she thinks her warning this morning landed, or maybe she's just tired of trying. Either way, I know I'm doing a great job self-destructing all on my own.

Two days without turning in homework, two days of zoning out during lectures— and apparently, that's the magic number. At least three different teachers pull me aside today, each of them giving me some version of the 'we're concerned' talk. But their concern feels about as useful as a paper umbrella in a hurricane.

But it doesn't matter. None of it matters. Not when I finally have a plan.

What I need is evidence. Proof. Something real enough that someone— anyone— might believe me. Galin will never be stopped if I can't show people he exists.

I have work to do.

By the time lunch rolls around, I'm practically vibrating

with nervous energy. I snag a croissant, skip my usual spot with the others, and settle at a table tucked behind one of the giant stone support beams. Out of sight, out of Joan's hair-trigger concern radar.

I pull a folded piece of notebook paper from my bag and start scribbling between bites.

Step one: I need to bring my phone tonight. *Need.* No way he's going to pause mid-abduction so I can grab it from my nightstand. I have to keep it on me. Maybe tucked in my waistband, somewhere I can reach fast. That way, I can try to record something. A photo. A voice memo. Anything.

Step two: Pictures might not be enough. Galin looks... normal. Weirdly perfect, sure. And maybe glowing but not enough that anyone would believe he's supernatural. And me? I come back every morning looking fine— annoyed and half-asleep, sure, but not injured.

Except... my uniform is still missing from last night. Joan's shirt is trashed. That has to count for something, right? I make a note to gather all of that.

Still, it might not be enough.

My stomach twists. I write it down anyway.

"Let them rough me up a little."

Just enough to show it's not a dream. A scratch. A bruise. Not anything too serious. Not death.

Even writing that feels gross. I want to gag, but I don't cross it out.

Step three: I need to call *while* I'm there. Or at least right before I vanish. If I can catch it live, someone might believe me; they won't if it sounds like some after-the-fact ghost story, especially with the missing girls case going around. They'll just file me under 'panicking teenager'. Which, okay, fair. But still.

I tap my pencil against my paper, chewing the end like it might help me focus. Then I grab my phone and search:

'Real fairy abductions folklore'

Might as well lean into it.

A million results pop up. Stories about people taken to the fae realm, missing time, strange lights, dreamlike states. Changelings. Rules. Warnings. There's even something about never eating their food or you'll be trapped forever.

Thanks for the heads up Cillian.

I glance down at my now half-eaten croissant and scowl. "Please don't let the cafeteria count as fairy food," I mutter.

There's one line that sticks with me, bolded in an old Celtic legend recap:

"Those taken by the fairies often feel drawn back—like a spell, or a promise they can't remember making."

My hand tightens around my pencil.

That's the part that scares me most. Because for all the panic and plans and late-night dread, part of me *wants* to see Galin again.

He terrifies me. But when I'm near him, it's like gravity shifts. Like I've known him longer than I've known myself.

I don't like what that says about me. About my brain. Or my heart.

Tonight will be the test.

Dinner tastes like cardboard and I eat it anyway.

Joan finds me halfway through it, plopping her tray

down with theatrical annoyance and eyeing me like I've grown an extra head.

"Okay. What's going on with you?"

I blink at her, halfway through chewing a too-dry piece of chicken. "What?"

She arches a brow. "You've been acting like a zombie all week. Your bed's cold. You've been weird. And now you're eating mystery meat alone like someone in a sad boarding school drama."

I shrug. "Maybe I'm just tired of you."

She snorts. "Cute. But I'm serious. If something's going on, you can talk to me."

"Oh yeah?" I lean forward, voice lower. "You're not going to rat me out the second you think I've broken a rule?"

"If it's real trouble, no," she says, her pout too rehearsed to be convincing. "But if you're sneaking out to parties and not inviting me? Then yes, absolutely."

Of course. Because for Joan, betrayal is less about danger and more about exclusion. If I was at some rager downtown and didn't tell her, she'd burn the place to the ground out of spite.

"I'm not going to any parties," I lie smoothly. Not the kind she's imagining, anyway. I've been dragged to ballrooms and thrones and flickering candlelit halls. But I didn't dance for fun, and I never got to leave on my own terms.

"Promise?"

"Promise."

She narrows her eyes like she's trying to read my thoughts. Good luck. I don't even understand what's happening to me.

"Then what's going on?"

"Nothing."

She doesn't believe me. I can tell from her scowl. But after a second, she sighs and stands, tossing her tray into the bin. "Fine. Keep your secrets. I'll figure it out myself."

I don't answer. I just watch her join her friends near the cafeteria exit, laughter trailing behind her like perfume. I should feel relieved she's gone, but all I feel is... alone.

As I push the remains of my dinner around with my fork, a new thought creeps in: *Maybe I shouldn't go back to my room tonight.*

Maybe I should stick with a crowd. Hide in the noise. The cafeteria is packed, full of witnesses and bright lights and that uncomfortable hum of too many conversations. He wouldn't dare take me here. Would he?

But I have a plan. I have to follow it.

Still, I move slowly— almost hoping something, anything, will delay me. The long stone halls are quiet this time of evening, the schools' ancient bones creaking with age. My shoes click against the checkered floor, the red runner muffling most of it. I climb the two flights of stairs like I'm heading toward my own execution.

My room waits at the end of the hall, dark and yawning like an open mouth.

I stop before the door, staring at it, like it might move. I don't want to go in. my whole body hums with the feeling that *something is wrong*. Like if I cross that threshold, I won't be me anymore. I'll just be another missing girl with an unbelievable story no one listened to in time.

I turn around, every step feeling like I'm trudging through sludge as I make my way back to the stairs. The hallway feels longer now, stretched by dread. I can hear laughter from a group of girls as they make their way toward me. I open my mouth to call out to them, the air around me smelling like stale perfume and old dust.

"You are late for our appointment."

Galin stands just feet away, more shadow than man in the flickering hallway lights. He looks out of place in a way that *somehow fits*— like this building was made for creatures like him, not students like me.

I clench my fists, my fingers stiff and slow. "You shouldn't be here. Someone could see you."

His lips curl into a smirk. "Is that what you're hoping for?"

"Maybe," I say. "Maybe I thought being around people would make it harder for you."

He tilts his head, amused. "Did you think I couldn't clear a room?"

I glance back toward the stairs— but the noise is gone. No laughter. No students. The hallway behind me is empty.

I whip around to face him again. "What did you do?"

"Nothing permanent." He steps closer. "You didn't really think safety was a simple as being seen, did you?"

I clench my jaw. "Let's just get it over with."

He gives me a mock bow, wicked and elegant. "As you wish."

The shadows around the hallway pulse and stretch, and then they reach for me.

The last thing I see is the glint in Galin's eyes— something between hunger and fascination— as the darkness swallows us both.

I'm not even impressed anymore when we land in Galin's room.

Maybe I should be. Maybe the fact that I'm starting to accept how *not human* he is should fill me with wonder— or fear, or *something*— but mostly? I'm just tired. Too many nights with too little sleep have worn away the awe. All I feel now is the weight behind my eyes and the dull throb of a growing headache.

"So," I say, dragging out the word as I flop into Galin's ridiculously elegant chair, "what are we doing tonight?"

He watches me with that unreadable expression he's so fond of, one eyebrow arched like I'm a puzzle he hasn't quite decided is worth solving. "I have business to attend to tonight."

I blink slowly. "What kind of business?"

"Nothing I will concern you with." He smooths the collar of his black tunic like that's the final word.

Ah. *That* kind of night.

I rub my temples and force myself not to sigh too loudly. "And what exactly am I supposed to be doing while you're off doing mysterious fairy business?"

"You may do as you wish," he says with a shrug, already moving toward the door. "Though I suggest you remain here. The palace can be... unsafe."

"So I'm free," I say, "but also not free. Got it."

He pauses, one hand on the doorframe. "There are politics at play here that you would not understand."

"Try me."

He offers the faintest smile. "You are a means to an end, Grace."

The words land heavier than I expect, even though I shouldn't be surprised. I cross my arms. "if you needed someone docile and disposable, you really picked the wrong girl."

Galine doesn't answer. He just gives me a faint, mocking bow and shuts the door behind him.

The lock clicks.

I wait a beat, letting my irritation settle before I move. Now isn't the time to fall apart— I have work to do.

Sliding my phone out of my skirt pocket, I press the home button. Nothing. I press it again. Then the power button. Still nothing.

"Come on," I mutter, shaking it slightly like that'll help. Dead.

I suck in a breath through clenched teeth, trying not to hurl my phone at the stone floor. All that planning and I forgot to charge my phone. No photos. No police call. *Perfect.*

Which leaves me with the one step I'd put at the very bottom of the list: get injured.

When I wrote it down, it was more of a last resort— some faint nail marks, maybe a bruise I could fake. Something to make the story stick. Something that wouldn't hurt too much.

But now? Now it's the only thing I have left.

I glance toward the fireplace, empty and cold, then to the door. The air in here feels thick, like the room is holding its breath.

The ballroom. That's where the real action is. Where the beautiful monsters gather and laugh like they're in on a joke no one else gets. If I want real proof— if I want out— I have to go in.

My hands shake.

I clench them into fists.

I can do this. I have to. No one's going to believe a tired girl with wild eyes and no evidence. They'll chalk it up to stress or fantasy or worse.

And I *will not* be just another girl who disappears.

I square my shoulders and smooth down my shirt. I don't feel brave, but I can look it. That's a start.

The doorknob is as cold as a corpse.

And I turn it anyway.

The hallway is empty. I don't think I've ever seen anyone else in here but me and Galin. I should be glad he's not waiting. I doubt he'd be thrilled about me wandering off. Not that I care what he thinks.

Because I don't.

...Right?

The music from the ballroom is louder than I remember. It pulses through the air, deep and slow, like a heartbeat you don't want to hear. My body draws back, my feet still moving forward.

This feels more dangerous than last night. More dangerous than any night before. There's something behind those double doors Galin didn't want me to see. I know it— in my spine, in the prickle crawling up my neck.

And in the fact that he didn't invite me.

But I don't have any other options.

The door opens on silent hinges, and I slip inside. Darkness swallows me, but there's just enough light to make out the twisting forms on the dance floor. My gaze lifts to the throne.

Tabitha sits on it like she owns gravity. Even in the

shadows, her silhouette is unmistakable. But tonight... she's not watching the dancers.

There's a line. A line of couples stretching across the ballroom, cutting the dance floor in half. Pressing my back to the wall, I watch, curiosity settling over the fear that's been crawling up my throat since I got here.

I recognize some of the creatures in line— the ones that don't try to hide what they are. Horns. Wings. Tails, fur. But next to them are others with human-looking shadows... and I know that can't be what they are. Not here.

The line moves slowly. At the front, elegant figures step up to Tabitha's throne. They speak to her in low voices, then peel off, disappearing into the dark.

From my place in the back I'll never figure out what's going on.

I start forward, carefull to avoid any motion that might look like dancing. That would be the worst way to die— crushed under some ancient dance curse before I even learn what this is. I tell myself I'm just here to get jostled a little, maybe spot Galin, then get out. No big deal. Just keep moving. Just keep breathing.

No one looks at me. That's worse, somehow. The mood is darker tonight, the music more jagged. This is the part in the horror movie where I'd yell at the screen: *Don't go in there*. But I've already gone in.

And this isn't a movie. This is my life.

And if any of these creatures actually *did* look at me, I don't think I'd leave with my body in one piece. Maybe not at all. I can already imagine Joan's face if they dumped my corpse on the floor of our room like a broken toy.

The closer I get to the throne, the heavier the air smells — sharp and metallic, like old blood and iron. I veer off to the side, careful to stay out of the line's path. There's a long table draped in something that *looks* like lace but clings like cobwebs. Of course, it's cobwebs. Delightful. These people are such freaks.

I crouch behind it, lifting the edge just enough to peek through. Tabitha glows. Her dress is some impossible mix of darkness and starlight, illuminating her face with an eerie shimmer.

A dryad steps forward— no hiding what it is— tugging along a second figure on a silver leash. Tabitha doesn't look at the dryad first. She looks at the other person. And her smile is the kind that would curdle milk.

She turns her attention to the dryad. They speak quietly. Then the dryad drops to its knees, leafed hands raised in a pleading gesture. Tabitha nods to someone on her left. Shadows shift. Guards emerge and take the leash, dragging the second figure away.

I lean in, trying to see. Whoever it is, they have a limp. Their movements are stiff and small, like they haven't been allowed to move in days. Torn clothes, dull brown hair hanging like wet string. Definitely not like the other fairies. Not dressed up. Not pretending.

Another pair steps forward. Same pattern. Then another.

I watch three more go by, and I still have no idea what's happening.

"You should not be here."

The voice right by my ear nearly sends me into orbit. I slap a hand to my chest and spin around.

"Cillian? Are you trying to kill me?"

"You should not be here tonight," he repeats, low and serious.

I press myself tighter to the table, ignoring the cobwebs

sticking in my hair. "I didn't exactly ask for a formal invitation."

"Galin brought you?"

"No, well-"

"Then you need to leave. Now."

I fold my arms, heart still racing. "Funny how you people are so good at dragging me into things, but so bad at explaining them. I already told Galin I'm not just going to do what I'm told. I'll tell Tabitha that too if I have to."

His eyes go wide. "Keep your voice down. If she notices you..."

He doesn't finish. He doesn't have to.

It's the fear in his face that stops me— not the threat. His forest green eyes are fixed on mine, not angry, just... worried. That same quiet protectiveness from last night, when he pulled me off the dance floor. He doesn't owe me anything. But he still came for me.

"I don't want to die here," I whisper, voice low and steady, even if the fear inside me is anything but. "What should I do?"

Cillian scans the room, lips pressed in a grim line, like he's just realized he's now in charge of my survival. His gaze catches on Tabitha, and his shoulders dip slightly. He's going to help me. Whether he wants to or not, I can see the decision settle in his expression. He didn't pull me off that dance floor last night just to abandon me now.

"Follow me," he says.

He gestures for me to keep close, weaving silently through the crowd toward an ivy-covered wall. I keep my hands stiff at my sides, ignoring the itch to brush the ivy like I would have a few days ago. I remember what Galin said about how every-thing here has teeth. Walking with Cillian now, Galin's threats feel less like exaggerations and more like warnings I should've taken seriously. There's something about having a literal faun as your guide that makes all the fairy tale dangers hit harder.

The trek across the room feels longer than when I entered. I keep glancing back at the line of prisoners still inching toward Tabitha's throne. I want to ask Cillian what it means, but even if he heard me, now isn't the time. Maybe later. Maybe when I'm safe in Galin's room.

Safe. In Galin's room.

I could slap myself. Those words have no business being strung together. And yet, somehow, here we are.

We're only steps from the ballroom doors when something massive and rocky steps into our path. It's twice as tall as Cillian, with skin like crumbling stone and eyes that glow like burning coals. I freeze, stomach flipping. Cillian, however, stands still— calm, even. He lifts his chin to meet the creature's gaze, expression unreadable.

"Leaving so soon?" the creature rumbles, his voice like an avalanche. His horns curl back over his skull, inch-long spikes jutting from his spine like jagged glass.

"Unless I'm needed elsewhere."Cillian's voice is smooth but hollow.

My stomach sinks. I don't know what game they're playing, but it's clear Cillian's giving ground— and that scares me.

"You know what I like," the creature purrs around a mouthful of fangs. "And it will not fetch itself."

Without a word— or even a glance at me— Cillian melts back into the crowd.

My mind stutters. Do I stay here with this fanged thing and hope for mercy, or follow the guy who didn't bother telling me his plan? Easy choice.

I shove into the crowd after Cillian. The creature hasn't

looked at me, and I don't want to give him a reason to. I'm betting he doesn't do polite conversation.

Cillian slips effortlessly through the dancers, but the moment I follow, the crowd swallows me like quicksand. He's a few heads ahead— then gone. I push forward, people jostling me, ignoring the pit blooming in my stomach. I should've stayed by the wall. Or with the creature. Or not come at all.

I duck between two towering beasts, only to feel something snag. I turn with a gasp, heart thudding. Not the creature— not again. Just a dancer, completely oblivious, its spiny leg tangled in my skirt.

A few frantic wiggles and I'm free, but now Cillian's completely out of sight. I let out a groan. Of course. Figures the one person who's even *sort of* on my side would lose me the second I need him.

But standing still isn't an option.

I try to retrace the direction he went, shoving forward with renewed urgency. Staying by the wall is no longer an option, not with that creature still lingering.

The crowd pulls at me like tar. I force myself to stand tall, keep moving, and not look scared. Don't let anyone see me panic. My heart beats with the music, faster and louder, like it's trying to drown me. The longer I'm in the center of this room, the more I feel the music dragging at my limbs, tempting me to move. My body remembers the dance, no matter how much I try to forget it. My heart pumps in time to the music, drawing me in. I can feel it in my blood, urging me to move, to join in the wicked throng around me.

But I can't. Not yet. I hold on to the memory of Cillian's face. He'll come back. He has to. With a final push, I stumble out of the crowd near the long banquet table. Fruit gleams under soft light, pastries shimmer with crystallized sugar, and drinks in carved bowls emit curling steam. The display is so heavy that the table threatens to sink in the middle. Cillian stands in front of it, holding a glass and a perfectly round and gleaming blue fruit like he has all the time in the world.

"What are you *doing*?" I gasp, breath coming fast.

He doesn't answer— just turns and walks back through the dancers. I grit my teeth and grab his arm, determined not to lose him this time. The crowd parts again, effortlessly, as if sensing who he is. And now that I'm right beside him, I'm safe in the wake.

The music dulls around us. Like it knows I'm not alone now. Like it knows better than to try.

We reach the edge of the room. The creature waits, eyes glowing red as he turns his attention toward Cillian. Before I can even flinch, he yanks the glass and fruit from Cillian's hands, snarling through flared nostrils like an angry bull.

Then it looks at me.

Claws extend. Spines rise. He reaches—

And Cillian steps between us.

"She belongs to the prince."

The creature grins with cracked lips. "Of course she does."

"You know the penalty for stealing from him."

"I do."

With one last look at me, he moves back through the crowd. I don't realize I'm shaking until I try to speak.

"Thank—"

"What were you thinking?" Cillian snaps.

My words die.

"What?" I ask, voice smaller than I'd like.

"You could have been killed."

He steers me toward the doors. His fingers are firm, not

cruel. I let him guide me, legs moving woodenly. He opens the doors and ushers me through, shutting them behind us like he's sealing off a nightmare.

"What possessed you to go in there *tonight*? Do you have any idea what kind of risk you just took?"

"What's so special about tonight?" I ask, trying to sound clueless.

Cillian mutters a prayer under his breath, like I'm a test of his patience. I cross my arms, resisting the urge to snap back. I might not be a genius, but I'm not an idiot either. I've been doing my best with what little anyone else tells me.

"Tonight is a revel."

"So? Isn't there a party in that room every night?"

"Some are just parties," he says, leaning against the ivy-covered wall. "But once a month, there's a revel. That is when the court shows its true nature. That is when they hunt. If anyone had looked at you long enough, they would have seen you for what you are. And that would have been the end of it."

My face goes cold, but I keep it together.

"You said something like that last time, too. So why should I believe this is any different?"

"Because tonight you wouldn't have danced yourself into nothing..." He hesitates, his little hooves making clicking noises as he shuffles on the tile. "You would have been *harvested*."

"Harvested?"

Something about the way he said it makes it feel like the worst word I've ever heard.

Cillian doesn't elaborate, and I don't push. My stomach turns just imagining it.

He shakes his head, brown curls bouncing against his temples. "I shall take you back to your room."

"My room?" I let out a breathy laugh. "I don't exactly have a reservation here."

Cillian's mouth stretches into a tight, polite smile, but he doesn't answer. He moves fast on his small hooves and I must walk quickly to match his pace as wind down the hallway, away from the chaos of the revel.

"Why are you helping me?" I ask, voice breathless from both the walk and the night.

"I had... strong encouragement." His hand moves briefly to his arm with a grimace. Did Galin send him after me?

He stops in front of a too-familiar door. My stomach dips as he pushes it open, and my feet sink into the plush rugs of Galin's room. Relief floods my body, washing away the last shreds of fear still clinging to me.

Cillian starts to close the door behind him, but I step forward and put a hand on it.

"Wait. Please— just give me something. I can't keep stumbling around in the dark."

I cross my arms, trying not to sound desperate, but it's hard. I need him. He's the only person here who hasn't lied to me or tried to enchant me. Galin may have claimed me, but Cillian is the one who's actually helped me survive.

His gaze softens. He glances down the hall, then back at me. "It is not my place to tell you anything. I am not your master."

I lift my chin. "I have no master."

Cillian's smile is kind and sympathetic on his lightly furred face. "If you truly had no master, you would not be allowed here. No human walks freely Under the Hill without someone powerful behind them. This place is not meant for you."

"Then why am I always in danger here?" My voice cracks more from frustration than fear.

He hesitates. "The protections here are for the fairies. You are not a part of them. Many of the creatures who live in this court— feed off things like you."

I blink, caught off guard. "Feed off...? What does that even mean?"

"I cannot tell you more than that."

"You mean you *don't want to* tell me more than that."

Cillian sighs. "If only it were that simple."

I lean against the door frame, only inches from his face. "Look, if you don't tell me something— anything— I'm going to keep making mistakes. That's not good for either of us. I don't want you constantly risking your life to pull me out of the fire."

He watches me quietly.

"Do you enjoy saving my butt every night?"

He snorts. "At this rate, I shall be forced to save you every time you are here."

I smile faintly. "You don't have to. If I knew even a little about the rules— how things work— I could stop walking into danger with a blindfold on."

His shoulders fall, tension easing a little. He glances down the hall again— still empty. Reluctantly, he extends a hand.

"Follow me."

I clasp his hand without another word. It's smaller than I expected, warm, and covered in short fur. He takes off quickly, and I stumble to keep up, breath catching in my throat.

The hallway darkens as we move away from the torches near Galin's room. This part of the palace is steeped in shadows, reminding me that night actually exists here, even in this strange, magical world.

Cillian slows down, picking his footing with more care as the wild pump of music trickles into the hallway in curling tendrils. I follow suit, trusting his instincts. He hasn't let me down yet.

The stiffness in his back tells me this isn't just caution —it's fear. Whatever he's about to show me, it's something dangerous. Something real. Something even *he* is afraid of.

"Not a sound," he whispers, pressing a finger to his lips. "I cannot tell you. But I can show you."

My stomach drops. I mouth, "*Show me?*" but he doesn't reply.

He slips into the shadows, hugging the wall beneath thick vines and greenery. I follow as best I can, careful not to touch anything. I'm not risking death by an enchanted plant. Cillian might be immune, but I'm definitely not. Galin warned me, and I actually paid attention— for once.

Movement shuffles in the hallway, and I immediately forget my own pep talk and press myself into the wall, plants rustling against my back. Voices echo through the hall, but I can't understand what they're saying. Cillian is stiff as a board beside me; I don't even think he's breathing. I mimic his posture, ignoring my hammering heart.

Black boots step into view, and I hold my breath.

"It has been so long since we could take what we wanted like this," says a voice, sharp and eager.

"Too long under rulers who bowed to human sympathizers. But we were here before the humans— and we will be here after. Why should we hide?"

"Exactly. Humanity has forgotten us. They will live to regret that."

"If the Queen has her way, they will not survive it," the other replies, laughing.

I bite my lip so hard I taste copper, heart racing. I've never really thought about being prey before. But now? I believe every warning I brushed off.

The men stop. One sighs. "If only the Queen were less stingy with the blood. I appreciate all she has bequeathed us, but would it not be better straight from the source?"

"Be patient, we have already been given more than we ever dreamed. Do not ruin it."

"As you say," comes the reluctant reply. "What will you do with your magic?"

They walk away before I can hear the answer. But the damage is done. Blood. Magic. Queens. I don't *want* answers anymore. I just want to be safe. I want to go home.

Cillian tugs my hand. I don't move.

He leans close, his breath warm on my cheek. "We cannot stay. You must come now."

That breaks the paralysis. My limbs unlock and I follow, my sneakers squeaking against the marble floor. Our steps are barely audible now, swallowed by the lingering music.

At last, Cillian reaches across the corridor and parts a thick curtain of vines. Behind them is a small wooden door. He doesn't say anything, just watches me with something like regret in his eyes.

"You will find your answers through here," he says softly.

My hand trembles as I reach for the handle.

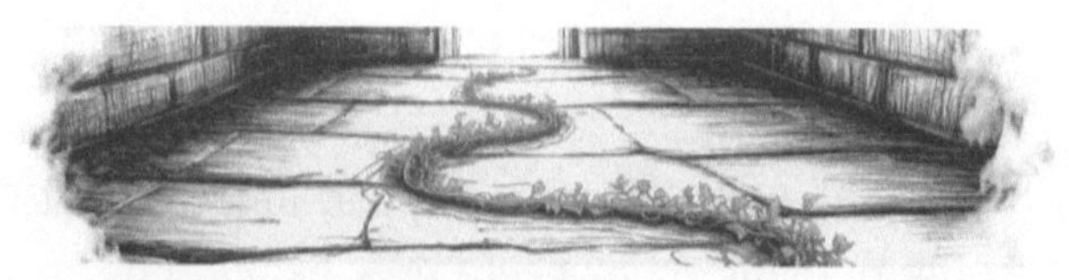

Chapter Seven

The music from the throne room thrums through the walls like a second heartbeat. I crawl into the cramped space Cillian shows me, and he follows close behind, shutting the door fast. It slams like a secret being locked away. He leans against it, one hand braced as if to keep the whole court out, then silently motions me forward.

But forward to what?

The room barely qualifies as such— it's more like a forgotten closet. The plaster walls are smudged and close, the ceiling low enough that I can't stand up straight without bumping my head. The back wall is paneled in old, dark wood, dry and flaking. There's no furniture, no light source, no sign of anything remotely helpful. No answers. Just air that smells faintly of mildew and dust.

I shoot Cillian a look. He doesn't meet my eyes, just nods again for me to go ahead.

Fine.

I take a breath and press my hands against the back wall. Cool wood, dry beneath my fingertips. I inch forward, toes nudging the baseboard. It feels like a dead end— until my fingers catch on a knothole, a real one, not just the suggestion of grain. The wood dips, and suddenly my fingertip slips into an opening just wide enough to feel like an invitation. I jerk back on instinct, heart thudding.

I glance over my shoulder. Cillian gives a single, solemn nod.

So this *was* the point.

I lower myself to my knees. Dust coats my legs and palms. There's a faint glow leaking through the knothole now that I'm closer. I lean in, slow and cautious, every inch of me braced for something horrible— like a stick stabbing me in the eye. Or worse. Fairy jokes can be cruel. But this doesn't feel like a joke. Cillian wouldn't have brought me all the way here just to laugh at me. I want to believe that.

I press my eye to the hole.

The view is limited, but the room beyond is nothing like the one we're in. Cold, damp stone lines the walls. A weak greenish light clings to the corners— moss, maybe, or some other strange fungus. It barely illuminates the space, just enough to make out movement.

At first, I can't quite believe what I'm seeing.

A girl leans against the wall directly opposite mine. Her pale hair sticks to her sweaty face, her eyes wide and glassy like a doll's. Her skin is too pale. Her body looks frail, like she hasn't had a proper meal in weeks. I can't recognize her, but there's no mistaking the human parts: normal ears, normal bones. No glamour, no trickery. Just a girl.

My breath fogs against the wood, heart hammering. I press in closer, almost forgetting to be quiet.

There are more figures. A cluster of humans, all slumped and silent. Some sit. Some stand, barely. No one speaks. If this is where humans are kept, why haven't I been tossed in there? Why did Galin dress me in a magical gown and take me to party while they rot in a dungeon?

A door opens on the far side of the room. All of them flinch.

A tall figure enters— hulking, bare-chested, with dark pants hanging low on his hips. I can't make out his face through the gloom. But the way he moves makes my stomach twist: like a butcher entering his shop.

"Who's next?" His voice is a grind of stone and gravel, low and hollow.

He doesn't wait. He grabs the nearest girl. She doesn't scream, but her mouth moves, whispering, "Please, please, no."

Her sneakers kick at the air as he lifts her effortlessly. A tag dangles around her neck— he snatches it, tugging hard enough to tear her tank top.

"A+. Just what we were looking for."

A+. Her blood type?

Oh my gosh.

The girl starts sobbing in earnest as he carries her through the door, which slams shut behind them with finality. The room stills. The other girls don't even look at each other. They just stare. Or cry.

One near the wall closest to me begins to rock, whispering for her mother. The sound is so soft it barely registers, but it cuts deeper than any scream.

I feel sick.

"Cillian," I whisper.

He doesn't move. Doesn't even look at me.

"Cillian, what is this?" My voice shakes, but I keep it low. I need answers, and he's the only one I trust to give them.

Still, nothing. His head snaps toward the wall like he's watching something, or listening to someone I can't hear.

So we're staying quiet. Fine. But I'm dying to ask those girls what's going on. If this is some holding cell, some sick farm for blood donors, they have to know more than I do. They're crying now, quietly, but not aimlessly. They know *why* they're afraid.

A crack from the other side draws me back.

The door opens.

The beast returns, grinning like he's proud of himself, holding the girl's limp body in his arms. She hangs there, still. Too still. Her hair drips onto the floor as he crosses the room and tosses her aside like garbage. Her body lands with a squelch.

No one looks at her. Not even the girls she sat beside. They're frozen, locked in place by terror.

I press in closer, searching for any signs of breath, of life. Nothing moves. I tell myself it's the light— it's too dim. I must be missing it.

The creature shifts, giving me a clear view into the semi-lit room behind him. I have to press my fist against my mouth to stop myself from screaming. In the center of the room is a stand that looks like an old-fashioned altar made from black gleaming stone with an axe leaning against it. Down the altar runs a river of red flowing into a metal bucket below. I glance at the limp girl and back at the red trickle running down the stone. Blood.

"Who is next?" the creature snarls.

The grin on his face is a thing made of nightmares. One girl breaks. She starts sobbing, backing herself into the wall. The beast sets his sights on her.

I can't watch this.

I stumble back, breath snagging in my throat. My legs

kick against the floor, and I try to crawl away, but panic is a thick thing in my veins now, choking reason.

Strong arms catch me before I hit the far wall.

Cillian.

His arms wrap around me, firm and steady. I freeze, my face pressed against the rough fabric of his shirt. He holds me there, not saying a word, just... being there. His eyes stay on the wooden wall, like he doesn't need to see what I saw — he already knows.

That's the part that shatters me.

I jerk back, scrambling out of his grip, landing hard on the floor as I scoot away, breath coming in quick, shallow bursts. I want to be anywhere but here. But even from across the cramped room, I can still hear the screaming. It rings in my head, louder than before, until I'm sure it's echoing off my bones.

I press my palms to my ears like I can force it all out— the sound, the blood, the limp girl's body. But it doesn't help. The screams cut off so suddenly it's like someone slashed the cord between life and noise, and that silence is somehow worse.

A terrible pressure builds in my chest. I have to do something. I have to help. I can't just sit here, knowing what's happening, doing nothing. There are girls in that room. Real girls. Scared and crying and being picked off one by one like cattle. And I'm just... sitting on the other side of the wall like a coward.

Cillian reaches for me again, eyes steady, mouth drawn tight. He motions for us to leave, but I shake my head violently. I can't— not while they're still in there.

"I can't," I whisper, more to myself than him. "I can't leave them."

He doesn't argue. Doesn't scold me or try to explain.

Just exhales a long, tired breath and steps forward. This time, he doesn't wait for permission. He grabs my forearms gently but firmly and pulls me to my feet.

"I'm sorry," he murmurs, and I don't think it's just about dragging me away.

He lifts me with ease and throws me over his shoulder like I weigh nothing, his grip secure even as I go stiff with resistance. I want to fight, to claw at his back, to scream that I'm not leaving without those girls. But I know better. I've already seen what screaming does here.

So instead, I bury my face in my sleeve, silent tears slipping down my cheeks. My fists clench and unclench as he carries me away from the horror, from the blood, from the hopelessness.

The hallway is empty. The palace is hushed, like the walls themselves know not to make a sound. Cillian walks fast, not bothering to hide us in the shadows this time. He knows no one's coming.

When he pushes open Galin's door, he sets me down without ceremony. I collapse onto the cold stone floor, too hollow to even brace myself. My limbs won't hold me. I feel like I've left part of myself back in that awful room.

Cillian stands in the doorway, backlit by moonlight, hands at his sides. He doesn't look like a smug trickster. He looks... tired. Haunted.

"Why did you take me there?" I croak. My throat is raw, each word a scrape. "Why would you show me that?"

His shoulders slump. "I'm not permitted to speak about it with humans."

"That's not an answer," I say, hating how weak my voice sounds. "I don't understand. What are they doing to them? Why do they care about blood types?"

"I cannot tell you."

"Why not?"

"Because my Queen forbids it."

There it is again. The Queen. Everyone keeps talking about her like she's some omnipotent being— but I've only seen one person on the throne, and she didn't look ancient or terrifying. She looked like someone who could have been my babysitter. Someone who wouldn't scare anyone in the real world.

"Do you mean Tabitha?" I ask. "She's barely older than me. Why does everyone act like she's some immortal goddess?"

"She is not what she seems," Cillian says softly.

"That is not comforting, you know."

I sit up slowly, every movement aching. "You don't have to do what she says. You don't have to be a part of this."

"If only that were true."

"Is it magic? A spell?"

"Something like that," he replies, and the heaviness in his voice makes it clear he won't elaborate.

I narrow my eyes. "So, you can't tell me anything directly. But you can... what? Give me clues?"

He almost smiles at that. Not a teasing smirk, something quieter. Sadder. "Sometimes a clue is all I can offer."

I glance at the wall again, the image burned behind my eyes. "Well, that one came with a side of lifelong trauma."

His expression shifts, and he actually laughs— quiet, and maybe a little pained— but it's the first real moment we've had that feels *human*.

"I'm not joking," I say, but my voice is lighter now. "I'm going to need, like, decades of therapy."

"I believe that."

"Do you even have therapy here? Or is it all just cryptic riddles and denial?"

Cillian doesn't answer, but the corner of his mouth twitches. That almost-smile again. I'll take it.

"So now what?" I ask after a long pause. "What am I supposed to do with that... *vision of horror* you just showed me?"

"You'll have to decide that yourself."

"Helpful."

He turns like he's about to leave, but I surprise myself by reaching out. "Wait. Do you have to go?"

He stops. "It would be... unwise for either of us if I were caught in these rooms."

"So you'd get in trouble?"

He doesn't answer with words, just shrugs— shoulders drawn inward like a child expecting a blow.

I nod, swallowing the tight knot in my throat. "Okay. Go. I'll figure it out."

He hesitates at the door, glancing back like he wants to say more. But then he steps out and closes it quietly behind him.

And I'm alone— with nothing but the weight of what I saw, and the certainty that something here is *very* wrong.

I slide to the floor and stay there, spine against the cold wall, my legs pulled tight to my chest. The fire crackles on, casting dancing shadows that stretch long and distorted. I can't tell how much time has passed— just that my heartbeat has slowed, and the ache in my chest hasn't.

The door creaks open. I don't look up.

Soft footsteps cross the rug, slow and deliberate. "Is this what happens when humans are left alone with their thoughts for too long? You unravel rather quickly." Galin's voice is mild, amused— but there's something underneath it. A careful note, like he's feeling for the edges of a wound.

I don't respond. I can't. I just stare into the fire until the flames blur. A stack of books leans against the wardrobe. The corner of a red spine catches my attention, and I focus on that. It's easier than facing him.

He crouches beside me, the heat of him curling into my space. "Grace."

Still nothing from me. He sighs, running a hand through his hair— it gleams like water and shifts like it too.

"Are you sick?" he asks, softly now.

He reaches out. His hand hovers before landing lightly on my shoulder, the barest weight of his fingers grounding me. Something about it breaks the dam— I blink, and tears spill down my cheeks.

A wrinkle mars his skin between his brows. "Something happened to you while I was gone."

I nod, just once.

He falls back into sitting, resting his arms on his bent knees. "I told you not to leave while I was gone."

That does it. I clench my jaw and push words through my teeth. "Is that what this is? Some grand experiment? See how fast you can break me?"

His eyebrows lift, not in mockery this time, but surprise.

I surge forward, fueled by anger and something more raw. "What's the point of dragging me here? Are you playing games with Tabitha, or do you just collect people like they're toys? Did it ever occur to you that I have a life before this?"

"Ah," he says slowly, "so it was them."

I blink. "You knew?"

He doesn't answer. That's answer enough. I dig my

fingers into the rug, letting the fibers work their way under my fingernails.

My voice sharpens. "Were you ever going to tell me there were other humans here?"

His expression shifts, a small crease forming between his brows. "Dear girl, do you not know? I do not lie."

"So you're admitting it?"

"I do not lie," he repeats, calm as ever, and somehow that makes it worse. "Fairies cannot lie."

I scoff. "Right. You just speak in riddles and metaphors until I give up trying to understand."

"It is not my fault humans don't ask the right questions."

I jab a finger at him, a weak and shaky thing, but it's all I have. "Then answer this: are those girls in danger?"

His body stills. "Yes."

"And you're okay with that?"

"I did not say that."

"You didn't say anything."

He leans back on his heels, watching me with something I don't understand. It's not pity. Not exactly. It's more like... regret. Or restraint.

"I warned you not to go wandering," he says finally. "Not all parts of the palace are meant to be seen."

"Then why did you bring me here at all?"

He pauses. "You intrigue me."

The simplicity of the statement makes my stomach flutter— and I hate that it does.

I look away. "That's not a good enough reason."

"For a fairy?" he murmurs, tilting his head. "It is better than most."

"I'm not some curiosity," I snap. "I'm not yours."

His eyes darken a shade, and when he speaks, his voice

has gone low and dangerous. "You made a bargain with me, Grace. You are mine. For now."

I want to hate him. But there's something about the way he says my name, like it matters. Like *I* matter.

"Fairies can't lie."

He smiles faintly. "You're learning."

I press my hand to my temple, thinking back over every conversation, every word he's said that felt like nothing but smoke and mirrors. "So you twist the truth instead."

"We find ways to be... selective."

"So when you said I couldn't leave—"

"It was entirely true."

"And you knew I didn't understand the rules."

"Of course." He tilts his head. "But tell me, would you have come with me if you had?"

The honest answer is no. I wouldn't have. But then I wouldn't have known about the others either. I wouldn't be sitting here, shattered and furious and *aware*.

Galin's smiles. Something about it makes him look younger... and even more beautiful. "I never would have guessed that humans were unaware of the strict nature of our agreements."

"Why would you think humans would know anything about you?"

"Humans are obsessed with us," Galin says, leaning back against the wall with an easy grin.

"Humans aren't obsessed with you," I say suddenly, grasping at something solid. "You're not gods anymore. You're barely bedtime stories. Sometimes you're the ones making cookies in trees."

His face twists in horror. "That is slander."

He shakes his head, pulling himself to standing. He runs

his hand through his hair repeatedly until even the long strands stand on end.

"I'm just saying, the world has changed."

"And yet," he says, inching closer, "here you are."

I hate how close he is. I hate how safe I feel when he's this close.

"I want a new bargain."

His brows lift. "Do you?"

"I do."

Galin smiles, his eyes darkening as he pushes off the wall and stalks closer to me. "You are not trying to get away from me, are you, Grace?"

"I wouldn't dream of it," I lie. "I'm just saying that maybe we should enter into an agreement that we're both aware of."

"I do not see how that would benefit me."

I cross my arms over my chest. "There has to be something you want that you haven't been able to get from me that we could switch things up for."

He raises a brow at me and kneels on the rug in front of me, hands loose where they rest between us. I hope he can't see through me.

"There are a few things I would like," he says, his voice deep, his hand creeping a little closer to my leg.

I try to ignore the way his words tickle along my back.

"So, you're willing to bargain with me?"

"Perhaps."

Resisting the urge to groan in frustration, I lean forward on my knees. "What do we do now then?"

He chuckles, the sound low and rich. His smile reveals his pointed canines. "Present your terms."

A log snaps in the fireplace, sending up a spray of red sparks. My breath catches. I remember the blood. I remember the silence that followed the screams. The help-lessness.

I scrunch my eyes closed and wrap my arms around my knees. Pressure builds in my chest as I teeter on the edge of panic. I'm going to end up just like those other girls. Harvested, forgotten, a source of fear for those left behind.

Galin frowns. "What is it? What just happened?"

All at once, I know what I have to bargain for. There's no way he'll give me my freedom. I already know that. Even while wheedling for it earlier, I always knew it was impos-sible. But there *is* something I can bargain for.

"I'd like to propose a bargain."

Galin sits up, the wrinkle still furrowing his brow.

"I want to work for you," I say, my voice shaking but firm. "In exchange, you ensure I remain whole. No lost limbs. No mortal wounds. No death. You protect me from this place."

He blinks. "That is a steep request."

"But not impossible."

His gaze drags over my face, and he scratches at his chin even though his face doesn't have a hint of facial hair. "And in return, you'll do whatever I ask?"

A vision of that nasty stable flits across my mind, but anything is better than becoming one of those girls, waiting for their turn for death.

I take a deep breath. "Within reason."

"Fairies do not deal in reason."

"Then make it a challenge," I say, a smile tugging at my lips despite everything. "If you're so clever, you'll find a way to keep me busy."

He leans forward, his face inches from mine. "You are dangerous when you are clever, Grace."

A tingle runs up my spine. "Deal?"

Galin grins. "Deal."

I reach my hand out for him to shake. He glances at it with a bemused smile and the world goes black.

My vision returns slowly, darkness still clinging to the edges of everything. The familiar outline of my room emerges from the haze, unchanged and deeply, unfairly normal. I don't even bother pretending to hold it together — I throw myself onto the bed like I've been running for miles, yanking the blankets over me in a heap of messy comfort and false protection.

It helps. Not much, but a little. The weight of the covers is something I can understand. Unlike what I've just seen. Unlike what I've done.

I burrow deeper, until the blankets become a cave, until I can pretend there's nothing outside but soft fabric and my own breath. The memories don't go away, not really, but at least down here they feel quieter. There's always some hidden basement in the mind where awful thoughts can sink, for a while.

The door creaks. Footsteps cross the floor. Light, cautious.

"Are you sick or something?" Joan's voice is tentative, unsure.

I seize the opportunity like it's a life preserver. "Yes!" I blurt. "Yes, I'm *so* sick!"

There's a pause. I imagine her blinking in confusion. "Are you sure? You don't sound very sick."

"It's my stomach," I say quickly. "Been upset all night. Couldn't sleep at all."

Joan sighs. It's the sigh of someone who doesn't quite believe me, but doesn't want to deal with it. "You never even came to bed last night."

"I was in the bathroom all night," I lie, willing my voice to sound pitiful through the fortress of fabric. "I swear."

There's a long silence. "Fine. I'll tell our teachers."

"Thanks." The words are muffled but heartfelt.

The door closes. I don't move until I hear her footsteps vanish down the hall. Only then do I let my body unclench, melting into the mattress. The panic uncoils a little, just enough to breathe.

I've bought myself time. A whole day, if I'm lucky. A day to sleep. To think. To figure out what I'm actually up against Under the Hill. There has to be something. Some clue. Some pattern. If fairy tales have rules, then those rules came from somewhere. Someone had to write them down.

I grope for my phone, hoping it isn't still completely dead. Maybe I can do some research. Maybe the internet has more to offer than the vague folklore I grew up with. Maybe there's more there than what I found in my quick search before.

But the screen flares to life instantly, lighting up my little blanket cocoon. I flinch at the brightness— and at the number on the battery icon.

56%

I stare at it. That's not possible. It was dead when I was Under the Hill. Absolutely undeniably dead.

I bury my head in my pillow and scream. Just one long, muffled groan of frustration.

I should've gotten pictures. I *planned* to get pictures. That was the whole point. I had a strategy— get proof, bring it back, figure out what's going on. But somehow, impossibly, the photos aren't there. The battery isn't dead. It's like none of it happened.

Except it *did*. I remember every detail too clearly.

I plug in my phone, though it feels more symbolic than practical. I roll onto my side and let the layers of blanket bury me again, hoping sleep will come.

Time passes in pieces. My sleep is shallow and broken, haunted by dreams I can't hold onto. I wake again and again, sweaty, tangled in sheets that should feel safe but don't. I keep waiting for the comfort of my own room to settle into my bones, to tell my body I'm home, okay— but it never quite happens.

Eventually, I just lie there, staring at the ceiling. There's a long wooden beam across it, the kind I've counted a hundred times when I couldn't sleep. I trace the cracks with my eyes, again and again.

What am I supposed to do now?

I got out. I *survived*. I tricked a fairy, used my wits, kept my life. But that sense of victory is gone now. Replaced by the echo of that axe falling, again and again, in my mind. The scream. The silence that followed it.

I can't stop thinking about the other girls. The ones in that cell. The ones I left behind.

Why are they down there? Why hold so many girls at once? Why the blood on the stone? Is it a ritual? A punishment? Some kind of twisted tradition?

It's not like any fair story I've ever heard. Nothing I've read in books or heard whispered at sleepovers involved blood sacrifices or underground prisons. Most of it was about circles of mushrooms and tricks of the light. Even the scary stuff had rules.

But if I can't trust the stories, I'll have to find new ones. There has to be something in the folklore— maybe old traditions, local legends. I need to understand what I'm dealing with. If I'm going to face it again— and I *will*— I need more than luck.

The light outside shifts. Afternoon sun begins to slope downward, warming the floorboards in golden streaks. I feel the change like a bell being struck. Something inside me hardens. Clears.

I can't leave them there.

I don't know how I'll do it. I don't have a plan, or allies, or the faintest idea how to fight fairies with nothing but a phone and a high school education. But I *do* know this: I won't be able to rest until I try.

They deserve better. All of them.

And if I was clever enough to survive once, maybe I can be clever enough to do it again.

They're going to make it out.

Somehow, I'm going to make sure of it.

Chapter Eight

I use what limited time I have left to research.

Setting my laptop up on my desk, I settle into the rickety plastic chair and take a few deep breaths, grounding myself in the clean stale air. My palms are still damp. My thoughts still scattered. But I need answers. I need *something* solid beneath my feet.

The internet, unfortunately, is not overly helpful. Most searches for 'fairies' pull up the cutesy stuff— tiny wings, glitter dust, flower crowns. Nothing remotely like what I saw Under the Hill. Nothing like Galin.

I don't know *what* he is, but it's definitely not that. Not unless he can shapeshift into a tutu-wearing pixie. I'd pay money to see that, actually. Scratch that— I'd pay a *lot* of money to see that.

I snort quietly to myself to keep going.

A search for 'blood fairies' yields even less useful results. Mostly edgy art and a few dubious RPG fan pages. Nothing about stone altars or sacrifices or imprisoned girls.

I lean back, frustrated, and try to recall what I *have* seen. The fire dancing in Galin's palm when we first met flashes behind my eyes. I refine the search: 'magic fairies'. This time, I get a flood of results— conspiracy theories, ancient folklore blogs, and the occasional crystal healing site with too many exclamation points.

I click on the first one. The background is a moody forest scene and the text is a glowing purple cursive that practically screams 'teen goth in 2008'. But I push past the cringe and read anyway.

Fairies and magic are terms that have always gone together. After all, a fairy without its magic would just be an elf (no offense, Legolas).

There are many theories concerning where their magic comes from. The most basic theory is that it comes from the earth. They absorb magic like trees absorb nutrients. This is the theory I adhere to as it makes the most logical sense. However, this kind of magic comes with its own problems, especially as humanity has taken over the majority of the earth's surface and toxified the ground with their overwhelming amounts of waste.

It's because of this that we find fewer accounts of fairy encounters in our day as opposed to our grandparents. The fairy community, as a whole, is struggling to adapt to the growth of its human counterparts. Fairy reproduction has been complicated at the best of times, let alone in their current struggle. As such, there are fewer fairies than there have ever been, and those that remain are more cautious in their interactions with humans.

I frown.

It's weirdly logical. If their magic is tied to the natural world, maybe that's why they've moved underground. Maybe they *have* to adapt to survive.

But then— how does that explain the sacrifices?

Still, the earth-magic theory sticks in my brain. If their power is drawn from the land, maybe there's a way to weaken it. Or disrupt it.

I tuck that thought away, chewing slowly on a granola bar from my desk drawer as I scroll. Crumbs fall across my lap as the lightly honeyed granola falls apart. At least it has the decency to deteriorate before it can cut the sides of my mouth like a million little razor blades, so that's nice.

I close the page and sit back, trying to digest all the half-information I've collected. None of it tells me what I really need to know: how to fight one. Or more importantly, how to *survive* one.

Because Galin is coming again tonight. And this time, I know better than to think I can weasel out of it.

What will he ask of me next? Scrubbing floors? Shoveling stable muck? Some other humiliating task designed to remind me of exactly how far out of my depth I am?

I sigh and press the heels of my hands into my eyes.

But he *did* promise I'd be safe. He said nothing mortal would harm me as long as I was under his protection. And somehow— I believe him.

I think of the way his voice curled around me like smoke. The sharp lines of his smile. The fire in his palm. The way he looked at me like I was some fascinating puzzle instead of just a scared girl who'd trespassed into his world.

I should hate him. I *want* to hate him.

But something about him draws me in. Dangerous and beautiful and unknowable.

And somehow, I trust him. Not with everything. Not even close. But enough to know that getting those girls out might only be possible if I keep him on my side.

If I survive whatever he asks of me next, maybe I can figure out how to use that strange, tenuous connection to do something that actually matters.

The thought lights a spark in me. I roll my chair over to the dresser and start digging through it, ignoring the neatly folded uniforms and tangled socks until I find what I'm looking for.

A birthday gift. Weird and unexpected. Something my dad gave me and I shoved away without thinking: a silver and black pocketknife, still pristine in its plastic sheath hidden under a previously folded pile of blue underwear.

At the time, I hadn't understood the gift—he was never one to remember birthdays— but now it feels like a lifeline. A tiny piece of control in a world that's spinning way too fast.

Standing in the middle of the room, I flick it open and closed a few times, getting used to the feel of it in my hand. The click of the blade is strangely satisfying. Grounding.

Galin promised I wouldn't be mortally harmed— but that doesn't mean there won't be danger. And if I have to face another clawed creature in a hallway that feels like it's breathing, I want to be ready.

At least it's not pink. That would've been the final insult. Instead, it's sleek and sharp, something that actually *looks* dangerous. Something that says, 'Take me seriously.'

I twist the blade through the air in slow, practiced motions, imagining a future where I don't just survive but *fight back*. Where I'm more than a pawn, more than a sacred girl with a camera and a vague plan.

I'm not going to be a passive observer.

Not anymore.

Especially not after what I saw.

I push the questions about the sacrifices out of my mind. I still don't know why they're doing it, or what they're gaining. But answers can come later. Right now, I need to be ready. I need to know the terrain. I need to gather proof.

The door creaks open and I freeze mid-swing.

Joan stands in the doorway, her eyes wide as they take in the scene: me in a ragged uniform, a knife in hand, my bed unmade and papers scattered.

"What's going on?" she asks slowly, setting her books down with deliberate care.

I close the knife and slip it into my pocket. "Nothing."

"This doesn't look like nothing." She crosses the room and sinks onto her bed, watching me with suspicious eyes. "And I thought you were sick."

"I was," I lie, too quickly.

Joan watches me. Her lips press into a line as her eyes follow the movements of my hand as I unplug my phone and slide it into my other pocket.

"You know you can talk to me, right?" she says, voice softer. "If something's wrong... I want to help."

"Are you sure?"

I nod, eyes on the darkening window. The sunlight is fading fast. My heart kicks up a beat. I've never been taken while someone else was in the room. Joan's always been out when it happens. I wonder if Galin's magic will still work with a witness. I almost *hope* it won't. It'd be the perfect loophole.

I imagine clinging to Joan like a very determined, very traumatized barnacle. She'd never be able to get rid of me. Not without filing an official roommate complaint.

The thought makes me laugh under my breath.

And then, without warning, the world goes black.

.

"Welcome back."

The cold marble floor bites into my spine as my vision returns, colors bleeding in slow waves from the darkness. Galin's voice greets me like a velvet thorn.

I groan and push myself upright. "Are you serious right now?" My voice is hoarse, shaky with lingering vertigo. "You couldn't have waited five more seconds?"

He leans casually against the fireplace, all self-satisfaction and indifference. "Time is slippery here. I didn't realize five seconds would matter so much."

"You took me while Joan was in the room. My roommate," I clarify, in case he's forgotten that I live with other human beings in a world governed by logic and consequence. "She's going to freak out."

He arches an eyebrow, like this is all amusing. Like I'm an overdramatic child playing at espionage. "Is that a problem?"

I clamp my mouth shut. A small part of me is relieved— now Joan will know something's up, and I didn't have to say a word. But the larger part of me is reeling from the reminder: Galin can take me whenever he wants. Wherever I am. Whether I'm ready or not.

That terrifying freedom of his— his total disregard for boundaries— should have me shaking in fury. And maybe I am. But it's tangled with something else. That same magnetic pull I keep trying to ignore. The way his eyes never stay on me too long, but never stray far either.

"Well," he says brightly, like we're just old friends meeting for brunch. He claps his hands once. "Are you ready?"

"For what?"

"You promised you would follow my orders tonight."

"And you promised not to get me killed." I cross my

arms. "You'll understand if I need a little more detail before I start marching to your tune."

His smile tugs higher. "Wise of you."

He strides to the intricately carved wardrobe in the corner — its door etched with weeping willows, so detailed they almost seem to sway. From the bottom shelf, he pulls a long, narrow box and sets it on the bed, motioning for me to open it.

I hesitate. This feels like a trap wrapped in a favor. Like he's luring me into lowering my guard.

But curiosity wins. It always does.

I lift the lid— and blink. Layers of silvery grey gossamer spill out, catching the firelight like moonlight on water.

"What is this?" I ask, though I already know. It's a dress. A very beautiful one. And that's what unnerves me.

"I require your presence tonight," he says, gaze on the steady fire behind me as his fingers pluck at an errant string on his black shirt.

"Define 'presence'," I mutter, staring at the fabric like it might sprout teeth.

He flicks his fingers at me dismissively and leans against the mantle. "Just put it on."

Suspicion coils in my gut like a living thing. But I don't sense danger— not like before. Not the edge-of-the-cliff kind. Just... something else. Something I don't know how to name yet.

The last time he dressed me, it had been someone else's will wrapped in silk. This time, the dress is clearly meant for me. It even has clasps I can reach myself. Small mercies.

I glance back— Galin has turned to face the fire, giving me his back. Respectful, or merely uninterested? The thought stings more than it should.

Still, I strip with practiced haste, tossing my ruined

uniform onto the bed. The dress slips over my head like water. It molds to me— not indecently tight, but close enough to remind myself I have a shape. Delicate silver embroidery spirals around my waist and down the skirt in silver leaves, pooling in a pile at my feet. The sleeves are sheer and fitted, the neckline modest. My hair spills over my shoulders like liquid gold, completing the illusion.

I look like I belong here. Like I could be one of them. That's the most dangerous part of all.

Galin turns. His eyes scan me, expression unreadable. "It fits. Good." He holds out his arm for me to take, but I don't move to take his offered arm.

"You're not taking me back to another *party*, are you?"

The memory slams into me uninvited, making me sway on my feet. I don't think I could handle going back to that room. Not right now.

Galin's brows draw together. "Not tonight," he says, voice quieter. "Tonight, I have business."

"That's supposed to make me feel better?"

He doesn't answer the door. Just opens the door and gestures for me to follow.

I hesitate a second longer, then trail after him.

The hallway beyond is dim and endless, all shadows and silver light. I jog to keep up with his long strides, sneakers squeaking embarrassingly against the marble tiles. So much for ethereal elegance.

"Would it kill you to slow down?" I snap between breaths.

Galin glances back, slowing just enough to keep me from collapsing. He does cut his speed though.

We move in silence. I want to demand answers— what his business is, why I had to dress like this, why he even bothers with me at all— but I hold my tongue. I need to pick my questions carefully. Galin isn't someone you waste words on.

We stop before a pair of towering double doors, carved with gnarled trees whose branches twine together like claws. He adjusts the collar of his tunic, casting me a sideways glance. He looks almost nervous, if that were possible, as he throws the doors open.

Whatever's behind them… I have the sinking feeling it's about to change everything.

Twelve people sit around a long oval mahogany table in a dimly lit room despite the chandelier overhead, its long tapered candles flickering without warmth. Their gazes shift to use with varying expressions of disapproval. At the head of the table, Tabitha lounges like a queen in repose, her crimson gaze lingering on me a beat too long.

Galin strides forward without pause. I hurry to follow, nearly tripping over the hem of my ridiculous, gorgeous dress. He slides into a high-backed chair to Tabitha's left— prime position, clearly reserved— and leaves nowhere for me.

I open my mouth to ask where I'm supposed to go, but he flicks his fingers casually toward the wall, not even looking at me. I take the hint. The wall is paneled with dark wood wainscoting that gives the room a kind of dignified gloom. No chairs. No place. Just a girl in a magic dress, feeling like I'm wearing borrowed skin, trying not to stick out any more than she already does. I move to the indicated spot and lean back against the wall, folding my arms to look as confident as I can fake.

"Now that Prince Galin has deigned to join us," Tabitha purrs, voice as slow as honey. "Where were we?"

"The magic deficiency," says a woman midway down the table, her long spiraled horns casting shadows across her face.

"Ah, yes," Tabitha says as she leans back into her chair.

"Any progress on identifying the contamination source?" a man at the far end of the table asks. His paper-thin wings twitch behind him like anxious thoughts.

"The source remains elusive," Tabitha replies, her lips dark red and gleaming. "But I am confident you are all managing on the replacement."

A muscle ticks in my jaw. Replacement?

"For how long?" another man demands, his tunic a rich emerald green. "We once drew power from the earth itself. Now we scavenge like beggars—"

"Especially after criminalizing our most potent source of magic."

Tabitha holds up a hand, silencing the crowd. "You all know just as well as I do that we could not continue the way we were. More potent though it may be, the blood of our brethren should not be considered a lasting source."

My mouth goes dry. Blood? Again?

It hits me like a rock— this might be what Cillian wanted me to hear. The senseless killings, the missing people... This is it. This is the rot at the root.

"They are only our brethren in the loosest sense," says a woman with nails tapered into sharp points says from her place at the end of the table. "They are not truly one of us."

"And so they deserve fewer rights than the humans?"

"I never said that," she snaps, a hand pressed to her chest. "I simply mean using the lesser fairies is... cleaner. Less risk of exposure."

Galin leans forward, looking interested in the conversation for the first time since we got here. "You fear the humans?"

The woman stiffens. "I will not be intimidated by you. You know what they've done. You know how dangerous they are."

"And yet your focus is interesting, Merida."

"My focus is on our continued survival," she says through gritted teeth. "Not patchwork solutions."

The room ignites into layered voices and brittle arguments. Galin leans back in his chair with a smirk, like this is all a mildly amusing performance.

I stay quiet, absorbing as much as I can.

Humans are the threat? Really? Everything I've seen here makes that feel backwards. And if magic is gone... what about Galin's little fire trick? That wasn't exactly subtle. Unless he's a magician on the side, which, honestly, would explain a lot. But why show me?

Tabitha stands, and the room stills like she's flipped a switch. She eyes each person around the table in turn, not bothering to flick her gaze towards me.

"The law is the law," she says, black-nailed fingers resting on polished wood. "There will be no repeal. If that's your goal, you may leave."

No one moves.

I almost hope Galin does. And almost hope he doesn't. If I can stay unnoticed, I might actually learn something. If I mess up...

I steel myself. I have to act like I belong here. Like I believe in the bargain I struck with Galin. Even if I don't understand it.

"The current system is holding." Tabitha sits back

against her chair. "There is no cause for alarm. Any further issues?"

Silence. The horned woman picks at her nails; the man in green studies the table grain like it holds secrets. Galin surveys the group, careful not to look at Tabitha.

"I have other matters to attend to," Tabitha says. "If no one has anything useful to add…"

She glides from the room, the train of her red gown whispering across the stone like a warning. No one follows. No one breathes. It's like the air has turned gelatinous, thick with tension and what they're too afraid to say.

The heavy door clicks shut.

Galin exhales softly. "Now. What do you really want to talk about?"

Still, no one jumps to speak. Which is strange. What's the point of showing up if you won't say anything?

I pick at the light layers of my dress, watching them float slowly back to my body. If this is what I've traded my safety for, I should have stayed locked in Galin's room.

"I have not seen this table full since the blight announcement," Galin muses. "Surely that's not a coincidence."

There's a long pause.

"I am not sure if I believe her anymore. The Queen. She says things are under control, but…" the man in the green tunic trails off.

"But she can't *lie*," I say before I can stop myself.

Too late.

The room turns to me.

Galin's gaze snaps to mine, curious. "Truth and deceit are not opposites. One may speak only truths and still obscure everything."

It clicks. He never said things would be fine. It just *sounded* like he did.

"Are you going to explain your human pet?" the green-tunic man sneers. "Why haven't you turned her in like the rest of us would have to?"

"My interest in pets is not why we are here and definitely does not help assuage the situation," Galin replies smoothly. "Let's stay focused."

Too late. I feel the weight of their stares, trying to decide what I am. I shift, eyes catching on a flower arrangement in the corner. At least this place smells good.

"We need to know," the horned woman presses. "Do you trust the Queen?"

"I trust that she *believes* she's in control," Galin says, his voice sounding bored.

"And that's enough?" she counters. "Because the humans won't stay quiet forever."

"Probably because they no longer believe in us," Galin says, tone sharp.

There's a stunned silence.

"What do you mean?" someone whispers.

He shrugs. "They see us as a myth now. Ghost stories. That grants us a rare kind of freedom."

He got that from me. And judging by the looks rippling around the table, this is news to them.

He didn't lie. He shifted the conversation. He turned uncertainty into control. Interesting.

"So, the threat isn't what it used to be," the honed woman says flatly. "Which means we could increase our collection rate. Why stop at one per month?"

"Because the Queen asked us not to," Galin says, eyes narrowing. "And she has her reasons."

"Yet she allows *you* to disregard her requirements?" The

man in the green tunic turns his attention to Galin with a smile full of poison.

"If you object to our arrangement, Matthias, I invite you to speak to her yourself."

He scowls, leaning back farther into his chair.

"Anyone else?" Galin asks in a lazy drawl. "And if possible, let's stick to business. Not bedroom gossip."

"We're done," the horned woman mutters.

Chairs scrape. Backs stretch. A few vanish quickly; others linger, revealing strange, hidden traits. A few have tails, some like mice and others like lions. There're more people with horns than I would have expected; they're just not as incredible as the woman who did most of the talking, several have veins of green running through their skin, and one has hair made up of flowers. Seeing them in the relative brightness of the room in their gowns and finery, they look less like predators and more like what a child might imagine fairies to be.

Which is somehow worse.

"Come."

I tear my eyes from the unnerving beauty before me and find Galin watching me with a raised brow. I duck my head and follow him from the room on quick feet.

He doesn't say anything to me as we move through chamber after chamber, conducting small business here and there and generally showing his face to the upper levels of his public. I trail behind like a shadow with sore feet and too many questions.

But the quiet gives me space to think. Not that I like where my thoughts go.

I'm.... drawn to him. I've known that from the start. Even before I knew who he was. And now that I *do* know, I should be planning. Plotting. Escaping.

But I'm not.

Why haven't I tried to hurt him? Why does the idea flit through my mind and vanish like it was never mine? Why have I not once tried to stab him or threaten him with the knife currently in my pocket?

Why do I feel *safe* around him?

My gaze picks up a bit to linger on the taut muscles of Galin's back. He glances back, that maddening smirk curving his mouth like he knows I'm staring.

I stick my tongue out.

He chuckles.

He opens a door and gestures me inside. Firelight flickers in the hearth. His room.

I shouldn't be relieved. But I am. My shoulders relax as he closes the door behind us.

"My business for the night is complete," he says, watching me

I blink. "Cool."

"Is there anything else you feel we should do?"

A thousand feelings pull in different directions. Anger. Longing. Fear. Attraction...

"No," I whisper, hating myself for sounding so breathless.

"Then you are free to go."

I stare. "I'm free to— what?"

Galin smiles, throwing himself onto his bed. "You are free to go home. I have no further need of you tonight."

"No further- I don't understand."

"You do not have to understand," he says, leaning on one elbow, his eyes heavy-lidded. "Sleep well, Grace."

"I— but—"

And darkness takes me.

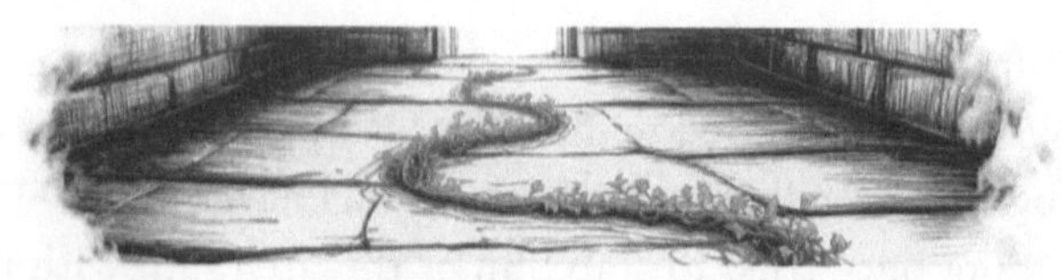

Chapter Nine

The next week's nights fall into a strange kind of rhythm. Every evening, I appear like clockwork, and Galin whisks me off to whatever cryptic 'business' he has planned. Afterward, he sends me home with the same quiet efficiency. There's always a new dress waiting for me— gossamer things made of shimmer and shadow, each more absurdly gorgeous than the last. I return before three in the morning, every time. A twisted little Cinderella, minus the pumpkin.

At least the dresses are stunning. They almost make up for the circles under my eyes that just keep deepening, a shade darker each day. Almost.

Joan stops asking so many questions about where I go. I guess getting home by what she calls a 'decent hour' means she doesn't think I'm still talking to strangers on the app— or worse. She hasn't brought it up again, and I haven't volunteered anything. It's easier that way.

The tiny sliver of sleep Galin insists I get is nice in theory, but I still feel like I'm always two steps behind. Homework stacks up like it's out for revenge, and my grades are circling the drain. I half-hope I start failing just to see if my father might finally show up to a parent-teacher conference. But I already know he won't.

Galin, for his part, doesn't give me any more attention than he did that first night after our bargain. I'm not a partner. I'm a prop. Something to be dressed up and posed, meant to stand still and look pretty while important people glance at me like I'm part of the décor. I don't speak unless spoken to, and even then, I measure my words like they're made of glass.

It's not a bad gig, to be honest. The places he takes me are absurdly beautiful. Every corner of the palace feels like the aftermath of a fairy tale— crumbling grandeur, faded elegance, all wrapped in a shroud of magic and memory. It's like wandering through a French palace with ghosts for company. I've even considered taking up sketching, just to try and capture a fraction of it. Not that I could— my phone always dies the second I step inside, no matter how fully charged it was when I left.

At least I haven't had to see Tabitha again. Just thinking about her makes my blood run cold. She doesn't just look at you— she *measures* you. And from what I've gathered, I'm not the only one who gets that reaction. Even the high fairies flinch under her gaze.

But finding this strange, glittering rhythm hasn't given me answers. If anything, the more I blend in, the easier it is to forget what I'm supposed to be doing. I still see their faces sometimes— the girls. The ones I swore I'd help. Their blank stares and twisted pain wrap around me like vines whenever I lie down at night. They haven't disappeared from my memory... just faded, like everything else in this place seems to.

At least I still remember to carry my pocketknife. It's a

pathetic comfort, I know, but it gives me the illusion of control. Like if something went wrong— *really* wrong— I'd have some tiny shred of power to do something about it.

I haven't tested it. Mostly because I'm terrified of what would happen if I did. Especially if it involved Galin.

I haven't seen much magic since that first night with him, but I don't doubt it's there. Waiting. Watching. And that strange mental lock— the one that keeps me from even *thinking* about hurting him— still holds strong. It's not fear. It's something else. Something I don't want to name.

The days grow colder as fall turns to winter, shimmering white mounds of snow blanketing the school in a forgiving sheet. Even under a fortress of blankets heaped on the bed, I still wake up every morning with numb fingers and aching toes. Under the Hill, the palace is covered in a sparkling layer of frost, the ivy that covers the walls shriveling back into brittle skeletons. It's still beautiful, but it's a cruel kind of beauty. The kind that doesn't care if I freeze.

When I show up in Galin's room tonight, I've taken the initiative to wrap myself in my coat. My tolerance has officially met its limit.

He raises a brow at my jacket but doesn't comment on it —just gestures toward the night's offering: another sleeveless, barely-there thing made of mist and thread. I stare at it, then shake my head.

"What's wrong now?" he asks, half-amused.

"I can't wear that." I fold my arms. "My fingers are on the verge of frostbite."

He smirks. "You cannot wear my extravagant gifts anymore?"

Of course he'd call them that. *Extravagant gifts.* I do get to take them home— except by morning, they've disintegrated into fine dust. Magic that doesn't survive the sunlight. Convenient for hiding secrets. I'm sure he designed them that way.

"Your extravagance is going to cost me a toe."

His gaze travels over my face, lingering on my quivering, blue-tinged lips. My shoulders shake with barely unrestrained shivers as I struggle to stay warm. Even the fire in the grate isn't enough to block out the ever-present chill inside the palace. I place myself on the chair set up beside it, hoping that feeling will start coming back to my fingertips.

"Don't you ever feel cold?" I wonder, not for the first time, if I'm the only one who's affected by the changing seasons in this crazy place.

His black tunic and tight pants have remained the same since I first met him, no changes to address the chill. The other high fairies haven't made many adjustments either. They bare their shoulders and feet with no care like it's the middle of summer. What would it be like to not have to worry about losing a toe to frostbite in a palace that quickly turns into an icicle? He hesitates, then looks down at his hands like he's suddenly remembering they're attached to him. "We do not react to winter the way you mortals do."

"Of course. Another point for the magical elite." I sigh dramatically. "Must be exhausting, being better than everyone all the time."

He doesn't smile. "I do not believe it makes us better. Not feeling the seasons... it is unnatural. A side effect of magic being drained from the earth."

"And you think that?"

"Think what?"

"That it's a curse."

He clenches his fists again, but nods slowly. "Yes. It is a curse."

Something shifts in the way I see him. He says it without drama, without trying to manipulate me. Just a truth, laid bare.

"I didn't expect you to admit that," I murmur.

His eyes meet mine, softer now. "There are many things I would not have admitted before you."

That does something funny to my stomach. I look away too quickly.

I wonder, not for the first time, what it would be like if he weren't what he is. If he weren't a fairy prince wrapped in shadows and secrets. If he were just... a boy. Someone who could walk in the snow and feel it melt on his skin.

At the last meeting, they spoke of lower fairies vanishing. No one knows if they're dissolving into the ground from lack of magic, or if they're being *harvested* by others. It's a brutal word, and no one said it outright— but it was there, heavy in the silence. This place looks like a dream. But the bones are showing.

"So," I say, keeping my voice casual. "What was winter like before all this? When things were normal?"

Galin shrugs. "Not much was different."

I narrow my eyes. "I don't buy that. Feeling winter has to change how you experience it."

"I suppose we wore more layers."

"Revolutionary."

"There were many more fires. Real ones. Especially in the throne room."

"Ones that actually worked, I assume?"

He laughs, a low sound like flint striking stone. "Yes. Ones that warmed more than the eyes."

I smile despite myself, rubbing my hands together near the grate.

Maybe I should be terrified of him. Maybe I was once.

But that fear has twisted into something else— complex and sharp, braided with curiosity and something far more dangerous.

Maybe I'm not falling in love with Galin.

But maybe I've started to fall *toward* him.

And I don't know how to stop.

Not that he's noticed. I'm just his little mortal tagalong, right? A walking promise, dragged from one strange place to the next. As far as his world is concerned, I rank somewhere below the lower fairies who are vanishing by the day.

Galin lifts a hand toward the fire and the flames leap higher, sending a wave of heat across the room. It should be dramatic and showy, but instead, it just feels... thoughtful. The warmth crashes over me like a tide, and my shoulders stop shaking. But then the real pain starts— the kind that blooms from thawing nerves. My fingers scream with pins and needles as they come back to life, the sting so intense I nearly cry out.

"What is wrong? Is this not what you wanted?" Galin asks, his eyes wide with genuine confusion.

"It happens when I've been too cold for too long," I manage, rocking on my heels and tucking my burning hands into my armpits. "It's a weird human thing. We're delicate, remember?"

"Forgive me."

I blink. "What did you say?"

"I..." His jaw works before he finishes. "I am sorry. For not considering your comfort sooner."

I stare at him, stunned. Of all the things I've heard in this world of glittering danger, an apology was not one I expected. Not from him. My heart lurches in confusion. It's not like I *want* him to care. But something about the way he looks— genuinely uneasy, even a little ashamed— makes me believe he might.

Before I can speak, he turns, disappearing into the wardrobe. A moment later, he returns with a box and places it in front of me. No words, just a pointed look.

With stiff fingers, I lift the lid. My breath catches. Inside is a heavy cream-colored outfit— soft, warm, and clearly expensive. I sink my fingers into the fabric. It's not fur, not wool, but something between the two. Like touching a cloud that decided to hug me back. Matching gloves and boots sit beneath the folds of the dress. He's never given me shoes before.

"Why didn't you give me this sooner?" I ask, unable to hide the awe from my voice.

"It did not occur to me," he says quietly, eyes fixed on the fire.

Liar. Or at least, *something* isn't adding up. He's hiding something— not in the obvious, mustache-twirling villain way, but in the soft silences and the averted gaze.

Still, he turns his back as I change, following our unspoken rule. I've stopped questioning how natural it feels to let my guard down around him. It should scare me. It probably did, once. But now... now I'm not sure if the calm I feel in his presence is magic, or just something more dangerous.

The dress hugs my skin like a second, better, warmer one— soothing and immediate, as if it knows exactly where I've been cold the longest. The heat spreads in soft pulses, comforting and alive. Even the boots feel like slippers, molded perfectly to my feet, but polished enough that I almost look like I belong somewhere important. Some-where royal.

A sigh escapes me before I can help it. Galin turns, probably to make some smug comment, but when he sees me, he doesn't speak. He just *looks*. His gaze lingers in a way that makes my cheeks flush and my fingers itch with the urge to fidget. I turn quickly, folding my school clothes neatly on the bed.

What is he hiding? What could be so important about a winter dress?

Not for the first time, I wish I had my mom to talk to. I never really got to know her, but I've always imagined she'd be the kind of woman who knew how to read a room, who would've understood things before anyone else said a word. Somehow, I feel it in my blood— she would've known what to do. She would've known how to see through this place, this dress, this boy who isn't a boy at all.

The material is soft like butter and has the weighted grace of something both luxurious and dangerous. It slides over my skin like a whisper, a promise. With bell sleeves and a flared skirt, I should feel overdressed, but instead I feel armored. Warmed in a way that reaches deeper than the chill in the air. The boots wrap around my calves like they were made for me, and the gloves cut the cold from my fingers completely. If someone asked me to trek across the Arctic in this outfit, I might actually say yes— and look good doing it.

Galin turns again, catching me mid-sigh. His expression halts between amusement and something else— something I can't quite name. I spin slowly, testing the dress, trying to look casual. His eyes don't leave me. Heat floods my face, and I turn away again, pretending to focus on folding my clothes.

"It suits you," he says quietly.

The words hit harder than they should. I bite down on the smile threatening my lips and push it away. I shouldn't care. I don't care. It's just— he's never commented before. Not on how it looked. Not on anything beyond what was required. It's like something shifted. Like I've suddenly become real to him.

I steel myself before facing him. "So," I say a little too brightly. "What are the big plans for tonight?"

He shrugs, a shadow of the moment we just had disappearing. "Nothing important."

"You're not going to tell me?"

"I did not think I had to."

"Of course you don't," I say, trying to keep my voice even. "But it might be nice if you chose to."

He frowns, the spell broken. "Come."

The word is short. Final.

Fine. I'm not surprised. Any time I push too hard, he withdraws. I know this dance by now. But it still stings a little. We're not friends— I remind myself of that as I follow him through the hallway. I'm just part of whatever this game is. Still, the warmth from the outfit clings to me like a shield. At least tonight, I don't feel like I'm walking through a frozen tomb.

As we walk, I smooth a hand down the front of the dress, tracing the tiny gold stitches and admiring the elegant construction. This one's different. Not just in look, but in intention. I can feel it. More care went into this than any of the others. Why?

We stop in front of the throne room doors. Galin inhales sharply, squaring his shoulders. I copy the movement before I even think about it. Reflex. Like I want to match him. That thought unnerves me more than the darkness that seeps out when the doors open.

But I hold steady. I'm not flinching tonight. This room doesn't get to win.

The revel looks like it always does. Mist. Music. Shadows that dance just out of reach. But the menace from the first night— the one I still dream about— feels dimmer. Duller. Maybe it left with the last round of victims.

Galin disappears into the crowd. That's fine. I can take care of myself. My pocketknife is in my boot. I've memorized the route back to his rooms. I'm not helpless here anymore. I repeat it to myself like a prayer.

My eyes scan the crowd. No sign of Cillian. Not that I expected him. But I miss him anyway. I shouldn't. I should want nothing from anyone here. Yet, I find myself searching.

"Hope you are not looking for me."

His voice slices through the noise, grounding me. I turn, grinning at the familiar green eyes. His tail twitches, but he doesn't smile back.

"What are you doing back here?" I ask.

"I was hoping not to find you."

I flinch. His tone is sharp, colder than I remember. "Galin brought me."

Cillian scans the crowd, searching for him, then looks back at me, his shoulders tight.

"I hoped I would not find you here again after what I showed you."

"It's not like I have a choice." I fold my arms over my chest. The heat rising in me is in part frustration, part guilt. I shouldn't take it out on him— but who else is there?

"You could at least stay hidden," he says. "It is not safe for you here."

"Not safe for you either," I mutter, eyes narrowing.

He jerks back. "You know nothing of what you speak."

"Try me."

"You still don't understand enough."

"Then maybe you should tell me instead of acting like I'm the problem."

He breathes hard through his nose. "You are not the problem. But you are tangled in it now."

"Are you just here to scold me?"

"I am here because I care," he says simply, and that stops me.

I don't reply. The air between us sharpens, thick with the tension of words we aren't saying. I turn my back and scan the room for Galin again. If Cillian wants to be cryptic, fine. I'll find my own way. I'm used to that.

"I'm not trying to offend you. I must protect you."

"From what? From Galin?" I turn back to him. "Because if that's it, you're too late."

"I fear you are already lost to him."

I swallow. The word 'lost' echoes too close to what I've been feeling— like I've been walking around in a fog that wears Galin's face. Like maybe I *am* slipping, inch by inch, into something I can't climb out of.

"What do you mean?"

"The dust," Cillian says.

I frown. "What dust?"

He glances around us, his eyes sharp and flicking like a rabbit's just before it bolts. No one is paying much attention, which I guess is the point. This dress, for all its unsettling magic, is doing its job. It makes me look like I belong. Or at least like I'm under someone's protection— Galin's specifically. It turns out that's enough to keep most of the fairies from looking too long.

Still, I hate the way Cillian's shoulders curl inward like he expects something dangerous to swoop down from the ceiling. Whatever he's about to tell me, it's dangerous.

"The dust," he says again, more quietly this time. "You know, the part of the app that makes it so potent."

My eyes narrow. "How do you know about the app?"

He lifts a brow, like I've asked whether birds know about flying. "Everyone knows about the app. It was created by us. For us. Designed by the higher courts, adapted for the mortal world. It was an ingenious idea— using your own devices against you. I will not say it was right. But it was... effective."

"You're serious," I whisper.

I inhale sharply, my lungs suddenly too small. *Of course.* That explains it. Why Galin has crept under my skin like ivy, coiling around my thoughts even when I try to pull him out. Why no other match even registered when I first opened the app. Why I keep forgetting who I am when he looks at me like I'm the only thing he wants to touch.

I should be furious. I *am* furious. But more than that, I feel... betrayed. And stupid. And a little scared.

"So," I say, struggling to keep my voice even. "You're telling me the app is... magic?"

Cillian makes a face. "Fairy dust is not quite the same as magic. It's older. More specific. It binds. Enhances. Addicts. Magic bends rules. Dust *writes* them."

"But it works the same way, doesn't it? That's what you're trying to tell me."

He gives me a grim nod. "Yes. It sinks into your body, your thoughts. It changes how you feel, then convinces you it was always that way."

I shiver. My mouth is dry, but my palms are damp. "I remember something," I whisper. "When I matched with him... there was this... feeling. Like something coated my throat. Like I swallowed static." I pause. "That was the dust, wasn't it?"

His gaze is soft, full of something like pity. I hate it. But I hate the confirmation more when he nods.

"And now?"

"It's adhered to you. Almost impossible to remove."

Almost.

"But not actually impossible," I press.

He hesitates. "No. Not impossible. But it will not be easy."

"Tell me how," I say, surprising myself with how steady I sound. Like I've already made up my mind. "I want to know."

Cillian's expression darkens. "We need to get the dust *out* of you."

"Out of me?" My voice pitches higher than I mean it to. I glance around, hoping no one caught that.

He nods slowly. "It's in your blood. We have to draw it out— undo the bond it's building."

I stare at him. "That sounds like the beginning of a horror story."

"It's more like surgery," he says gently. "But less... sterile."

I bark out a laugh before I can stop myself. "That's *reassuring*."

Cillian's mouth twitches. Not quite a smile, but close. "It will not be pleasant, but you will be free."

Free.

The word knocks around in my chest. I'm not even sure what it means anymore. What does it look like to *not* want him? To stop dreaming about Galin's voice, his eyes, the way he always seems just on the edge of telling me something that matters?

I glance sideways at Cillian. His posture is still tense, but his expression is honest, open in a way I'm starting to recognize as rare here. There's no trick in his voice. Just concern. Real, raw concern.

"Why are you helping me?" I ask quietly.

He doesn't hesitate. "Because I like you. Because you try even when you should not have to. And because I have seen what happens to humans who cannot fight the dust."

There's a lump rising in my throat. I nod, just once.

"Okay," I whisper. "Let's get it out."

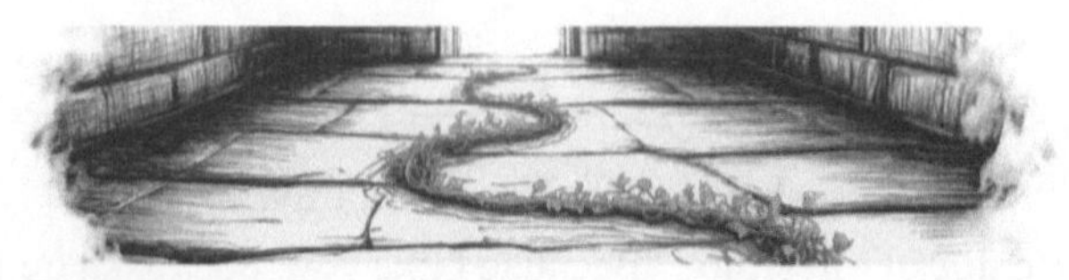

Chapter Ten

illian leads me down— farther and deeper than I want to go— through a narrow spiral stairwell that feels more like a tunnel carved into a cliffside than anything that belongs in a palace. Each step echoes with a low thud, and I can't help but count them as if it might delay what's coming. He hasn't told me yet what this 'extraction' will entail. Just that it's the only way to get the dust out of me. And I need it gone. I *want* it gone. But the unknown presses against my ribs like a weight.

The deeper we go, the dimmer the light gets, until I'm reminded— vividly, uncomfortably— of the last time I followed Cillian somewhere underground. That memory still lives sharp-edged in the back of my mind.

Girls behind doors. Blood on stone.

The sound of someone sobbing softly into the dark.

By the time we reach a low-ceilinged chamber, all dirt walls and musty chill, my skin prickling. There's only one candle already lit in the room, perched on a short, black stone table that gleams like it's already wet. Cillian doesn't speak as he lights a second candle, its flame stuttering to life with a hiss. Then, wordlessly, he pulls a small knife from his belt.

Immediately, I reach into the folds of my dress and snap open my own blade. Galin's wardrobe might make me look fragile, but I've never liked the part where I play defenseless.

Cillian startles slightly, then lets out a short, amused breath. "I am not interested in hurting you," he says, raising both hands. "And if I *were*, I wouldn't drag you to the very bottom of the palace to do it. Violence," he adds dryly, "is hardly a foreign concept in the throne room."

"Charming," I mutter. I don't lower my blade. "You'll have to forgive me for being a *little* jumpy when you pull out a knife without warning."

He winces, giving his forehead a light smack. "Of course. But this is the only way to drain you of the dust."

I blink. *Draw out.* That word alone is enough to make my skin feel tighter. "You're talking about blood, aren't you?"

He nods once, expression suddenly solemn. "It is in your blood Grace. That is how the dust works. If we can drain enough of it out— safely— it should lessen the bond. Maybe even break it."

My face grows cold. Not from fear, exactly, but from memory— sharp and brutal— of a girl thrown into a room like she didn't matter. Her blood painted on the floor. I blink hard, force the thought away. I've had to get good at that. At pressing trauma into neat little boxes and shoving them somewhere I can't see.

Still, I don't sheath my knife. "You can't have my blood."

The answer is automatic. My mom drilled that into me early. *No one sees your blood. No one touches it. No matter what.* Not doctors. Not friends. Not anyone. I never understood why. I still don't, not really.

Cillian sighs, his brow pinching in concern. "If we cannot let the blood, Grace, then I do not know how to help you."

"I'm sure there's some other way."

He thinks for a long moment, face furrowed with genuine effort. And when he says nothing, my stomach tightens. *Think harder*, I want to snap. *Try again.* But I stay quiet.

Because the truth is— I'm not sure *he's* wrong. I just don't want him to be right.

My mom's voice echoes through my head. *Special blood. Special rules.* She used to panic over scrapes like they were bullet wounds. Even minor injuries turned into whispered crises behind closed doors. It wasn't just caution— it was *fear.* But she wasn't exactly herself before she died, was she? Still, the real trouble came with deeper bleeding, and with her warning, I've been able to keep out of any serious injuries. Not that I would have gone looking for them anyway. I'm not crazy.

What if she was wrong? What if I've lived half my life terrified of something that was never even real?

Cillian's voice pulls me back. "The dust has fused with your life force. It is bound to your life force, buried in your blood. The only way to remove it is to *remove* part of *you.* We have to do it in sessions. Little by little. Until you are clean again."

Clean. Like I've been infected.

And maybe I have.

I study his face— those green eyes that look more goat than human, the earnest set of his brow. He's always been honest with me. Protective, even. The only one in this cursed palace who's never tried to own me.

"All right," I say in a tight exhale. "But make it quick."

I slide my knife back into my pocket and let him push up the cream-colored sleeve of Galin's dress. His fingers are gentle, apologetic almost. He stretches my arm out across the dark stone table. The surface is cold against my skin, and polished so smooth it reflects the flicker of candlelight like water. Like something *waiting*.

"I wish we did not have to do this down here," Cillian murmurs. "But your blood would have drawn attention upstairs. *Too* much attention."

Of course. In a world where blood means magic, and magic means power, of *course* they've learned how to sniff it out.

I keep my gaze fixed on the far wall, trying not to look as Cillian positions the blade. I don't want to see it. Don't want to think about it.

But when the knife cuts through my skin, I don't flinch. The pain is real but distant, like it's happening to someone else. I've lived through worse.

My blood pools quickly, sliding across the black stone in fat, glistening droplets.

Cillian gasps and I glance at him, startled. His eyes are locked on the wound, wide as saucers.

"What?" I ask, my voice hoarse. "What's wrong?"

He doesn't answer.

I look down.

And freeze.

What's flowing out of my arm doesn't match the bright red blood staining the stone beneath it. No, it's not just blood. It's laced with something else. Something bright. *Gold.* It glimmers in the candlelight like molten metal, thick and surreal, pooling on top of the darker blood like oil on water.

"Is that... is that the dust?" I ask, barely breathing.

Cillian shakes his head slowly. "I have never seen it do that before. I have heard rumors of something like this... but it would not apply to you. Not even most fairies..."

I search my memory, unwillingly dredging up the scene I've tried for weeks to forget. The girl. The bleeding. Nothing glowed then. No gold, no shimmer.

So this... this has to be something else.

"My mom warned me," I whisper. "She said my blood was different. That no one could see it. I thought that she was just—" I stop. *Crazy*. I'd nearly said it. I won't now.

Cillian's jaw tightens as he watches the stream of gold coil across the stone like it's alive. The image is entrancing and sickening all at the same time.

"Should we stop?" I ask, heart racing. "If it's not supposed to look like that?"

He nods and quickly pulls out a strip of white linen. His hands are shaking as he wraps it around my arm. The bleeding stops almost immediately, like the blood— whatever it is— *chooses* to stay inside me.

"Has it always looked like that?" Cillian asks with a frown.

"I don't know," I say. "It's not like I go around bleeding on purpose."

"You have never seen this before?"

"This isn't the 1700s," I mutter. "We've got antibiotics and ibuprofen now. Bleeding people isn't a normal Tuesday."

He huffs a breath— half frustration, half amusement— as he presses another cloth to the pool of gold and red. But he doesn't move to clean it.

Just stares.

Like it might whisper answers if we're quiet enough to hear them.

I glance from his face to the glimmering blood and back again. "Are you trying to divine my future in it, or are you just admiring your handiwork?"

Cillian doesn't smile. Doesn't even blink. "There is power in blood. I am just trying to understand what kind of power yours holds."

"You're the expert," I mutter. "You tell me."

Cillian misses the sarcasm in my tone as he taps a finger to his chin, genuinely considering my answer. "What blood type are you?"

"A+?" I offer, voice light, like it's a joke. It kind of is. I mean, it's the same answer I put on the questionnaire. But I doubt any of that applies when your blood glows like it was spun out of dying star.

Cillian reaches for the other cloth, holds it over the mess... then lets it fall uselessly back to the table.

"You can't just leave it there," I say, sharply now, the sight making my stomach churn.

"It feels... wrong to clean it up."

"And what, you're going to leave it for someone else to stumble on? That seems safe."

"It is not about safety. There is something about you, Grace. Something rare."

I shove myself upright and press my fingers over the wound, both to stop the blood and to stop myself from yelling at him. "So what? You've *honestly* never seen anything like this? You're not just playing into some long game to freak me out or manipulate me?"His face crumples slightly at that, like I've just smacked him.

"Have I ever done anything to hurt you?" he asks quietly. "Truly?"

"No, but you've also never told me *why* you help me."

His jaw tightens. "The why should not matter."

"It's *all* that matters," I snap, and then immediately regret it. "I'm sorry. I just... I'm not good at being in the dark. Not about people."

Cillian steps back from the table. "You think I am like them. That I am like Galin."

I pause, his name a shock in the quiet. "I think I don't know how to tell the difference sometimes."

He studies me, his eyes sad and sharp all at once. "We all have our secrets, Grace. Even you."

That stings. Mostly because it's true. I want to argue, but instead I nod, and the tension between us softens a little. Enough for him to finally begin cleaning up the blood.

I don't watch. I can't. Instead, I sit down against the wall, feeling woozy and useless and like I've somehow failed my mom, myself, and every single rule I've lived by up to this point.

Cillian grunts and gestures toward the door. Time to go.

I pull myself to my feet, still lightheaded, and attempt a smile. "Same time tomorrow, then?"

He raises an eyebrow, but I catch the ghost of a smile before he turns away. I'll take that as a win.

The hall is darker than it was before, shadows deeper and sconces sputtering like they're being snuffed out one by one. Something cold and heavy settles in the air, pressing into my lungs.

Cillian walks faster. His silence is louder than any alarm bell. Something's wrong.

Mist slithers across the stone floor when we reach the

main level. It swirls at our ankles, curling like fingers trying to find a grip. A shiver runs down my spine.

Cillian says nothing, just watches it warily. Of course he doesn't explain. He never does.

I expect him to leave once we hit the main corridor— he usually does— but tonight he sticks close, matching my shaky pace as I wind my way toward Galin's room. The thought of the throne room makes my skin crawl. It's too open. Too dangerous. Too... hers.

I hug the wall, the ivy brushing my arms while I do everything I can to avoid the creeping mist. I'm not ready to find to find out what it does. Or what lives in it.

Shapes move through the fog. Some pass by like they don't even see me. Others pause. Watch. Wait.

I stay upright, but the world spins and my pulse is a roar in my ears. Cillian stays close, his presence steadying but not enough to fight off the rising tide of panic.

Then comes the sound of breathing— low and wrong and far too close.

I bolt.

My legs move before my brain catches up. I run blindly, adrenaline burning away the fog in my mind. Cillian shouts behind me, but I don't stop. I can't. I can't be caught out here. Not now. Not like this.

I don't hear footsteps behind me anymore. Just my own ragged breath and the slap of my shoes on stone. I reach Galin's door, nearly collapsing against it as I wrench it open and hurl myself inside.

The door slams behind me. Silence. Blessed silence.

I slid down the wood, pressing my cheek to the cool surface. No matter what else has happened Under the Hill, Galin's room has always been safe. It's the only place I've ever been able to breathe.

The floor creaks. I freeze.

No fire burns in the hearth. No candles glow. The shadows are thick in here— too thick. A figure steps forward, and I fumble for my knife with hands that don't want to obey.

Then I hear his voice.

"Where were you?"

Galin.

I blink, trying to find him in the dark. "I— I had to—"

"I didn't say you could leave," he says, his voice like ice on bare skin.

My lips part, but no sound escapes.

"You made a promise to obey me. And what I wanted... was for you to stay in the throne room."

"Not *with* you though," I say, surprising even myself. The words tumble out, blood loss making me bolder than I should be. "You haven't looked at me once in days. I'm just there for decoration."

He stalks closer, shadows clinging to him like a second skin. "You think I do not see you?"

"You act like I don't matter."

"You matter more than you could possibly understand," he snaps, his voice low and dangerous.

That should scare me. Maybe it does. But my heart skips anyway. Because there's something else beneath the fear— something undeniable. The way he says it, like the words are dragged out of him against his will, like he *hates* that they're true, makes something fragile and reckless unfurl inside my chest.

Hope, maybe. Or something more dangerous.

"I don't want to be your prisoner," I whisper.

He is a few paces from me. I still can't see his face through the clinging shadows, but I feel him— feel the magic humming in the air between us, like the breath before the storm. His presence wraps around me, not like chains, but like silk— soft, seductive, and no less binding.

"You are not," he says, quietly this time. Like it costs him.

And somehow, that's worse. Because if I'm not a prisoner... then I've been choosing to stay. Choosing *him.*

I straighten slowly, heart thundering, chin lifting as I search the darkness for his face. "Then what am I to you?" I ask. My voice shakes a little, but I don't look away.

There's a pause. A long one.

He exhales, the sound rough, uneven. His breath ghosts against my cheek, curling like fog, and the shadows shudder as if pulled by an invisible thread. With a soft. Almost reluctant sigh, the dark recedes, crawling back into the corners, lifting like a veil.

When I blink, I can see him.

Galin stands just in front of me, his chest rising and falling too fast, head bowed like he's barely holding himself together. His eyes are closed, and for the first time, I can really *look* at him.

He's... beautiful. That unfair, impossible kind of beautiful you only find in stories or paintings. His tunic clings to him like water, black as ink, open at the throat to reveal the sweep of inked skin I've only ever glimpsed in pictures— the runes etched into his chest curling downward, ancient and ominous. He's always seemed untouchable, unreadable, some polished weapon carved out of moonlight and menace. But right now?

Right now, he looks like someone unraveling.

The quiet stretches between us like a wire, strung tight.

"You use your looks like a weapon," I say softly. "You know that right?"

His eyes snap open. And they are not right.

They're not his usual black with a hint of gold, the way they are when he's amused or annoyed or scheming. They're pitch black. Absolute. As if someone took a brush and painted out every part of them. No light. No emotion. Just void.

My breath catches. "Galin?"

He doesn't answer. Doesn't blink. Just lifts his head slowly, gaze pinned to mine like a predator scenting weakness.

Something's wrong.

The temperature drops. The walls narrow in. Every part of me screams *run*.

I take a step back, and my shoulder hits the door with a soft thud. My hand scrabbles behind me, fingers fumbling for the handle. I'd rather face whatever waits in the hallway than... whatever this is.

He *roars*.

It's not even animal. It's raw power, cracked open and bleeding into the room. The sound tears through me like a physical force, vibrating in my bones, freezing my blood.

I can't move.

I want to. I *need* to. But my body won't obey. It's like the air itself has locked around me, holding me in place, forcing me to *feel* every second of his fury.

I clench my fists. I *will not* scream. I will not cry. I will *not* collapse into some helpless, shivering mess like I did the first night. I'm smarter than that now. Stronger. I've learned to mask terror with sarcasm and strategy.

But there's no mask strong enough for this.

Just when I think I'll shatter under the sound, it cuts off.

Silence crashes down.

Galin falls to his knees. Not gracefully like a prince. Like a man whose strings have been cut.

He kneels in the center of the room, arms hanging limp at his sides, head bowed. Breathing hard.

The spell breaks.

I lunge for the handle, gripping it like it's the only real thing in the world. I half-expect him to lunge after me, to snarl or vanish or beg or *anything*.

But he just lifts his head.

And his eyes— his *real* eyes— are back.

Dark and furious and so achingly human it steals the air from my lungs.

I should run. I should.

But I can't move.

Because in that moment, he looks not dangerous, but devastated. Not like a monster trying to devour me, but like a man trying— and failing— not to destroy himself.

"I never wanted you to see that," he says hoarsely.

"You didn't give me a choice," I whisper back.

His head dips, and I catch it then—the tremble of his fingers and the rawness in his voice: shame. Not regret. Not anger. Shame. There's a vulnerability to him that makes my pulse quicken.

Then, so low I almost miss it, he murmurs, "Let the others burn. You are the only one I have ever wanted to protect."

The words hit harder than his roar.

I should run. I should.

But I falter.

Because yes, he looks dangerous. But also broken. A man unraveling, choking on the very darkness that rules him. A man who doesn't know how to stop breaking everything he touches.

And still, my treacherous heart stumbles over itself.

Even now— even after everything— I can't stop wanting to understand him.

Wanting to believe there's more to him than the monster I just saw. Wanting him.

But that's the problem, isn't it?

He's not human. No matter how much he tries to act like it, no matter how much he makes me feel like I could be safe with him... he never will be.

Wanting him means losing everyone else. If there's the faintest chance I can save them—save anyone—I have to go.

So I turn the handle.

And this time, I run.

Chapter Eleven

The twisting mists in the hallway dissolve like breath on glass, leaving behind the half-frozen ivy crusted along the walls and the steady burn of sconces casting golden light. My footsteps fall too heavily across the marble despite the soft-soled shoes Galin gave me— shoes chosen, I realize now, so I wouldn't make a sound.

The irony burns.

I've barely made it past the first turn before my breath starts to tear from me, shallow, and painful. Each inhale scrapes my throat like knives. My limbs are heavier than they should be— sluggish from blood loss and panic— but I force them to keep moving. Faster. Quieter. Smarter. I strain to hear anything beyond my own ragged breathing. Any whisper of pursuit. Any footfall echoing too close behind.

I have to get out. I *can't* stay here, waiting for morning and pretending I'll be safely delivered back to my world like this was all just a dream. No matter what Galin says— no matter how tender his voice can be or how careful his touch has been— he can't protect me. He couldn't even protect me from himself.

My hand tightens over the bandage on my arm. It's warm now, damp again. Not enough to bleed out, probably. But enough to remind me this body has limits. And I'm nearing them.

Nothing happened in that room— but it felt as if the air itself was ready to snap. I don't know what exactly would have happened, only that if I'd stayed another second, something inside him—something fragile and dangerous—would have shattered.

The corridor veers sharply into a new wing, ending in a staircase I've never seen before. Then again, the palace feels different tonight—warped somehow, like it's folding in on itself. Still, the sight of something new makes me hesitate.

The staircase is metal, winding like a spiral vine. The banister branches into curling limbs, and the steps themselves are enormous leaves of hammered bronze, each one unique. Beautiful. Unnatural. Like everything else in this palace.

For a breath, I pause. I *want* to admire it. Even now. Even as my pulse crashes through me. But beauty has teeth here, and I've learned not to stand still in its presence. Not anymore.

My feet hit the first step with a clang, then the next. Down, down, deeper into the palace. I know heading underground isn't the logical choice when you're trying to escape, but it's the only path left to me. And I don't have time to be cautious. I just have to hope I don't find myself back in the throne room—or worse, that stone chamber where Cillian bled me.

The metal echoes fade into silence as I descend. No voices. No footsteps. Just the rasp of my own breath and the whisper of blood pounding in my ears. I tell myself no one is following me. That Galin isn't. But that doesn't slow my pulse.

He wouldn't hurt me. Not intentionally.

But that version of him—black-eyed, trembling with fury and power and something close to grief—*that* version wouldn't care what he mean to do.

The stairway finally empties into a level of soft earth. I stumble forward, nearly losing my balance as the ground shifts beneath me. Dirt instead of marble. Cold instead of warmth. I recognize the sensation—like the unfinished basement in one of my friend's houses back home. The kind with exposed beams and mothballs. I used to find it creepy.

Now, it feels like a blessing.

This level is darker. What lights remain are no longer sconces, but flickering torches wedged into the walls like afterthoughts. The air is cooler, but heavy. Not with threat —but with emptiness. Unlike the misted hallways above, this darkness doesn't press in like it's watching.

Still, I don't trust it. A soft scuff behind me makes my heart seize. My body reacts before I can think—sprinting forward again, pain lancing through my thighs and calves. I run from torch to torch, the glow burning in my periphery as the curved ceiling lowers just slightly overhead. My vision blurs. My lungs feel tight. The blood loss is catching up to me now.

There are no doors here. No alcoves. No turns. Just a straight, terrible corridor. I don't have anywhere to hide if something is chasing me. And I'm in no shape to fight.

Not that I was ever much of a fighter.

Another step. Another burst of light. The hallway looks like it ends in shadow, like the earth simply swallowed the rest of it. I don't slow. Because there *has* to be something else. A door. A trap. A way out.

Palaces don't build ornate staircases to nowhere.

But when I reach the end, my pace falters.

There's nothing.

Just solid packed earth. A dead end.

I stand there, chest heaving, staring at it like if I look hard enough, it might dissolve. My legs shake beneath me. My hand instinctively reaches for the wall, grounding myself. I turn back toward the long, torchlit tunnel, but the staircase is no longer visible. No glint of metal. No gold. No light. Only the long, dim corridor stretching into the dark.

Something is there. I can *feel* it. That pull again. Like gravity. Like memory. But it's not Galin.

I'd know if I were him.

Unless... unless he's hiding from himself too.

I press my back to the wall and close my eyes. Maybe it's childish, but I don't care. The moment they shut, I pretend—for half a second—that I'm home. That I'm curled up on the floor of my bedroom, clutching a pillow and not my wounded arm. That I'm not falling for something ancient and angry and half-broken. That Galin is just a boy I met online.

Scrape.

The sound of dirt shifting against stone.

And I'm falling. The wall gives beneath me like wet paper, and there's no more ground. Just air. Darkness. Cold. My scream doesn't even make it out of my throat before the world disappears.

My body hits the ground hard, the impact knocking the breath from my lungs.

But I'm alive.
And I'm alone.
For now.

The fall slams the air from my lungs. For a moment, I can't move—I just lie there on my back, gasping like a fish thrown on the shore. My ribs ache. My arm throbs. Everything inside me feels misaligned.

Above me, a sky studded with faint stars slowly sharpens into view. Black, endless, beautiful. The quiet is so complete it feels unnatural.

Eventually, I manage to roll onto an elbow, grimacing as pain flares through my arm. My breath comes in shallow stutters, but at least I'm breathing. That counts as a win.

I blink the spots from my eyes and take in my surroundings.

Tall, silent trees stretch up into the sky like pillars in a cathedral. Their trunks are wide, ancient, thick with moss. A soft carpet of pine needles cushions the forest floor, stretching in every direction without interruption—no shrubs, no underbrush, just trees and needles and silence.

There's no sign of the palace. No doorway. No tunnel. No hidden mound to mark where I might have fallen through. It's as if I've simply... appeared here. Like I was plucked from one world and set down in another.

I slowly push myself to my feet. My legs tremble under me and my shoes sink slightly into the bed of needles. Everything is still. Too still.

But the stillness brings a flood of relief.

I'm out. I actually did it.

My heart surges, warm and wild. I wrap my arms around myself and laugh—half-mad, half—exhilarated. A dizzy little spin escapes me, the joy too sudden to suppress.

I'm out. I made it.

I did what no one else could do—I got out of Under the Hill.

The euphoria is probably a little premature. For all I know, this could be some magical holding cell for escapees, or a dreamlike trick meant to lull me. But it doesn't *feel* like the palace. No golden halls. No mist. No pressure against my skin like invisible eyes watching me. Here, there's only the hush of trees and cool air on my face.

A grin stretches across my cheeks despite everything. "Maybe this place *does* have emergency exits," I whisper.

The joy flickers. Confusion creeps in.

What *was* that room I fell through? A secret passage? A trapdoor no one expected me to find? Did the palace make it for me—or did it fail to close something it should have?

And why does nothing in this palace ever look like what it is? Walls become doors. People become monsters. Kindness becomes a mask. I want to ask someone if they ever get lost in that place, or if fairies just instinctively know how to navigate its chaos. Maybe they're born with a mental map I'll never get access to.

Well, it doesn't matter now.

I spin in a slow circle, scanning the endless trees. I don't recognize this forest, but I don't need to—not yet. It's real. It's *not* the palace. That's enough.

There are a dozen old forests near school, probably more. I've barely set foot in any of them, but I'm still hoping one leads somewhere human.

Still, my practical side whispers that I should be careful. I remember someone –maybe a teacher, maybe a book—

once saying that if you get lost in the woods, you're supposed to stay in one place so rescue teams can find you.

Except no one's looking for me.

No one *human*, anyway.

If I stay still, the only people who might find me here are the ones I just escaped from. And I'm not about to lie here like a beacon for Galin's court.

So I pick a direction and start walking.

The forest floor makes for easy travel, smooth and soft. But every step sends a dull ache through my legs, and my arm stings where Cillian made the cut. My chest is tight, like my ribs are cinched with rope. I try to draw deeper breaths, but my lungs keep fluttering short.

My ears are tuned for danger, but the silence presses in like a thick blanket. No birds. No rustling animals. No distant chirps or hoots or the flapping of wings.

Nothing.

The absence prickles along my spine.

Shouldn't there be owls at least? Or bats?

The forest *feels* old. Sacred, maybe. Or cursed.

I try to shake it off, but the stillness gnaws at me.

It doesn't take long before my legs decide to give out. My muscles buckle, and I collapse into the pine needles, the thick layer catching me like a too-thin mattress. I lean against a tree, its bark rough against my shoulder, and I let my head rest there. I don't care how long it takes to get back. I made it out. That's what matters.

The nightmare is almost over.

And now that I know bleeding is what lets me break Galin's hold on me, I can do that myself. It's not ideal—I'm not exactly looking forward to slicing open my own skin, but it's doable. I won't need Cillian or anyone else to help me. I can keep myself clean of it. Of him.

He's not coming for me. I know that.

He let me go.

Or maybe he didn't know I left. Maybe he's still up there, furious and gold and terrible, scouring the palace for a girl who slipped through a crack in his kingdom.

A branch snaps in the distance.

Sharp. Loud. Deliberate.

I should leap to my feet. I should run or hide or get ready to fight.

But my body is done. It has nothing left to give. The ache in my bones is deeper than tired—it's something like hollow. My mind tries to scream danger, but the edges of my vision are already blurring, and my eyelids feel like lead.

I *know* I shouldn't sleep here.

Not in the open. Not now. Not with who might be watching.

But my body doesn't care. It's been asking for sleep since the first drop of blood hit the stone.

And finally, I stop fighting it.

My eyes drift closed, and the last thing I hear is the forest breathing around me—quiet, waiting.

And then—nothing.

Rustling along the ground jerks me into wakefulness.

I bolt upright, eyes snapping wide in the gloom, my body already tensed to run even before my mind catches up. The forest looms around me, darker than I remember, but the light hasn't changed much—so I couldn't have been out for more than a few minutes. A tiny mercy.

Then I hear them.

Voices. Low and sharp. Not far behind me.

A chill slices down my spine.

Galin?

No. My heart gives a single, painful thud at the thought —it's too soon to hope for him, and something about the tones is all wrong. Too clipped, too coarse. My breath stills as I press flat against the tree behind me, its bark scraping through my dress and into my spine.

There are three voices, but I can't understand what they're saying. The words are jagged, monkey-like chattering that grates against my ears. Nothing human. Nothing good.

Where am I?

Was that wall a one-way passage to somewhere even stranger? Some deeper pocket of fairyland? Some place not even Galin could reach?

I hold my breath and ease around the tree trunk, just far enough to try and glimpse them. If they're human, then maybe—I don't know, maybe I'm still near the edges of the human world. Maybe I've fallen into some weird wilderness preserve, and these are just creepy hikers. Anything but more fairies.

But the forest plays tricks. The sounds shift, move, refuse to settle in one place. Then—movement.

Something thin and long and wrong slinks from behind a trunk. A bony, bark-colored arm veined with green. I squint, trying to piece together what I'm seeing—who it belongs to—but the forest swallows their shape like it wants to keep their secrets. Still, I can just make out a face when one of them finally emerges.

I blink. Once. Twice. Three times.

No luck. He's still horrifying.

His nose is knobby, his grin too wide, filled with

crooked teeth. His eyes are sunken and gleaming. A heavy brown hood shadows the rest of his face, but there's no mistaking it.

Not human. Not even close.

My nails dig half-moon crescents into my palms as I slowly ease back into place, praying they'll pass me by. But fate doesn't deal in mercy, not with me.

My hand brushes against a twig—and it snaps.

It's barely a sound. A whisper. Surely they didn't—

The leader stops.

He raises a hand, and the other two freeze instantly. His head tilts, sniffing the air like a hound on a scent. His gaze scans the trees, and I shrink tighter into mine, lungs burning from how hard I'm trying not to breathe.

Please. Please let them think it was a squirrel. A fox. A branch falling.

But I know better. I've never been lucky. Not once. A lucky girl wouldn't have ended up Under the Hill in the first place.

Soft boots pad silently across the pine floor. If they hadn't been talking, I wouldn't have known they were there. They move like ghosts, silent and sure, and I press harder into the tree, wishing I could melt into it. Wishing I could vanish like I used to pretend I could as a kid, hiding under blankets from monsters I thought weren't real.

My heart is a drumbeat in my throat. Any second now, they'll give up. They'll turn away. Any second now.

A voice, low and oily, cuts through the silence.

"What do we have here?"

A strangled scream bursts from my throat before I can stop it. The leader's hand grabs around my neck, lifting me off the ground like I weigh nothing. His carrion-coated breath cascades down my face as he grins, lifting me to his eye level.

"A human beast?" the creature behind him asks, staring at me with sunk eyes.

"Smells like a fairy," the other one asks, large nostrils flaring as he takes a whiff of me.

"Shut up," the leader snarls, not taking his gaze from my face. His face is even uglier up close, barely resembling anything human. "Whatever it is, it's ours now."

I struggle to breathe, to say anything against the heavy pressure of his cold hands on my neck. Grabbing onto his arm, I try to lift the pressure off my throat before my head pops off like a daisy.

"It's not often we get fresh meat in this part of the woods," he breathes. "What brings you to the cursed forest?"

Cursed forest? Of course, I fell into somewhere just as dangerous as I left. I try to speak to him, the sounds coming out sputtering and weak around his grip, and his lipless mouth curves into a grin. He takes a long sniff of me, his nose brushing against my cheek.

"She has the smell of one of the Claimed. None of them have ever been left to explore here. Must be a mistake."

"I-it's not a mistake," I rasp, though the words scrape my throat like glass.

The leader's face shifts, his forehead a mass of wrinkles. "Then what are you doing in the cursed forest?"

"I got lost," I wheeze, wriggling in his cement grip. "I—I was in the palace, and I got turned around. Then... then I was here."

Not a lie. Just not the whole truth.

"The curse keeps others out. Humans do not just end up here." His smile turns evil, his yellow eyes glowing.

"I didn't mean to come," I blurt. "I swear. I didn't even know this place existed."

"Then your master does not value you very highly," he says with a smile that reveals each one of his jagged teeth. "Seems like you are fair game."

He barks something at the others. They grab my arms and hoist me off the ground, just as the leader finally releases my throat. Air floods in, sharp and cold, but my feet dangle uselessly.

They carry me through the forest, away from everything I recognize. Each step feels heavier, harder to breathe through. What will Galin think when I don't show up? Will he even care?"

He has to. He *has* to care.

Because whatever we are—whatever this pull is between us—there's something real there. He saved me once. Fought for me. and I—

I can't stop thinking about him.

Not even now, when I should be thinking only about escape. My throat aches where the leader grabbed me, but my arm where Cillian cut me, burns even worse.

The forest floor blurs as we walk. My arms go numb. Cillian's cut reopens on my skin, bleeding red then sluggish gold into my cream sleeve.

The faint blush of morning crests the trees, sending rosy light across the ground.

My heart lurches. *Dawn.*

I've never stayed in fairyland past sunrise. That was the deal. No matter how late I was, Galin always sent me home before light could touch me.

So why... why am I still here?

I shut my eyes, bracing for the rush of magic, the tingling sensation of something to tell me I'm leaving.

Nothing happens.

Why am I still here?

Was our bargain broken when I fled?

Or... has he chosen to end it himself?

The ache in my throat thickens. But I won't cry. Not now. Not when I still have a chance to think, to plan.

The forest shifts. A house appears ahead. It has to be. It's rounded like a tree trunk, but wider, using decaying pine boughs as a pointed roof and curving branches twisted together to make walls. A curl of grey smoke comes from a hole in the center of the roof. The leader in the front picks up the pace as he moves towards the house, and I can feel the palpable excitement wafting off the creatures next to me.

Dread pools in my stomach. Whatever's in there, I don't want to find out.

A rounded section of the house opens, revealing more creatures inside. Some are tall like the ones carrying me, but many are small as they hold onto the sagging brown clothes of the creatures closest to them. Children.

They brought me home.

"Welcome home," a creature with a rounder face than the ones I've been with for the last few hours says as it opens the door wider.

"We found something," the leader says with a grin that sends a chill down my spine.

The creature looks past him, its gaze landing on me. A small smile quirks at the side of its mouth. "It has been a long time since you brought something so substantial home with you."

"It is time we were truly fed," the leader says, passing through the wide door without a glance back at me.

I keep watching him, calculating. Because I'm not

giving up yet. Not on myself. Not on Galin. Not on the magic between us.

If he *did* choose not to call me back, then I'll find out why.

And if he didn't –if he's looking for me even now—then I need to stay alive long enough for him to find me.

Chapter Twelve

The creatures tie me to a post in the center of the room—thick, barkless wood that smells faintly of rot. A bonfire the size of a Volkswagen crackles nearby, casting flickering shadows across the packed dirt floor. More of the creatures cluster around the flames. The smaller ones—children, judging by their high-pitched clicks and unfiltered curiosity—creep closer. One of them prods at my leg with a stick.

I flinch, twisting away, but my limbs are stiff and uncooperative. Everything aches from being dragged here.

The leader of the group stands to the side, barking commands in that same guttural language I heard earlier. He gestures at me, and several of the larger goblins turn to stare. I bristle under their gaze. The leader barks something else and they laugh—a high, sharp sound. I don't know what was said, but my face burns.

Why do I even care? It's not like their opinion matters. They probably want to roast me like a marshmallow. Let them laugh. It's not going to matter when I'm smoke and bones.

My arms are twisted behind the pole, wrists bound by coarse cord that feels like jungle vine. Another strand coils around my ankles. I wriggle uselessly as another jab from a stick lands on my side. My skin throbs and I wriggle like a worm to get away from them.

I bite my tongue instead of snapping at them. No point wasting energy. If I'm going to get out of here, I need a better plan than yelling at children.

I would even take Galin's fury right now if it meant I was out of this new nightmare. At least with him, I wasn't about to be someone's dinner.

Closing my eyes, I count to ten and take inventory of everything I have on me. I have a pocketknife, one that's probably still halfway open, in the pocket of my dress. That's something.

I also have Galin's promise. He swore I wouldn't get hurt, so long as I followed his instructions. And technically... I haven't broken any rules. He never explicitly told me not to leave the palace. Never told me to stay in the throne room. He gave me space. That should count for something.

Unless none of this was trust at all. Unless he assumed I wouldn't be stupid enough to wander into the unknown.

Still, a promise is a promise—and Galin seems like someone who keeps his word. Or at least takes it seriously. Which means, assuming I'm not already on a spit, that he'll be looking for me.

Assuming he even knows I'm gone.

I grit my teeth. That line of thought isn't helpful.

Focus.

There has to be a way out. I've gotten through worse. Maybe not literally tired-up-and-threatened-by-cannibal-goblins worse, but still. I've survived this far.

The creature with the round face—the one who opened the door when we first arrived—shuffles toward me. Its forehead wrinkles as it studies me. It shoos the children away. They giggle, poking me once more before they scatter.

Its moss green hands are cool and clammy, like wet stone. It grabs my chin and tilts my face side to side, studying me like I'm a piece of fruit it's not sure is ripe. I try not to recoil.

It pulls back. Turns away.

"Wait."

I don't know why I say it. Maybe desperation. Maybe instinct. Maybe I just need someone—anyone—to see me as a person and not a snack.

The creature pauses, halfway to standing, watching me with narrowed yellow eyes.

"What are you? Where am I?"

Its head tilts. Maybe the question surprises it. Maybe no one's ever asked. Or maybe it's just surprised I can still talk.

It scuttles closer on spindly legs and folds its knobby arms. "You do not know what we are?"

I shake my head. "Should I?"

Its eyes narrow further. "Then how did you end up in the Cursed Forest? Mortals do not stumble in by accident."

"I didn't exactly plan a trip," I mutter. "There was a portal or something. I... fell through it."

That gets a reaction. It stares at me, then glances toward the larger group.

"We are the goblins of the Cursed Forest. I am Nioss."

Goblins? I guess it makes sense. Their skin looks like what I might have imagined a goblin would look like. I just didn't think they'd be so...big? The adults are easily a foot taller than me. For some reason, I'd always thought goblins were something smaller. Like a creature I might find in the bottom of a drawer or something ridiculous like that.

"Grace," I say.

She—Nioss apparently—nods and stands. She puts her triple jointed fingers on the leader's arm, whispering something into the thin flesh of its ear. The leader glances at me with a frown, turning to say something more to Nioss. Seeing them together, I realize Nioss must be a she and they must be partners.

I can't help but wonder... if she advocating for me? Pleading my case?

More likely, she's suggesting how to spice the meat.

Still. It's something.

The leader smiles, the points on his teeth glinting in the firelight as he comes closer to me. My back presses into the pole, my arms straining as I push to get away. The cut in my arm is a constant screaming pain as my body tenses. I stretch my fingers towards my pocket, wishing they could reach my knife even while knowing such a feat is impossible. Instead, I claw through the hard-packed dirt until the space under my fingernails is black.

"You say you are one of the Claimed," he says, crouching in front of me.

I swallow. "Y-yes."

The word shatters in the air. I hate how shaky it sounds. I want to be brave, but fear coats everything in my throat.

"Depending on who claimed you," he says, "my wife believes you may be worth more alive."

I blink. "Alive?"

He nods once. "Tell me who claimed you. We will consider."

"Galin," I say quickly. "His name is Galin."

His eyes narrow, considering my words. I don't know

what there is to think about. From what I've seen, Galin is a powerful guy. Wouldn't that immediately make me more valuable alive? He scratches at his smooth chin.

"I do not know of a Galin."

My stomach drops.

"He spends a lot of time with Tabitha," I try, grasping for anything. My voice stays steady and I'm grateful. I doubt any show of weakness would make me look any less appetizing at this point.

"The Queen of the Underhill?"

"The.. Underhill?"

He stands. "You lie."

"No—I'm not lying!"

But he waves me off, already turning away. "You had your chance. Too bad. You could have been valuable."

The words hit like a slap. The tiny hope I'd been cradling snuffs out.

I sag against the post, my wrists burning. No. no, I won't let it end here.

There's going to be a moment—a mistake, a slip, something—and I'll be ready.

I think of the room with the prisoners. Should I have said something to them? Offered comfort, a promise? Told them I'd come back?

What would that have helped? Nothing. I haven't done anything yet. Haven't even figured out how to return. And now that I've found a way out of the palace, it led me straight into a death trap.

Still, I'm not done.

I won't let this be the end of my story.

Not tied to a pole in a goblin hut, waiting to be someone else's dinner.

I chew my lip, heart hammering as I think. There has to

be a way out. Just because I haven't found it yet doesn't mean it doesn't exist. I've made it this far—I won't give up now.

With that decided, I push the swirling panic into the back of my mind and zero in on the most pressing problem: how to escape.

Wiggling my hands against the cord, I try to make more room in the knot for me to slip my hand out of. My hands can fold up pretty small when pressed up against something. The problem is that my wrists are abnormally small. They've been a feature I was proud of, my delicate wrists. It only makes it ironic now that they're going to be the thing that keeps me bound. The cord is tied so tightly around my wrists that there's no room for even a folded hand to slip out of.

Shifting against the pole, my hair comes out of its elastic, falling in gold sheets over my shoulders, blocking my field of view. If I were alone, I might twist myself into some horrible shape to get my hands near my feet, but the goblins haven't made that easy. I'm right in the center of the room—tied like a warning sign. Any suspicious movement and they'll be on me. I need a different plan.

A log shifts in the fire beside me, shooting red sparks toward the ceiling. I glance at it, and an idea flickers, dangerous and absurd.

It's a bad idea.

But it's *something*.

Before I can talk myself out of it, I swing my legs toward the flames and hook my feet onto the rim of the fire ring. Heat slams into me like a wave. I bite down on a scream as my shoes start to bake. It's agony—but the cord's cotton. If I can weaken it...

Sweat slides down my back. The goblin leader looks up

at my muffled groan and laughs, pointing me out to the others like I'm some kind of circus act. I can hear the words he doesn't say: how thoughtful of the girl to cook herself for us.

Let them laugh. I grit my teeth and twist my legs apart. The cord strains. Heat curls around my ankles. Just when I think I can't take any more, the cord gives with a snap. I yank my legs free with a gasp, smoke trailing from my scorched shoes.

My feet scream with pain. The white satin slippers Galin gave me are ruined—burnt, blistered, blackened. It shouldn't matter, but it does. They were a gift. A soft thing in a hard world.

I hope you understand, I think, not sure who I'm saying it to—him or myself.

My legs are free. That's something. I brace my hands behind me and try to stand—but my feet collapse under me. The pain is too sharp. I suck in a breath, fighting tears.

Thud.

The door shakes.

Silence falls.

Dozens of goblin eyes swing toward the door. The children stop whispering. Even the fire seems to hold its breath.

There's not much worse that can happen to me right now—but I've been wrong before.

Seconds drag by.

A knock hits the wood door. Polite and deliberate. Somehow this is even more terrifying than a crash.

I curl in tighter, heart thudding. The air feels too still. Even the goblins are tense. Something waits on the other side of that door—and it *isn't* turning back.

The door explodes inward with a bang, scattering dust and pine needles across the dirt floor. A dark silhouette, tall and sharp-edged, stands backlit by the morning light.

Galin.

My breath catches.

His name lives on the edge of my mouth, but I don't say it. I don't trust my voice not to crack.

Chaos erupts. Goblin children scream and their mothers scoop them up and retreat to the back of the room. The warriors form a loose wall between me and the door. Their leader grips a club in one green hand, his bulging with inhuman joints.

"You have something of mine," Galin says, his voice low and lethal.

"We cannot get anything that does not come to us in the forest."

Galin tilts his head to the side, his dark eyes falling on where I lie tied up. His eyes narrow, and he flicks his attention back over to the leader.

"Crel, you know your confinement here is due to your own actions."

"More like a punishment for being goblin."

"If you really find it that impossible to tame some of your... bloodier urges—"

"Like you do? We've heard what you fairies have done. Even the forest hears rumors."

Galin's jaw clenches. Crel smirks, pressing the insult deeper.

A flash of blue-white fire bursts from Galin's fingers, hissing as it hits the dirt. "Enough."

Crel shrinks back, the only sign of his fear. He hefts his club higher. "You cannot come into my home and talk to me thus."

"I can when you have taken what is *mine*."

Galin steps forward and the line of goblins shifts back instinctively.

For the first time, I notice a sword at Galin's hip. He never carries one. Not for show, at least. My eyes snag on it —smooth silver pommel, faintly glowing. Something old. Something real. I should be afraid. I'm still tied to the pole. Still bleeding. Still cornered. But curiosity burns hotter than fear.

Crel raises his voice. "We only take what the forest offers. If you have lost something, that is your fault."

"She is *marked*," Galin says, his voice colder than his flames.

"Marked makes no difference if they end up here."

Crel steps forward.

Before I can react, his hand knots my hair, yanking me upright. Pain explodes in my scalp. I'm forced to my feet, ankles wobbling, arms still tied to the pole.

The blade he pulls from my own pocket gleams as he presses it lightly to my throat.

"How much is she worth to you?" he asks Galin, stroking the knife against my skin. A whisper of steel. A warning.

My breath hitches. I go still.

Crel drops his club, winding his free hand through my hair and gripping my arm. I'm locked in his grasp, sharp pain shooting down my spine.

"How much is your life worth?" Galin asks, his voice terrifying in its softness.

"I would bet it has a higher value than hers."

"And more than *theirs*?" Galin glances towards the crowd of innocents that huddle farther into the back of the hut.

Crel hesitates. "They have nothing to do with this."

"Neither did she."

The blade bites deeper. I feel the burn as it slips through my skin. Warm blood slips down my neck.

Galin's gaze snaps to the red line blooming across my throat. His eyes widen—just a little—but I see it. Recognition. Understanding.

He has to see it now.

"You will release her," he says, "or you will burn."

"You would not dare."

Galin smiles and flicks his wrist, letting a small spark of blue flame land against the dry bark lining the walls of the hut. It catches immediately, the walls turning blue in the heat of his fire. They catch fast, too fast. Screams rise behind me.

"Do you believe me now?"

Crel curses in his native tongue. He yanks the knife away from my neck and stares at the flames climbing toward the roof.

"Stop this!"

"Let. Her. Go."

Crel swears again and slices the cord binding my wrists. I collapse to my knees, hands finally free.

He throws my knife into the ground beside me. "End this!"

But the fire keeps growing. Smoke curls toward the ceiling. Children sob behind me.

Not all of them deserve this. Not the ones cowering behind their leader. Not the ones who didn't choose this.

I twist and crawl toward my knife, fingers scraping the dirt until I find the handle. I drag myself upright, heart pounding, smoke stinging my eyes. Blood drips from my throat, dotting the front of my ruined dress with gold splotches.

Crel stares at Galin, oblivious to me. I take a shaky step away, scanning the room. Too many people. Too little time.

An arm slides around my waist.

I scream, twisting—

"Grace."

Galin's voice is low, steady.

It's him.

His arms wrap around me, and the world disappears into mist. Cool, dense, swallowing the fire, the goblins, the blood, the smoke.

The last thing I hear is the fire crackling behind me as the darkness takes me.

Chapter Thirteen

The mists peel away in slow, silvery tendrils, revealing first the plush rug beneath me and then the rest of Galin's room. I collapse to my knees, hacking smoke from my lungs, my chest heaving like I've run for miles.

I'm still gripping the pocketknife. My knuckles are bone-white around the handle, muscles locked in place. Even if I wanted to drop it, I couldn't.

Forcing a long breath through my nose, I uncurl my shoulders and lift my chin. Galin stands above me, tense and silent. His lips are pressed tight, jaw rigid as if he's physically restraining the words trying to claw out of him. His eyes rake over me—my ruined dress, streaked with ash and blood, the gash at my throat still weeping slowly. The cut on my arm has soaked through my sleeve and begun to drip, dotting the fine carpet with bright stains.

"What were you thinking?" he says finally, his voice low and sharp.

I flinch. Not because he yells—he doesn't—but because there's something frayed and frightened beneath the anger.

"I didn't know where I was going," I say quietly.

"Is that meant to comfort me?" His tone hardens. "You were warned, again and again, what lies beyond this place. And still, you ran."

My fingers tighten around the knife. "Being near you felt like the greater danger."

That stops him. He steps back, as if the words strike something buried deep. He turns away from me and walks to the cold hearth, planting one arm on the mantle. His head bows low, breath shuddering against the stone.

"I made a promise to protect you," he says, barely audible.

"I didn't think you cared," I murmur.

Galin turns, showing me the side of his sharp jaw. "We made an agreement, and I am bound to it."

I straighten, chin lifting with slow resolve. "Then why am I still here? It's already daylight. Shouldn't our deal be finished?"

I hear the edge in my voice. It's colder than I meant it to be, ignoring the fact that his fury earlier was about me vanishing. That he came for me. Fought for me. I should be grateful, but I'm too tired and too hurt to say it aloud. Right now, I need answers.

He doesn't look at me when he speaks. "You left the palace. The magic only works within its boundaries."

"Oh."

The truth hits with a hollow weight. I'd thought it was proximity to Galin that mattered. That his anger had somehow rewritten the rules. I hadn't realized just *being outside* the palace would strand me there.

If I'd stayed—even just a little longer—I'd be home by now.

"Will you send me back?" I ask, almost before I've finished the thought.

It's not pleading. Not quite. I'm already calculating what I'll need to do if I want to make it to class. The blood loss might make that hard, but if I can clean up fast enough, maybe I'll avoid a full disaster. I'll deal with Joan. With school. I just need to get back.

Galin turns back to the fireplace and the silence between us stretches long.

"No."

The word hits like a slap. "No? What do you mean, *no*? I need to go home—"

"You are in no condition to leave."

I grit my teeth, fighting the tears burning behind my eyes. "I'll manage. I'll change, cover the worst of it—"

"Changing clothes will not stop the bleeding," he interrupts.

"It's not that bad." My voice cracks. I reach up and brush my fingers over the cut at my throat, trying to prove my point—but the gesture makes him turn. Really turn.

His gaze slides from my neck to my arm, tracking the blood that drips from my sleeve and puddles at my feet. I step off the rug and onto the tile, where the bright droplets hit the marble like falling stars. No use hiding it now.

He's going to know.

Know that I asked Cillian for help. Know that I was trying to undo whatever magic Galin left inside me. Know that I didn't trust him.

And still—still—I'm afraid of what he'll say.

"Will you let me help you?" he asks.

"Will it cost me something?" I shoot back. "Another bargain? Another debt?"

His face remains calm, but I see the slight recoil in his shoulders. "No deal. Just help."

My fingers slip, trying to press against the worst of the cut. "You really expect me to believe that?"

"You should," he says. "You are already under protection. This falls under the same promise."

He's watching me too closely. Reading me. I hate that I want to believe him, that I want his help even though I'm still furious.

"You said I broke the deal by leaving," I argue. "Shouldn't that make your promise invalid?"

He exhales a quiet breath, something like amusement softening the edge of his jaw. "You are clever, Grace, but you are wrong. I never said you *had* to stay. Only that I would keep you safe. That failure was mine."

I stare at him.

"So you're... what? Holding *yourself* to the bargain?"

"Yes."

There's no hesitation in his voice. No pride, either. Just truth.

I let out a long breath, pain and exhaustion unraveling my defenses. I glance down at the blood staining my fingers, the torn edge of my sleeve, the knife still clutched in my hand.

I look back up at him.

"Then help away."

I half expect him to do something to make this worse—another clever barb, a cruel smirk—but his hands are gentle as he guides me to the chair in front of the fireplace.

With a flick of his fingers, flames curl into life. The warmth unfurls across my skin, chasing the deep chill I hadn't even realized had set into my bones. I sink into the chair's plush embrace, letting it cradle me, soft and safe. Or as safe as anything here ever is.

Galin tilts my head with the barest touch, coaxing my chin up to inspect the damage. The firelight gleams off the blood still drying on my throat, warming it, making it feel strangely alive again.

I should be more afraid. A cut across the neck is never trivial. But I'm not scared. All I can think about is how I must look—wild-eyed, bloodied, a far cry from the polished girl he brought into his court. The thought flickers through me like shame, and I hate myself for it.

I barely breathe as he presses a cloth to my throat.

"You are fortunate," he murmurs, dabbing gently. "It does not appear to be deep."

"I don't know. It feels like any neck wound kind of cancels out the 'fortunate' part."

He huffs, but it's not quite a laugh. "You are right. I should have prevented this."

"That's not what I-" I start, but he lifts a finger to my lips, silencing me with a featherlight touch that sends a shiver straight through my spine.

His expression is unreadable as he resumes wiping away the blood. Then he pours something sharp-smelling onto a clean cloth and presses it to the wound. I gasp as it stings, but don't pull away.

"It needs to be cleaned."

His voice is low and careful. I close my eyes to avoid the way his jaw clenches every time he finds a new scrape. He shouldn't have to do this. He's a prince or a predator or both, and yet here he is, tending my wounds like it matters.

"You don't have to be the one to do this," I say, opening my eyes. "There's probably someone else—"

"I know." He doesn't look up. "But I *am* the one doing it."

"It's your job to keep me alive, not...this."

"Would you prefer I leave you to clean your own wounds?" His eyes finally meet mine, dark and unreadable. "Would it be easier if I did not care?"

My heart skips, stumbling over the question. "But you don't—"

I stop too late. My mouth betrays me faster than my blood ever could. Heat floods my face, and Galin's mouth curls into something small and knowing. A near-smile. He doesn't comment, just dips the cloth in water again and continues his careful work.

I'm grateful for his silence—for the way he pretends not to notice the mess I'm becoming inside.

I keep reminding myself it's the fairy dust. That's all. That's why I feel drawn to him, why every brush of his fingers feels electric. Logically, I know this isn't real. But logic has nothing on the way my pulse jumps when he leans closer.

"You should bathe before returning home."

"I'm sorry, what?"

Will my blush ever go away? At this point, all the blood left in my body has to be pooling in my face.

He raises an eyebrow, unfazed. "You are caked in forest grime and ash. Even in this light, it is obvious."

"I'll shower when I get back."

He shrugs, setting down the cloth now stained red and gold. I stare at the smear of my blood—unnatural, glittering. He doesn't comment. Doesn't ask. He must know. He *must* be wondering.

And yet...silence.

Maybe if he asked, I could lie. Or not lie, exactly. I could say I didn't know. Maybe we could figure it out together. But he's not asking. So I won't offer. If this doesn't matter to him, then I'll pretend it doesn't matter to me.

Even though it does.

He picks up a soft wrap and winds it gently around my throat, careful, his fingers brushing against my jaw, my collarbone. The intimacy of it makes it hard to breathe.

Too distract myself, I blurt, "Too bad it's not the 90's. This would make a killer choker."

He blinks. "A...choker?"

I suppress a laugh. "Never mind. Time-bound fashion joke."

He tilts his head slightly, amused and confused. Everything he's given me to wear looks like it was pilfered from a history drama. I guess chokers weren't a thing in the fairy courts.

"Thank you," I say quietly.

"It was only what was owed."

"You could just say, 'you're welcome'."

That earns me a rare smile. "You are welcome."

The words land more softly than they should. Softer than what I want to admit. And suddenly, I don't feel quite so fogged by magic. This—this feels real.

His eyes lower to my arm. "You have another wound."

"I can manage that one myself."

"I am positive I can do a better job."

"That's not the point."

"You would leave me still bleeding?"

I cross my arms—awkwardly, one of them still throbbing. "I want to go home."

"I'll send you," he says, his tone even. "After we dress this."

His patience is wearing down my resistance. With a sigh, I slump back. "Fine. Do you want me to change first?"

"You will only bleed through clean clothes. Pull your arm out if you can."

The dress is low-backed enough that I can tug the fabric down on one side, baring my shoulder and arm. Still, the motion feels strangely intimate now, with his gaze steady on me.

The bandage Cillian left is soaked through. The golden blood still drips slowly, traitorously, down my skin. Galin peels the cloth away with careful fingers. He doesn't speak.

He must know now. The wound was too clean, too old, too deliberate. Not goblin-made. What does he think I was trying to do?

He picks up a fresh cloth, dips it into the murky water, and begins to clean the gold sheen from my arm. His touch is slow, almost reverent. I watch his face, waiting for judgment, curiosity—anything.

Nothing.

"I'm sorry," I say finally.

His eyes flick up to mine. "For what?"

There's a dangerous closeness to him now. His breath brushes my collarbone.

"For running."

He pauses, his hand still warm on my arm. "Mortals run from what they fear."

"I still shouldn't have. You promised to protect me. I should've trusted that."

He's so close. If I turned my face, just slightly…

"You had no reason to trust me," he says quietly. "Not

yet. And not when you don't know the rules of our bargains."

"Is that it? I just need a better fairy rulebook?"

He lets out a soft huff. "Perhaps. But even then, you might still assume the worst. Fairies...we have earned our reputation."

"So you *do* find ways out of bargains?"

"Often."

"That's reassuring."

He dips his head, not denying it. "It is who we are. We were made that way."

"Made cruel?" I ask, harsher than I mean to.

"No," he says, brushing the last of the blood away. "Made to survive."

"And you think humans aren't?"

"I think you burn too brightly and too briefly."

The words strike something deep. I sit still, heart skipping.

"You mean mortals in general," I say, voice tight.

He doesn't answer.

My stomach twists. "What do you know?"

Still nothing. Still, silent.

"What aren't you telling me?" My voice cracks, desperate and afraid.

Galin presses the cloth gently to my arm, but I pull it away, clutching it to my chest. His face is full of something unspoken. Anguish? Regret?

"Tell me what's going on," I whisper. "The full truth this time."

Galin's voice is quiet, almost tender. "I brought you to every meeting. Have you truly not pieced it together?"

My heart stutters. "I..." My mouth opens, then shuts again.

He repeats himself, voice heavier now, sadder. "Do you not know what is happening now?"

No. I don't.

And I hate that I don't.

In those meetings, I'd half-listened, letting my mind drift toward more comforting distractions—the shimmer of gossamer sleeves, the way that one courtier's voice curved around his sentences like music, how another laughed too loudly, trying too hard to impress Galin. I'd watched the fairies and tried to understand who they were, what they wanted—except not the important part. Not the part that mattered.

I'd listened like a tourist at a foreign play, trying to guess the plot from the costumes alone.

I'm an idiot.

"There was nothing I could do about bringing you here," Galin says. "A human was required. But there is a reason you are still alive when others are not."

His words hit me like a blow to the chest. "The others aren't..." My thoughts fall into a dark spiral.

Dead?

All those girls—the ones I left crying alone in that dark room—gone...

I should still have time. I *had* time. Didn't I?

But my brain refuses to finish the thought. Some protective instinct wraps my mind in fog, refusing to let it go there.

Galin steps closer. "Do you not know? Everything I have done has been to change this."

"Change—?"

"Grace." His hands are suddenly on my shoulders, grounding me, anchoring me. "Are you listening to me?"

His voice echoes like it's coming from the end of a

tunnel. None of this makes sense. None of it fits with what I thought I knew—about him, about me, about those girls.

He shifts his hands, cupping my face now. "Grace."

"Wh-what are you saying?" My voice is paper-thin, but it's a start.

"I am saying I need you. I need your help."

I blink at him. "Why would you need *me*?"

I pull away, the motion nearly topples me from the stool. Galin lets me go, arms falling to his lap, face drawn with something I can't name—guilt? Pain?

"I have told you—I had to take you. It was a requirement."

"Then why are you saying everything like it's some grand confession?" I snap, regaining some of my voice. "If you're trying to enlighten me, this is the worst possible method."

He reaches out again—just one finger this time, pressed gently against my lips. The sensation is lightning in my chest. My heartbeat staggers and the pine smell of him fills the air around me, blotting out conscious thought.

"Because," he says quietly, "this is bigger than just you and me. The law requires that we offer Tabitha blood each month. Our own kind is protected, which leaves one obvious source."

"Humans." The word barely makes it past his finger.

"I found a loophole," he continues, lowering his hand. "I am required to *claim* blood, not deliver it. Having you here has technically fulfilled my obligation. I have delayed the worst of it. For you."

I should feel relieved. But all I feel is cold.

"So that's all I am?" I ask bitterly. "Blood on a technicality?"

He presses on, voice thickening. "It is more than that. I

am trying to show my people that *they do not need blood at all.* That we can return to what we once were."

"What do they even want?"

Galin smiles—but there's no real joy in it. "Magic."

And suddenly, something clicks.

A flash: that meeting with the golden-robed fairy, her voice cutting sharp across the table. *"Our reserves are dwindling. We must find a more sustainable source, or the court collapses."*

A second memory: the quiet, lean one—his name started with a T?—murmuring, *"There are rumors that blood type alters the potency. That human blood... could align with ancient rites."*

I'd been half-listening. I thought they were talking politics, old legends. Not *murder.*

I force myself to focus. "And our blood gives them that magic?"

"Each blood type holds different strengths," he confirms. "Tabitha drains her offerings, then gives the power back to her favorites. But the magic doesn't last. It burns quickly. So she gathers more."

A terrible thought worms into my chest. "Is that where *your* magic comes from?"

I picture the way he summoned flame like it was breathing, how mist curled at his fingertips. All the times he whisked me through corridors like I weighed nothing. How many people had to bleed for that?

"No," he says quickly. "I draw my power from the earth, the way we were meant to. But fewer do now."

"Because the earth is contaminated."

"Yes. But not dead. Just harder to reach."

I nod slowly. "And blood is easier."

He watches me carefully. "Too easy. And it has changed us."

"Changed you how?"

"We used to live in balance—danger and joy in equal measure. But now the danger is the joy. The cruelty feeds them. They have forgotten what it is to live without hunger."

"That's why you care?" I ask. "Not because the humans are dying, but because the fairies are acting differently?"

He flinches, just slightly. "I will always prioritize my people. That is the truth."

My heart dips. Of course he would say that. Why had I expected more?

But he adds, quieter, "That does not mean I do not care what happens to you."

I cross my arms, ignoring the sting of my cut and the fact that I'm still half-dressed. The memory of the dress and what it did to me lingers, and Galin's presence doesn't help.

"You're not a savior," I say. "You're just another one of them."

"But you are not one of *them*," he says, his voice sounding almost desperate.

"I might as well be. If I'd been swooped up by any other fairy, I would have been a mess of blood across an altar by now."

"No," he says. "I would not have let that happen."

"You wouldn't have had a choice. I would have belonged to someone else."

"You only ever could have belonged to me."

The world stills around me. Galin's eyes are dark, his gaze wavering towards my lips. I swallow slowly, trying to rid myself of the lump in my throat. He leans in closer, sending a wave of his earthy scent over me. My arms relax, sending a stab of pain in my arm from the freed blood flow. The pain wakes me to reality, and I pull farther away from him. The sound of the fire comes rushing back in, and Galin stops himself from coming any closer.

"I belong to *no one*."

He smiles faintly. "I think I am beginning to understand that."

"Then tell me. What do you *actually* need me for? You already have magic."

Galin pauses, using his long fingers to massage his temples. "It is not as simple as you make it out to be."

"Try."

"I am still trying to figure that out. But I do know this—we cannot take just anyone. Our reach is limited. But you... there was something about you. I was drawn to you."

"Lucky me," I mutter.

"It is not nothing," he says softly. "Maybe it started as a necessity, but that is not what this is now."

I close my eyes. Without the fairy dust clouding my thoughts, the truth hits harder.

I didn't matter. Not at the start.

"What really matters," Galin says, "Is that I need to stop what Tabitha's doing. And I cannot do it alone."

I want to stay angry. I want to hate him. But our goals are just starting to overlap, and that makes the rage harder to hold.

"What do you need me to do?"

"First," he says, "you need to learn how to use that knife."

I glance down at my pocketknife where it lies discarded on the floor, a line of gold burned into the metal.

"What does it matter to you if I know how to use it or not?"

"A weapon you are holding that you do not know how to use can be used against you. I would rather have you somewhat prepared to defend yourself instead of being at the whim of any fairy you meet down here."

"How charming."

Galin shrugs. "It is my attempt to be honest with you."

"I thought that's all you *could* do."

"I am trying to be *clear*," he corrects, running a hand through his silky hair. "What do you want from me, Grace?"

A hundred thoughts whirl in my head. Freedom. Power. Revenge. Safety. But all I say is—"I want you to release me."

Galin sighs. "If I release you, then I have to start all over."

"You haven't even started."

He stands suddenly, muscles taut, blood dark against his tunic like a galaxy of stars. He paces back and forth, a hand constantly working at his hair until it's sticking up in a million directions. "You think I have done nothing? Just waited?" he snaps. "Then maybe you are right, and this *is* all wrong.

Even furious, he's beautiful. I hate that I notice. I hate *him*. I hate that I can't stop.

"Will you work with me or not?" he finally asks, standing with fists clenched on either side of his body.

"Will you release me first?"

"If I do, how can you work with me?"

"You'll have to trust me."

His eyes narrow. "Nothing about this conversation has made you look trustworthy."

"Right back at you."

He stares at me, and his knuckles whiten as he tightens his fist.

I take a deep breath, the copper smell of blood mixing

with his smell of pine as I brace myself for the fight that is sure to come. I don't expect him to take me up on this, but I want to at least get more from him than what I've had. If he wants us to work together, then I'll do it as his equal, not his prisoner.

"Fine." He breathes out a long breath. "You are free of our bargains."

"All of them?"

"As many as you want. I would recommend you keep the one forcing me to protect you in place. That is as much for your safety as anything else."

"Even though it binds me to your orders?" I raise my brow.

"If we are allies, then that should not be a problem."

"Fine."

"Then will you let me teach you how to use that knife now?" he asks.

I exhale slowly. "As thrilling as that sounds, it's daylight now. I need to go home."

I'm already going to be in huge trouble for going missing. My phone is probably blowing up with texts I'll never be able to explain. But when they see my injuries—when they see what's been done to me—it won't matter what story I tell. I might as well have been killed tonight.

None of that will matter to Galin. He doesn't understand consequences the way humans do. So I keep my mouth shut and wait while he considers my request.

"Tonight then," he says finally, his voice careful.

"Sure," I say, even though I don't know if I'll be able to stand up, let alone fight.

He adds, "If you are healed enough by then."

Something flutters in my chest, wild and unwelcome. I crush it.

He doesn't care what happens to me. He just needs me to be functional. I'm only useful to him if I can stand upright, hold a weapon, and bleed on command. I repeat those thoughts like a mantra, trying to kill the flicker of hope his words stirred.

"I am... grateful you are willing to help me," Galin says, gaze dropping to his hands.

The quiet in his voice surprises me. There's something unfamiliar about him now—a gentleness I haven't been able to see before. A softening. He seems...human. Almost.

Is it me? Is it the absence of fairy dust in my system that's stripped away the glamour and let me see him more clearly? Or is *he* playing another angle, trying to make himself seem safe enough to trust?

I narrow my eyes. "I'm not doing this for you."

He nods, solemn, and doesn't ask why. He doesn't need to. He already knows what I'm thinking.

That I'm doing this because people are dying. Because I don't want to be complicit. Because I want to *matter* in a place where everyone treats me like I'm disposable.

Even if I'm not entirely sure that's the whole truth anymore.

Galin speaks again, this time without looking at me. "I recommend you keep your injuries... to yourself."

His eyes flick to the bandage at my neck, then away. The look on his face is unreadable. Guilt? Regret? Calculation?

I raise my chin. "It's my injury to worry about."

This gets another nod from him. Smaller this time. Like he's shrinking inside himself. He's not the same male who threatened to burn down an entire hut full of innocents to protect me. Not the firestorm in velvet who bent the air around him like it wanted to obey. He looks... smaller now. Tired. Worn thin.

Is that real?

Or is it just another illusion?

I study him. There's something about the way his shoulders curl inward, in the way his hands twitch like he wants to reach for me but doesn't dare. There's power in him, still. But it's laced now with something hesitant. As if *I* could hurt *him.*

And for a second—just a second—I want to.

Because it would be easier than this. Easier than letting him crawl into my chest and make a home there with nothing but silence and the ghost of a look.

"Send me home, Galin," I say, my voice as sharp as steel.

His hands still. His jaw tightens. But he says nothing. Doesn't argue. Doesn't beg.

Doesn't even look at me.

And then—

The world lurches sideways.

The palace, the dark velvet air, the smell of moss and roses—it's all yanked away like a curtain torn down in a storm.

And I'm gone.

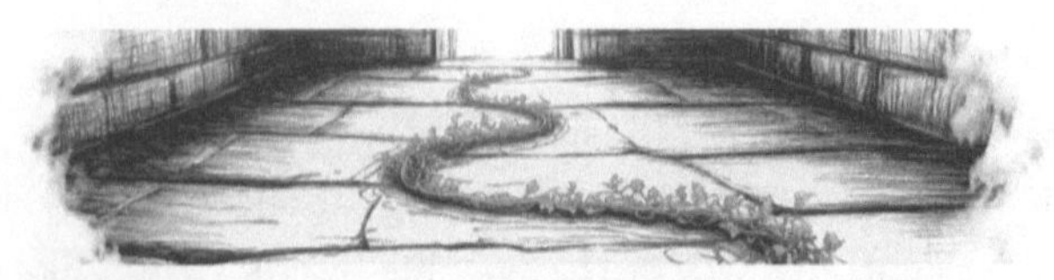

Chapter Fourteen

I fall to my knees before the darkness fully dissolves. My hands hit the carpet and I don't even feel the pain. The weight of the night descends on me like a thick, suffocating blanket, pressing down until my lungs feel like they're folding in on themselves.

All I want is to crawl under my blankets, bury my head in my pillow, and pretend none of this ever happened. Pretend I never met Galin. Never bargained. Never bled.

The blinking red numbers on the clock by my bed reads **9:00am**. If I can move now—if I can move—I'll have only missed one class. I could still make something of the day. Technically.

But my limbs don't listen. My muscles have turned to soaked wool, heavy and useless. Every cell in my body is screaming in silence.

I glance down—and freeze.

I'm still wearing *that dress*. The cream silk thing Galin conjured last night. Somehow, it followed me back. There's no sign of my uniform. No shoes. No explanation. Just the soft, expensive fabric that clung to my body like magic, now stained with ash and dried blood. My blood.

The sight breaks something in me.

Tears slip down my cheeks—slow and hot, carving paths down my skin like acid. I cover my mouth with both hands to keep the sob from escaping, but my shoulders shake with the effort.

"Grace?"

Joan's voice. She sounds more surprised than concerned. A moment later, the edge of her pristine sneakers appears in the corner of my vision. Her socks are perfectly folded, as usual. I must look like roadkill next to her.

I still can't move.

She crouches beside me and her hands—warm and oddly clinical—lift me off the floor. I don't protest. I don't have the strength.

Joan's eyes narrow as she scans me from head to toe. Not with worry. With calculation. Like she's trying to work something out.

"What happened to you?" she asks, her voice barely above a whisper.

I shake my head. Not because I can't answer—but because I *won't*. Galin doesn't need to warn me to keep this a secret. Even if I tried to explain, who would believe me? The police didn't. My own father wouldn't. Joan? Not a chance. She'd report me, or worse—try to *help*. The wrong kind of help. The kind that puts people in padded rooms.

"I'm fine," I whisper, and even I don't believe it with the tremor running through my voice.

Joan doesn't press. Instead, she lets out a breath and says, "Let's get you cleaned up."

She strips the dress from my body with an efficient

grace, not flinching at the dried blood or the faint smell of fire. I wonder if she's seen worse. The thought sends a chill crawling up my spine.

Without a word, she grabs a pack of makeup wipes from her dresser and starts scrubbing the ash on my arms, not the crushed blood at my collarbone. Her movements are practiced. Detached. Not *kind* exactly. Just... thorough.

The wipes are freezing against my skin, but I don't complain. I sit, trembling, as she peels away the evidence. Bit by bit.

When she's satisfied, she walks to the closet and pulls out a fresh uniform. It's mine. One I remember folding before all of this mess ever started.

You're lucky," she says, sliding the shirt onto my limp arms. "No one's come looking for you yet."

"I guess I'm not important enough to miss," I murmur.

Her lips twist, but she doesn't answer.

Once she's forced me into the full uniform, she steps back with a winkle of her nose. "There's nothing I can do about the bonfire stench coming from your hair," she says. "But you look alive now. More or less."

She glances at the clock. "We need to go. Before the headmistress gets involved. You really want her calling your dad?"

I flinch.

Getting my father involved would be the worst-case scenario. He's not the kind of man who listens—he fixes. Which usually means pulling me out of school and dropping me into some other one the second a problem arises. That, or a punishment designed more for his convenience than my growth. When I signed up for the app, I wanted to get his attention. But not like this. Not through blood and fire and bruises I can't explain.

"I'll walk," I mumble, but Joan is already grabbing my bag, already guiding me out the door like I'm a toddler.

She says nothing as we pass other students in the hall-way. But I feel their eyes. My neck burns with it—my bandage, my sunken eyes, my silence.

I tug my collar up over the wound Galin took care of. It's probably obvious. Too tight, too deliberate. But no one says anything.

Joan shepherds me into class and deposits me in my seat like a handler with a broken bird. She takes the desk beside me, cracking open a bubblegum pink notebook that's disgustingly cheerful given the circumstances.

I want to thank her. I think.

But every time I look at her, there's a question I can't quite put my finger on. She didn't ask *nearly* enough ques-tions. She didn't even blink at the dress. Or the blood. Or the bruises.

Why not?

Our teacher breezes into the room, already droning on, but I don't hear a word. My mind is a haze of fatigue, fear, and suspicion.

Joan doesn't say anything the entire period, but she doesn't need to. She's watching me. Carefully. Casually. Like she's memorizing my tells.

When the bell rings, I push up from the seat with stiff limbs.

"I'll catch up," I tell her. "I forgot something in the room."

She shrugs but doesn't argue. Doesn't ask what.

Of course she doesn't.

As I make my way down the hall, I feel the weight of the morning pressing harder on my shoulders. If I'd made better friends—if I'd *let* people in—maybe someone would have pulled me aside and asked the right questions. Maybe someone would have *cared*.

But I didn't.

And now Joan is the only one watching.

And I'm not sure if that's a good thing—or the beginning of something worse.

Standing in front of the mirror mounted to the back of the door, I barely recognize the girl looking back at me. My shoulders droop, hunched in a posture I don't remember learning. There's a stark white bandage stretching across my throat—bright and sterile against skin that's too pale. And my eyes... they're sunken, lost in bruised circles that speak more honestly than I ever could. Weeks of restless nights have etched themselves into my face. I look like something half-dead, dragged out of a grave.

Fairyland has been kind to me. And the worst part is, I let it happen. I went looking for magic. I wanted something *more*. And I got it. I just didn't understand the cost.

With a sharp breath, I tear my gaze away. There's only so much truth I can take in one sitting. I turn my back on the mirror and kneel in front of my closet, rummaging through the wrinkled mess of dress codes and uniforms until I find an approved sweatshirt. It's navy and shapeless and smells faintly of laundry detergent, which feels like a small mercy.

I tug it over my head and pull at the neckline, trying to stretch it higher. But it doesn't come close to covering the bandage. I scowl at my reflection in the mirror's corner, already judging me.

Then I remember.

Last year, my father sent me snow gear. It arrived in the middle of spring, like he'd only just remembered I existed and didn't bother checking the season. I never used it. Where would I go? But I think I shoved it under the bed in a burst of frustration. Or maybe guilt.

Shifting to my knees, I peer beneath the bed. There—a plastic tub wedged against the wall. I reach for it, and pain sparks in my shoulder. A hiss escapes my lips. Even that small movement lights every nerve in my arm on fire. I grit my teeth and keep going, dragging it out one awkward inch at a time.

The lid sticks. I wrestle with it until it pops open and the contents slouch forward like they've given up too. Hats, scarves, mittens, all never used. They look as tired as I feel, crumpled and forgotten.

Somehow, it feels like a metaphor I didn't ask for.

I shove the thought aside. There's no time to spiral.

The first scarf I pull out is dark navy wool, just barely matching the plaid in my uniform skirt. Not perfect, but better than nothing. I wind it around my neck with shaking fingers, tucking the ends carefully to hide the bandage. The fabric brushes the wound and I flinch.

I still haven't looked at it. Not directly. Galin bandaged it, and I told myself that was enough. The idea of peeling that wrap away, of seeing what the Goblin *really* did to me, makes bile rise in my throat.

Maybe I'm a coward. Or maybe I'm just not ready. If I wait a week—two, maybe three—the shock won't be so sharp. That's the logic I tell myself. It sounds reasonable when I say it in my head. But deep down, I know the truth:

A slice across your throat never becomes normal. It never stops being terrifying.

The clock flashes at me from the dresser, and panic jolts through my system. I've wasted lunch.

I shove the tub back under the bed and stumble to my feet. My body aches in protest, every step like dragging bricks. I grab my bag and race for the door.

Joan is already waiting in the hallway, arms folded around a neat stack of textbooks. Her face is unreadable, mouth neutral, eyes cool. She doesn't say anything at first —just falls into step beside me like a second shadow.

Her gaze flicks down, skimming over my scarf, my stiff posture, the way I hold my arm a little too close to my side. She doesn't ask questions. But she sees *everything*.

I'm not sure which is worse.

The scarf won't fool her. Probably won't fool anyone. But it's not supposed to. I don't need people to *believe* I'm fine. I just need them to stop asking. Teachers are too busy to investigate why I've decided to pull out winter gear in early fall. And the other students? They're more used to me being weird.

It's my father I'm worried about. If anything gets reported—if a teacher decides I'm enough of a liability— he'll get the call. And if he shows up, it'll be with demands and punishments and the kind of attention that hurts more than it helps.

So no, the scarf isn't for comfort. It's for survival.

Joan walks silently beside me, but I feel her attention like static electricity. Too aware. Too quiet.

"You look like you got hit by a truck," she says at last, her tone dry but not exactly unkind.

"Yeah," I mutter. "I feel like it, too."

She hums, like she's filing that response away. And then she drops it. No questions. No pushing. Just quiet observation and a careful neutrality that sets my nerves on edge.

Why doesn't she press? Most people would. Most people *should.*

We slide into our seats and Joan opens her notebook with precise fingers. Her handwriting is bubble-curved and neat. Mine is a disaster lately. I haven't taken proper notes in days.

I glance sideways at her.

She's helping me. Guiding me to class. Covering for me when I can't function. But her patience isn't limitless. And I keep wondering—what does she want? People don't offer help without strings.

And Joan? Joan *not* asking questions is starting to feel like the biggest question of all.

I shake the thoughts away. Not now. That's a problem for another day.

Right now, I have to survive.

I have to survive and find a way to get those girls home.

Because whatever bargain I've made, whatever damage I've taken—it can't be for nothing.

I barely make it through my classes. My head feels light and heavy all at once—a paradox that makes me nauseous, like my body can't decide whether I'm about to faint or implode. Everything around me is too bright, too loud. The noise of pencils scratching paper and chairs scraping linoleum might as well be fireworks in my skull. I force myself to nod like I'm listening, jot down notes I won't remember, even raise my hand once just to prove I still exist.

After dinner, I don't even pretend to socialize. I mumble

something to Joan, something polite and vague, and head back to our room on autopilot. My pulse beats in odd, off-rhythm stutters, like it knows something is coming. It always starts around this time—just before the sun dips too low, before the veil between their world and ours starts to thin. My body remembers even if I don't want it to. This used to be the hour Galin came for me.

But the deal is over. I broke it. That should bring relief.

Instead, it brings terror.

Because now there are no rules. No schedule. No warning. Will he come tonight? Tomorrow? Or not at all?

And-and this is the part I won't admit out loud-do I want him to?

I collapse onto my bed, curling on my side beneath the covers. The warmth and weight are too much. After a night with no sleep and a day spent pretending I'm okay, the soft darkness under the blankets is dangerously tempting. Just a short nap, I tell myself. Ten minutes. Maybe twenty. Just to feel human again.

The door slams open, I jolt upright so fast my vision tilts. I swipe at my eyes, heart lurching in my chest. I'm already half-expecting to see Galin, that strange shimmer of his magic pressing into the room.

But it's not him.

It's Joan.

My chest feels tight and I pretend his absence doesn't mean anything.

She stands at the foot of my bed, arms crossed, face sharp with suspicion. The room feels colder with her in it. The air too still.

"Are you going to tell me what happened?" She folds her arms over her chest, watching me with narrowed eyes. "I let it go before, but I think you owe me some answers."

"You wouldn't believe me even if I told you."

"Do you really have so little faith in me?"

"Not in you," I hedge, shifting upright and clutching the blanket closer. "Just.. in your ability to suspend your disbelief long enough to hear what I have to say."

"I think my ability to believe might astound you," she says dryly, hands braced on her hips.

There's something careful in her voice. Something she's not saying.

I hesitate. There are a thousand ways this could go wrong. But the truth is, I'm tired of being alone in this. And if anyone's going to press me into honesty, it's Joan.

"It has to do with the app," I murmur.

She exhales sharply and flops down on her bed, letting her hair fall into her eyes. "Of course it does."

"And...someone I met through it."

Joan's gaze slides to the scarf around my neck. "Did he hurt you?"

I shake my head. "Not him. Someone else. He—he saved me."

She frowns, chewing on her thumbnail. "So what kind of trouble are you in, Grace?"

"The kind I probably should've seen coming," I mutter.

But Joan doesn't jump on the chance to say *I told you so*. In fact, she looks strangely...conflicted.

"What did you know about it?" I ask cautiously.

She stiffens.

That's all the answer I need.

I sit up straighter, my blanket sliding down my shoulders. "You knew. Didn't you?"

Joan hugs her knees to her chest and avoids my eyes. "I could've been more honest."

I stare at her. "Why weren't you?"

She doesn't answer right away. Instead, she tucks a strand of hair behind her ear and sighs. "I thought I was protecting you."

"By lying to me?"

"By not telling you everything. You were already in deep the moment you downloaded the app. I didn't think scaring you more would help."

I stare at her in disbelief. "You let me walk straight into it."

Joan shifts. "I didn't know it would be *you*. Not at first. You think I have control over any of this?"

Her voice cracks slightly at the end, but I'm not sure I buy it.

"You still could've warned me," I say, quieter now. "Told me the truth instead of acting like I was just being reckless."

"I *did* warn you."

"No." My voice grows firmer. "You hinted. You judged. You guilt-tripped. But you never said what you knew. You never gave me a chance to choose."

Joan looks at me for a long moment. "Would you have listened?"

"I don't know," I admit. "But it would've been *my* choice."

She shifts on the bed, moving her feet under her as she glances back up at my face. There should be more vulnerability there, but instead, I see hardness. A crisp fall breeze blows through the window, brushing her hair out of her face and exposing more of her hard jaw.

"I can help you now," she says finally. "If you want out, I can help."

"Why now?" My voice is soft. "Why didn't you say something weeks ago?"

"I didn't think you'd survive long enough for it to matter."

It's honest. It's brutal. And it makes my stomach twist.

"But I did."

She nods slowly. "You did."

I pull my knees to my chest and sit with that. Let it settle into the quiet.

"I need to know everything," I say at last. "No more secrets."

Joan hesitates. Her eyes dart to the door, then back to me. "I know what the app is," she says finally. "Because I helped build it."

The world shifts sideways.

"You—you *what?*"

"I didn't know what it would become," she says quickly. "When they came to me, they were beautiful. Kind. They said it was about connection. Magic. Belonging. And I wanted to believe them."

She looks younger now, like someone pulled out the scaffolding that held her upright. The light seems to fade from her eyes.

"I'd done some dabbling in apps before. They're fun to come up with if you know what you're doing. When they told me they were having a problem with getting people to come visit them, I suggested that this might be a good solution. I didn't know they were going to use it like this. That girls would start disappearing. That they'd make deals— real ones. Blood-bound, bone-deep."

I stare at her, struggling to reconcile the cold, composed girl I've known with the one sitting in front of me now. This isn't some casual mistake. It's betrayal.

"You've known this whole time."

"I've suspected," she admits. "But after what happened to you—I knew for sure."

I shift to the far side of the bed, putting space between us. "And you didn't do anything?"

"I couldn't." She sounds desperate now. "If I came forward, I'd be next. You don't understand what they can do."

"But I *do*." I press a hand to the scarf at my neck. "I understand *exactly*."

Joan doesn't speak after that.

The room stretches into silence, the kind that fills every crack in your resolve. I pull the blanket around myself again, shielding my skin from the cold that's slipped back in. The sky outside our window is fading into that last shade of dying blue. The color of twilight. The color of choices.

"I'm getting those girls back," I say into the quiet.

Joan doesn't answer.

I don't expect her to.

"But you knew," I continue, voice low, shaking off the blanket and standing in the narrow space between our beds. "When they started disappearing. When we started realizing they weren't coming back—you knew something."

She looks up, eyes shiny. "It took me a while to understand what was causing it. They were...kind to me, Grace. You have to understand."

"I don't have to understand anything." My hands are balled so tight my nails dig half-moons into my palms. "How did you even find them?"

Her gaze shifts toward the window, to where the neatly trimmed lawns bleed into the creeping edge of the forest.

"I had a hard transition when I came here," she says finally.

I tilt my head, not because I'm sympathetic but because this doesn't sound like the confident, calculating girl I've been living with for four months. It sounds like someone else entirely.

"It's hard," she continues. "Coming to a school where everyone already knows each other. Where you're just this new thing, a curiosity for five minutes, and then...nothing."

"No kidding." I've said the same thing to her. More than once.

"So I stopped trying. I'd go outside, wander. The woods behind the school—have you ever really walked them? Old trees, so much older than anything built here. There's something steady about places like that. Like they've already seen everything."

Her voice has gone somewhere distant. The glassiness in her eyes is too well-practiced to fully trust, but there's something real behind it. Or something real enough to be dangerous.

"I'd been going out there for a week before they approached me," she says. "Not the powerful ones. Not at first. Just the little ones. The ones that blend in. You wouldn't notice them unless you'd been watching long enough to know which mushrooms don't just appear overnight."

She looks at me, tears now slipping freely down her cheeks. "I was so alone, Grace. I know it sounds stupid, but they talked to me. They remembered my name. I hadn't heard my name spoken with kindness in weeks."

I cross my arms, but my posture softens slightly. I *want* to believe her. Maybe some part of me does. But that doesn't make any of it okay.

"So what?" I say, trying to keep the sharpness of my voice from cutting deeper than it should. "You met a magic mushroom, made some friends, and decided to help them lure girls to their deaths?"

"No! It wasn't like that!" Her face twists. "I've known them for years now, both the low and the high. They trusted me. It was *never* about sacrifice."

"But you and me?" I ask. "Was our relationship based on lies?"

Joan's eyes narrow. "I told you not to go. It's not my fault you decided to be stupid anyway."

"Oh, so that makes it okay? For the others to go missing, for them to die, so long as it wasn't me?"

"What do you want me to say?" She throws her hands down at her sides. "But I can help you now."

"Your help," I say coldly, "comes with a body count."

She flinches, but I keep going.

"If they were your friends, if it wasn't about being liked—then why help them hurt people?"

Her mouth opens, then closes. Her eyes go distant.

"They told me they were dying. That the earth wasn't feeding them anymore. That it was *our* fault. That the magic they needed was slipping away, and they were scared."

I sit back on the edge of the bed, watching her closely. "So they asked you to help."

"They didn't ask for blood, not at first," she says quickly as her cheeks redden. "They said they needed...essence. Life force. I didn't know what that meant."

Of course not. Of course the fairies didn't say 'blood'. I press my fingers to my temple. My head is starting to pound.

"Did you offer yourself?"

"They said it would make me sick. That they didn't want to do that to me."

"How generous," I mutter. "So what made them change their minds?"

She shifts uncomfortably. "They didn't. It wasn't until Tabby showed up."

My stomach tightens.

"Tabby?" I echo, a chill spreading into my bones. "What does she look like?"

Joan shrugs, almost sheepish. "Small. Maybe to my hip. Long black hair. Violet eyes."

My heart rate slows—Tabitha is tall. I've seen her. She looms. But...

"I didn't meet her right away," Joan says, voice quieter. "The others said she was different. Special. She only came when I started offering to help."

I lean back against the wall. "What was different when she showed up?"

"They were nervous. I could feel it. The low ones wouldn't even look at her. They told me to be respectful. Quiet."

"And were you?" I ask through clenched teeth.

"Or course," she says, chin tilting up. "She said she was grateful. That she appreciated my willingness to help despite being human. That it meant something."

None of this bodes well. None of it feels *safe*. I've seen how Tabitha smiles. I've felt the weight behind her words.

"Tabby smiled at me, and I remember feeling like everything was going to be okay and I had nothing to worry about—which was nice because I'd been getting a little worried about how strange everyone was acting.

"Tabby told me that before they could accept my help

that they needed to do a fingerpick, that it was part of their traditional initiation rites."

I sit up. "Had they never asked you to do anything like that before?"

"No," Joan looks up at me with sunken eyes. "They never said I'd have to do that to be friends, but they said Tabby was different and that I should do what she said."

"And you did."

She nods slowly. "I didn't want to offend them."

The pieces are falling into place. Not cleanly, not fully, but enough. Joan may not have known what she was doing —but she didn't stop once she found out either.

Tabitha. She was the one that wanted blood from the beginning. But why? Was Joan the first? What was it about Joan's blood that made her interested in getting more? My gaze drifts to the window where the sun is already below the trees.

"She asked me how we could meet more humans," Joan says. "Ones like me. Willing to help. I said I could build an app. It didn't seem dangerous. I thought it would help."

"But you built a pipeline," I say. "You gave them a menu."

Her mouth opens to argue, but she falters. "I didn't know they'd spike it with dust. I didn't know what it would do. If I had—"

"But you didn't stop," I interrupt. "You *still* haven't."

She folds in on herself, arms hugging her sides. I can feel the rage building in my chest, sharp and hot. But I keep it in. She's my only link to the ones behind this.

"Are you still in contact with them?"

She nods.

"Then here's what you're going to do," I say, voice

clipped. "Find out how to shut it down. The app, the network. Whatever's powering this. Find it. Kill it."

"I can't—"

"You can try," I cut her off. "And you *will*."

Joan hesitates, but then nods, her lips pressed into a thin line.

One step. One move forward. It's not enough, but it's something.

She stands, jaw set, and walks to the door. For a moment, she pauses—like she wants me to stop her. To forgive her.

I don't.

I hope she goes to them. I hope she's stupid enough to walk into that nest of vipers and come back with something useful.

The door clicks shut behind her, and I'm alone.

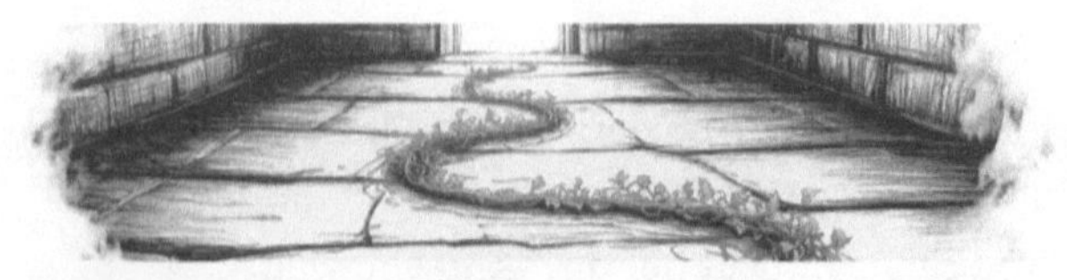

Chapter Fifteen

Picking up the dress Galin left me—the one Joan dropped carelessly between our beds—I turn it over in my hands, searching through the hidden seams and inner pockets for my knife. No luck. It's not there.

Of course it's not. It must still be Under the Hill. I mutter a quiet curse under my breath, fingers tightening around the expensive fabric. These are the first clothes he's given me that haven't vanished the moment I took them off, and I'm grateful I didn't materialize at school naked. But gratitude only goes so far when I'm defenseless in a place full of people who smile while plotting your death.

I glance around the room, scanning for anything I could conceivably use as a weapon. Hairspray and bobby pins are the best I can come up with. The Joan of last week would've told me that was enough—with the right intent, anything could be a weapon. She would've winked while saying it, like it was a private joke we shared. Thinking about that version of her stings more than I expect.

This—whatever it is—won't be forever. I won't always

be this vulnerable. I won't always be unsure of who I can trust. I repeat it in my head like a prayer.

Behind me, the floor creaks. I spin around fast, fists raised like I know what I'm doing. I probably look ridiculous. But I'm ready to try something if I have to.

Galin stands by the window, a lean shadow outlined in the moonlight, arms crossed and eyes gleaming. A smirk plays at the corner of his mouth.

"What was your plan?" he asks, cocking his head. "To frighten me with your trembling fists?"

"Shaking was never what I intended to do to you," I shoot back, crossing my arms even though my hands are still clenched tight. I hold his gaze, daring him to keep teasing.

His low chuckle warms the air. "You are in a good mood."

"I'm in a lot of moods," I say. "Pick one."

"I like this one." He gestures vaguely at me, gaze flicking over the rumpled dress in my hands and the tension still held in my shoulders. "Angry. Determined. Beautiful."

I roll my eyes hard enough it should leave a mark. "That's what happens when people keep trying to kill me."

He nods, not missing a beat. "An excellent response. Many would simply collapse."

My thoughts flicker to Joan, how she folded in on herself when I confronted her. There was no fight in her, not anymore. Maybe I am growing. Changing. Surviving. But I'm not about to bask in Galin's approval.

"What exactly do you like about it?" I ask, lifting a brow. "Because I'm just as likely to at you as I am your Queen."

That's not true, not entirely. I know who my enemies are. I know Galin doesn't make that list—at least not yet.

But he doesn't need to know I've started thinking of him as something other than a threat.

"Good," he says, a slow smile spreading over his face. "It would be... dangerous for you to become too comfortable in my presence."

Something about the way he says it makes my spine stiffen. His calm makes me restless, like I'm the one playing a game without knowing the rules.

"Why are you here?" I ask. "Our deal's dissolved. You don't have a reason to be lurking around my room."

His smile sharpens. "A delightful idea, but I seem to recall we made a new agreement."

"Are you trying to give me a headache on purpose?"

He plucks a piece of lint from his black tunic with the kind of slow precision that makes me want to shake him. "Are you trying to tell me you were not expecting my presence?"

"That's not what I'm saying."

"Then what are you saying?"

"I don't know," I snap, flinging my hands up. "Just tell me what we're doing and get on with it."

His mouth curls in a side smile, the kind that makes heat flicker in my chest despite myself. His gaze drifts down to the dress in my hands, the gold splashes of blood staining the beautiful fabric.

"I would say I owe you a uniform, but it seems you have destroyed my dress," he says dryly. "What a waste of an heirloom."

"I assure you, I had help."

"I seem to remember," he murmurs, his voice soft now, almost fond.

I sink onto the edge of the bed, dropping the ruined dress beside me with more force than necessary. Arms crossed, I tilt my head and wait. I'm not filling the silence. Not this time. If he wants something from me, he can speak first.

He sighs, dragging a hand through his dark hair. The moonlight from the window spills across the floor and into his eyes, streaking them with silver. Something in him is quieter tonight, stripped of his usual sharpness. From his pocket, he pulls out my knife and flips it open. His long fingers move over the blade with practiced ease—open, click, close, click. The dull stones in the rings on his fingers catch the light in turns, glinting like old bruises, like storms long past.

He looks different tonight. Cleaner. Sharper. His tunic is pressed, lined with intricate silver embroidery in the shape of curling leaves. A silver circlet rests low in his hair, barely visible unless you're watching him closely. Which I am. Too closely.

Something's happening. Something important. Probably why it took him this long to come back.

I force myself to sit still, to let my questions pile up behind my teeth. I can wait. For a little while. Maybe.

"I promised I would start teaching you how to use this." He nods at the knife in his hands. "But I am not at your disposal tonight."

It's something. A start. I weigh my response, then decide to risk it. "Is there something I should know?"

He doesn't answer at first. Just keeps flicking the knife open and closed like it soothes him. "There has been a calling of the court."

He's deliberately vague, and it makes me want to scream. "Okay. And what does that mean?"

"I must stand before my Queen. With the entirety of her court."

"Does this happen a lot?"

He shakes his head. "Not for centuries."

"Is that... normal?"

"No. These gatherings are rare—reserved for monumental events: royal marriages, coronations, births. Or calls to tithes."

I frown, sorting through what little I know. Tabitha isn't married. She's not handing off the crown, and she definitely isn't pregnant. That leaves—

"She's demanding a tribute?"

He nods. "This is more formal than the revel you attended. It will not be... festive. This is ceremony. Obligation."

"And you think it's a sigh she's making an announcement?"

His frown deepens. "I do."

His uncertainty hits harder than I expected. If he's unsettled, then something is truly wrong.

I hesitate. "Do I get a choice here? About what happens next?"

"You always have a choice," he says, though there's a strange coolness in his voice that makes me wonder if he means it.

"So what are we doing if not weapons training?"

"You may accompany me. Stand with me at court. Or you may stay behind."

Just like that. No pressure. No guidance. No hint of what he wants.

He rises smoothly, every line of him composed, distant. I'm on my feet before I can think twice, chasing the space between us.

"Do you even care what I choose?" I blurt. The words hang there between us, raw and real.

He looks at me, his eyes dark. "Do you?"

I want to lie. I want to pretend I'm fine either way, but my chest aches. My cheeks burn. I remember the way he tore through the goblins to get to me. How he looked when he saw me bleeding. How I let myself believe, just for a moment, that I mattered.

I was a promise. A debt paid. Nothing more. And yet...

"I'll come," I say. My voice is steady, even if I'm not.

He doesn't smile. But his nod feels like something heavier than agreement. Like relief he won't admit.

The shadows curl around us, thick and velvet. They rise to claim me, but this time, when they touch my skin, I don't flinch. I open my arms to them. To him.

If I'm walking into danger tonight, at least I'm not walking alone.

The fire in Galin's room is out. Darkness pools in the corners like spilled ink, shadows clinging to the walls where warm light used to flicker. The air is cold and still, stale with the absence of burning wood. I wrap my arms around myself, chilled in a way that has nothing to do with temperature.

Nothing has happened—yet—but my instincts squirm like worms beneath my skin. Something is wrong here.

Galin moves beside me, his profile a grim line as he turns away. He goes to the wardrobe and yanks it open, tossing something dark onto the bed with a casual flick of his hand. Then he pulls out a long, black jacket, one I haven't seen before. He slides it on in one fluid motion, and the change is immediate. Regal. Dangerous. He looks like a prince carved from night—inhumanely beautiful, sharply drawn, and unshakably in control.

My breath catches.

He doesn't look at me. "Get changed. I have no wish to be late."

Late for what, he doesn't say. There's no explanation, no context. Just a command wrapped in velvet.

I don't ask. I already made the decision when I agreed to stay. Now I just have to follow through no matter what waits on the other side of that door.

The dress on the bed gleams in the low light. It's the same shape as yesterday's—long, elegant bodice fitted to flatter—but this one is darker than midnight, with a spill of starlight sewn down the back. When I touch it, the fabric slides through my fingers like cream and shadows.

I lift it with care. "Do I leave the bandages on, or will it ruin the aesthetic?"

He doesn't answer—just grunts, already half-turned from me.

Fine.

My pulse kicks up, responding not to his indifference, but to the tension radiating off him like heat from a forge. Whatever has Galin on edge is likely to be worse for me. I'd ask for my knife back, but I doubt he's thought to return it, and even if he had, I'd still be outmatched in a place like this.

I pull the dress on anyway.

The gown settles over me like liquid armor, soft but impenetrable. Warm. I smooth the fabric over my hips, straighten my shoulders, and look toward the warped silver mirror in the corner. I spin once, and the skirt fans out around me like black smoke.

Galin appears behind me in the reflection—tall, still,

watching. For a breath, we're twin shadows in the glass, two creatures of the same strange world. I can almost imagine it: us, aligned, together, safe in a way I've never known. We could almost belong together.

Then he turns and gestures to the door, and the spell shatters.

The hallway beyond is silvered with frost, every surface glittering faintly in the low light. Whispers drift like smoke through the cold, and reflections twist in the gilt surfaces lining the walls. Ghosts of people flicker where no one stands. My sneakers squeak against the marble as I follow Galin, cringing at the sound.

He walks like silence itself, each step calculated and smooth. I follow like someone wearing borrowed skin.

Ahead, the corridor curves toward the throne room. Bodies gather in near-silent chaos—pressing close to the ivy-covered walls, eyes bright in the dim. Galin scans them like a blade cutting wheat. He ignores their order entirely and strides toward the massive doors, his expression unreadable.

I hurry after him, nerves buzzing.

He throws a sharp glance over his shoulder, and for a heartbeat, our eyes meet. Something unspoken passes between us, a shiver of heat threading through the cold, before he turns again, all shadows and command.

Inside, the throne room is full. Fairies are crammed into every inch of space, clinging to walls, hovering overhead, perched on bannisters and beams. They all face forward, toward the throne.

Toward *her*.

Tabitha.

She gleams like something holy—light-wreathed, commanding, dangerous as she sits proud on her throne.

Her gown is a rust red that clings like melted wax, her dark hair falling in perfect waves over her bare shoulders. Her lips curl into a smile as she sees Galin standing in the open doorway.

Her gaze snags on me. Lingers.

I freeze.

No logic, no cleverness, no inner strength can save me from the flood of fear that locks my limbs. I am prey caught in a spotlight.

Galin glances back. For a heartbeat, I expect him to walk away. Instead, he reaches for me—quiet, steady—and takes my hand.

He doesn't speak, just pulls.

Somehow that's enough. My legs obey, stumbling after him even though my heart is thudding a panicked rhythm in my chest.

The crowd parts reluctantly around Galin, closing tight behind me. Wings brush my arms; long fingers graze my back. I choke on the thick air, sweltering with heat and perfume and magic.

I scan the room for other humans. I both hope and dread the idea of finding them. If I'm alone, I'm vulnerable. If I'm not, everyone else is in danger.

Galin squeezes my hand as we near the throne. His grip is damp, his tension unmistakable. We pass the dias —and instead of approaching the throne, Galin veers into the shadows behind it. There, a single wooden chair sits in the gloom, plain and unremarkable, like it doesn't belong.

He drops into it with a creak. The moment stretches taut. Then, with his hand still clutching mine, he guides me behind him.

I let my fingers rest on the back of his chair. It's not

much, but it helps anchor me. From here, I'm nearly out of sight. Hidden. Safe-ish.

For now.

Galin's knuckles go white on the armrests. Something's coming.

Tabitha rises and silence descends like snow.

"Thank you for responding so promptly to my summons," she says, her voice as smooth as glass and just as sharp. "It has been too long since our court stood united."

The crowd watches her as if entranced.

"I had hoped to call you together with glad tidings. Alas, our fates twist cruelly."

I grip the chair harder.

"You know of the earth's retreat. Without its gifts, we wither. Our immortality frays. Our magic thins. This I will not accept." Her voice grows low, intimate. "It is this defiance that has led to... necessary sacrifices."

A ripple of discontent stirs. A group of fairies in swan-feathered cloaks exchange tense glances, their discomfort obvious. I've never seen them before. They don't look like partygoers. They look like rebels.

Tabitha raises a hand and they fall silent at once.

"Blood has given us what the earth would not. New powers. Healing. Strength."

"It's not giving," a voice calls. "It's *taking*."

A man steps forward—broad-shouldered, arms crossed, face lined with quiet fury. "Maybe the earth is humbling us for a reason. Maybe we should listen."

Galin leans forward on his knees, watching the man intently.

Tabitha's smile becomes something feral. "You think we should lie down and die? Accept weakness as a gift?"

"No. I think we should accept change with grace."

Her power pulses from the dias like heat. "And what lesson would the earth be teaching us, Lord Briarleaf?"

He falters. Drops his gaze. He shakes his head, blonde braids swinging over his shoulders

"That's what I thought," Tabitha says, honey-sweet and lethal. "Now, as I was saying..."

She draws a slender vial from her sleeve filled with thick, golden liquid. She tips it back and forth, letting the light catch it.

"This is no ordinary blood. It is the key to our future. My assistant did not reveal the source, but I believe the donor is among us tonight."

My breath catches.

Golden blood.

That's what mine looked like when it was allowed to bleed a little. That shimmer. That glow.

I don't know what fairy blood looks like, but my stomach drops anyway. I'm the only human I know with blood that color. I attributed it to the fairy dust working its way through my system, but what if I'm wrong? What if there's something wrong with me?

"I have gathered us all together in an attempt to find the human responsible for producing this special blood. It would not be wise of me to share exactly why this blood is so special, but suffice to say, without it our race will be doomed."

How would she know?

"What is she saying?" I whisper to Galin.

I glance at Galin but his face is unreadable. He hasn't said a word. He leans against the back of his chair and runs the fingers of his left hand along his jaw.

He hasn't *told* her, has he?

Tabitha lifts the vial. "Find the human whose blood this is, and you will be rewarded beyond imagining. Fail... and our people fade into dust.

The silence that follows is immense.

Then movement. The fairies begin to drift out, their gazes calculating. Hungry.

I shrink further into the shadows.

Tabitha watches them with a predatory glee. She doesn't turn her back once.

Galin stands as well, his hands forming loose fists at his sides. If not for the tension in the back of his neck, I would think he had no feelings about what just happened at all.

"Wait," Tabitha says, lifting one elegant hand.

Her voice halts Galin mid-step. His spine goes rigid and he freezes like a puppet with its strings pulled taut. I stop too, caught between them, every hair on my neck prickling.

The queen does not raise her voice, but the power in it thrums through the air. "I expect you to follow this order. You would do well to remember that you are my prince. Any power that you have is because I have given it to you."

Her tone is smooth, almost lazy, but the threat underneath it is sharp enough to draw blood.

Galin turns, slow and deliberate. "And I have always acted with your interests in mind, my Lady."

He says it with the kind of cold, formal grace that could be mistaken for obedience. But I can see it—the tightness around his eyes, the small twitch of muscle along his jaw. The fury leashed just beneath his skin.

Tabitha descends the stairs from her throne. Each step she takes is deliberate, her long dress whispering like a flame over the frost-laced floor. Her bare feet leave no prints, as if the cold dares not touch her.

She stops just before him. Galin doesn't flinch, though

he has to look down to meet her eyes. The air between them shimmers with tension.

"You forget yourself," she murmurs. Her hand, adorned with rings like tiny knives, lifts to trace the collar of his coat—almost affectionate. "I see you sulking in shadows. I hear the whispers. Do not mistake the patience of a crown for weakness."

"I've made no mistake," Galin says quietly. His voice is even, but I feel the weight of every word. "I know exactly who wears it."

"Then remember," she says, and this time, her voice softens with something that could almost pass for fondness. "You owe me everything. If I wanted to I could *ruin* you."

"I haven't forgotten."

"Good." She smiles, and it's all teeth. "Find the source of the blood. Bring them to me."

For a terrifying moment, her eyes flick to me.

My breath catches. A dozen thoughts barrel through my mind—how still I've tried to be, how Galin didn't flinch when she looked my way, how I don't *know* what she suspects. I force my expression blank, even as my pulse stammers in my throat.

Galin moves then—just a slight shift, as if putting himself a fraction more between Tabitha and me.

She notices.

Her smile doesn't falter, but her eyes harden. "Sentiment will undo you, Galin. You should know that better than anyone."

He bows again, deeper this time, but not low enough to be real submission. "Of course, my Lady."

"Don't disappoint me," she says.

"I never do," he replies.

Then he grabs my arm—not gently—and pulls me after him. His steps are longer now, faster. He doesn't speak as we pass back through the thinning crowd, past curious eyes and the lingering echoes of Tabitha's command.

But I glance back once, just for a heartbeat. Tabitha stands where we left her, arms crossed, her dark eyes glowing faintly in the low light. She is still watching us.

No—watching *me*.

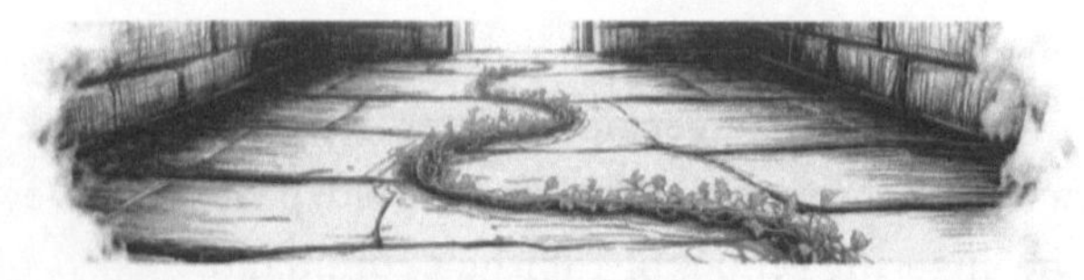

Chapter Sixteen

My heart beats a furious rhythm as Galin pulls me farther into the dark. I can feel Tabitha's gaze like fire crawling across my skin.

She knows.

Not suspects—*knows*.

So why the spectacle? Why summon a glittering court, stage a dramatic blood-hunt, set the palace itself to hunting shadows—when she already has the truth? Why not just say it? Drag me forward and name me what I am?

Unless...she doesn't want everyone to know.

Not yet.

A chill creeps along my spine, colder than the stone walls around us. This isn't a hunt—it's a performance. One with an audience. One with a purpose I haven't figured out yet.

But the bigger question gnaws at me with sharper teeth. *Why does she want my blood so badly?* How did she get it in the first place? And what makes it valuable enough to cloak in so much theater?

I'm drowning in a sea of questions, and no one here

seems eager to throw a rope. No answers—just riddles wrapped in smiles.

Galin's grip tightens on my arm as he veers off into a side corridor, his steps swift and purposeful. He doesn't speak. His jaw is rigid, his eyes storm-dark and far away. I don't know what he's thinking right now, and I don't care. As long as he keeps dragging me away from that throne room, he can sulk in silence.

Just don't leave me behind again.

The corridor curves, and suddenly, we're somewhere I've never been. It holds the same marble bones as the main hall, but none of its splendor. No ivy coils across the walls, no gilded sconces light the way. The air is heavy, stale, like a room that's held its breath for too long. Dust veils the floor, undisturbed by anything living.

"Where are we?" I whisper.

"The abandoned wing," he says.

"Why was it abandoned?"

Galin doesn't answer. His jaw clenches tighter, and he pulls me through the drifting dust.

The ground shifts under me. My foot catches. My knee slams into cold stone.

Pain flares, bright and brief, and I suck in a sharp breath.

For a second, I just stare at the floor. Part of me wants to laugh—hysterically. Girls are being killed, I've been bled like an animal, and now I'm falling over like a child. On the scale of today's disasters, a bruised knee barely qualifies. But the absurdity of it sits heavily on my chest.

"Is it bad?"

The words jolt me. Galin crouches beside me, his brow furrowed with something I can't name—worry, maybe. Not frustration. Not annoyance. *Worry.*

It throws me. I can't remember him ever asking me like that. Not directly. He's patched up my wounds before, but always with the detached efficiency of someone fixing a broken weapon, not comforting a hurt person.

I blink, trying to find my voice. "It's fine," I manage, a little too quickly.

He gives me a long look like he doesn't believe me but won't argue. Instead, he moves without a word—slides his arm under my legs and lifts me into his arms like I weigh nothing.

"I can walk," I murmur, more out of instinct than pride.

"I know," he says, his voice quiet.

But he doesn't set me down.

I don't fight him.

Instead, I let my head rest lightly against his chest. His heartbeat is steady and strong, like the calm at the center of a storm. The warmth of him seeps through the layers between us, anchoring me in a way I hadn't known I needed. His arm tightens slightly around me, subtle, protective, and I feel it—not as fear, but as something dangerously close to longing.

I *could* insist he let me go.

But I don't.

And maybe that's the most dangerous choice I've made all night.

The hallway stretches ahead, flooded with pale moonlight from towering windows set into the walls. Without the torches and the movement and the buzz of living things, it feels like we've slipped out of time entirely.

Like a place forgotten. Or maybe *abandoned on purpose.*

"Why did they leave this wing?" I ask again, softer now.

Galin hesitates.

"Some rooms are easier left closed," he says finally. "Some memories, too."

A non-answer, but not a lie. I tuck it away.

He shifts again, tightening his hold with one arm while pushing open a warped door with the other. The hinges groan in protest, and darkness spills out like smoke.

Despite everything, my pulse stays steady. I should be afraid. Of the dark. Of where he's taking me. Of him.

But I'm not.

That might scare me more than anything else.

He steps through, and I follow him into the dark—not because I'm helpless, not because I have no choice, but because, for once, I trust him more than the world I left behind.

And that's a truth I can't afford to examine too closely.

There is nothing but black.

If not for Galin's arms wrapped firmly around my waist, I might believe I've been swallowed whole by the void. Like I'm not just lost in the dark, but that the world never existed at all—no throne room, no blood, no Tabitha. Just this...suffocating emptiness and me.

And him.

Galin whispers something in a language I don't understand—low and smooth, like water curling over stone—and a cool blue flame flickers to life in the palm of his free hand. It glows like moonlight through water, spreading outward until the room brightens enough to reveal the tunnel around us. The earthen walls arch high above, carved by hands long forgotten. Thick roots drip from the ceiling like skeletal fingers, brushing the crown of Galin's head.

"Where are we?" I whisper.

He gently sets me down, one hand lingering on my waist as if he's not quite ready to let go. His warmth fades as his fingers slide away, and I remind myself to breathe.

"This is an old escape route," he says, brushing dirt from his hands. "Built by the last king before he was murdered in his sleep. It's been long forgotten by most. Except me."

"Convenient," I murmur.

He smiles faintly, but his eyes remain distant. "It was used for the king's secret guests. People he didn't want anyone to know he met with."

My stomach knots. "And what are we doing here? Should I be flattered or worried?"

"You need to leave the palace," he says flatly, stepping ahead.

My feet stay rooted. Then why the whole dramatic court scene? Why let Tabitha put on her show? Why not just do your little shadow thing and poof me home?"

He doesn't stop walking. "Because if I did, she would know exactly where you are. She can track any magic cast within the palace if she chooses. This way, there's a chance she won't follow."

I swallow, my stomach feeling unsettled. "Has she been watching us this whole time?"

He doesn't answer.

My voice sharpens. "What aren't you telling me?"

The tension that pulls across his shoulders is like a drawn bow. Secrets practically bleed from him, coiling through the damp air.

"I mean it, Galin. What does she want with me? Why am I the one she's obsessed with?"

He stops. Slowly, his fingers curl into fists, and the flame in his palm leaps higher, bathing the tunnel in ghostly light. "As soon as I saw your blood," he says hoarsely, "I knew."

The words hang there, thick as fog.

"Knew what?"

He turns. The flame catches the edge of his profile—his angular cheekbones, the pointed tip of his ear, the flicker of something haunted in his eyes.

"That you were what she's been searching for."

My heart skips. I take a step back, my spine colliding with the cold curve of the wall. "What does that mean?"

"She's not trying to gain power," he says. "She's trying to...replace something. I don't know why. I only know she's been searching for a long time. And that she thinks it's you."

The silence presses in between us, and I brace a hand against my hip as I wait for him to continue. His shoulders are so tight that they shake, his shadow appearing to dance against the wall.

I stare at him. "Did you give her my blood?"

His eyes widen, and for the first time, I see something like real pain etched across his face. "Never. I would never betray you like that."

"You've betrayed me once before," I say, softer than I intend.

A long silence falls between us.

"I told you already," he says at last, voice low, "you are mine.

It should scare me. Maybe it does. But not enough.

"She doesn't seem to care who I 'belong' to."

"No," he agrees. "And that is why I am taking you home."

"Tabitha's not stupid. When you stop showing up to meetings with me, she'll know something's off."

Galin turns away. "I will not be attending the meetings."

A startled laugh slips out of me. "So what, you're going to ghost the queen of fairyland?"

"Something like that," he says with a grin.

"She made it very clear what happens to people who cross her. Did you not hear the venom in her voice? Because I did. She was practically spitting teeth." I poke my finger into his firm chest.

"And that is why I shall be staying with you," he says calmly.

My jaw drops. "You can't be serious."

He shrugs, and the movement is so casual, so unnervingly confident, that my stomach flutters. "You are not safe alone."

"You didn't make me sign up for that stupid app. I walked into this world on my own," I protest, even as my pulse betrays me.

His voice softens. "That does not mean I should let you walk out of it alone."

My heart stutters at the tone, and I want to believe him —I want it more than I want almost anything—but I've learned not to trust so easily.

"I have a roommate," I try. "Joan's not exactly the share-the-bathroom kind, let alone the hide-a-fairy-prince-in-the-closet' type."

His face darkens, and the shadow that falls over his features makes my pulse spike in a way that has nothing to do with fear. "She will not be a problem."

Something in his voice makes the hairs on the back of my neck rise. "What did you do to her?"

He says nothing.

"Galin."

"I did not harm her," he says finally. "But she is...no longer your concern. Those she owes have come to collect."

A chill steals down my spine. "Is she in the palace?"

"I do not know. But we cannot help her now. You will only make it worse."

I lurch toward the tunnel mouth, but he grabs my shoulder, his fingers cool against my skin, and pulls me gently back. "She is alive. And she will stay that way. Her value lies in her usefulness, not her blood. She is not like you."

My stomach clenches. "She made the app. She brought all those girls here."

"I know."

Of course he does. Everyone seems to know everything but me.

"I won't forget her," I mutter. "You don't get to decide who I care about."

"I would not dare," he says, and there's a softness in his voice that makes the hair on my arms stand on end. "But right now, we have to move."

His fingers curl around mine, strong, deliberate, and the touch makes heat bloom up my arm. He guides me forward, and I can't help but lean just a fraction closer, the brush of his hand against mine electric in a way I'd never admit out loud. The tunnel looms endlessly before us as I follow him through its stale and earthy air. His steps are sure as he leads the way. Maybe it helps that he's carrying his own flames and can handle any threat that comes our way.

Maybe the ability to be dangerous gives the confidence I'm lacking.

My legs ache as I stumble after Galin's long strides. He reaches out again, fingers entwining with mine, anchoring me with a touch that is both a command and a reassurance.

If I were willing to accept his strength, I might be able to make it through this. But at what cost? Do I give over my soul for a taste of safety? I can't do it. My heart can't handle it anymore. Not after all the times my father let me down. What would make Galin any different?

"Do you need to rest?"

Galin's voice echoes through the caves and into my mind. Shaking my head, I push past the ache in my legs, in my heart, in my mind, and shove past him so I'm in front. It's all shadows everywhere I look, but that matches my mood just fine. Galin doesn't comment on my move, and I'm okay with that. I wouldn't know what to tell him anyway.

The tunnel tilts upward, my calves straining against the new terrain. The angle steepens, and my breathing sharpens.

I keep moving, refusing to stop or slow down. I must get out of here. I must get out of this. If I can just make it out of here. If I can just get home. My mind circles around this solitary goal, the only thing holding me together.

Keeping my gaze on the ground just in front of my feet, I count my steps to quiet my mind. If there's only numbers in my head, then there's no room for anything else. 1, 2, 3, 4… it keeps me breathing.

I'm in the 30s when my head knocks hard against a wooden door. Galin comes up behind me on silent feet, flames going out as he wraps an arm around my shoulder. He grabs the knob and flings it open.

Daylight spills through the opening.

Snow blankets the ground outside, fresh and white beneath a pale winter sun. My lungs ache as I inhale the first clean breath in what feels like forever.

We step into the clearing. A massive boulder sits in its center like a marker stone, surrounded by naked trees and pale sky. Behind us, the wooden door vanishes into the bark of a pine, almost like it was never there.

"Real," I murmur, brushing a hand along the mossy trunk. "It's all real."

"Of course it is," Galin says softly, and the way his gaze lingers on me, not on the trees, not the boulder, makes my chest tighten.

He paces around the boulder, eyes sweeping the clearing, but something in the tilt of his head, the subtle flex of his stance, draws my attention back to him again and again. I'm aware of the way he moves, the quiet strength in each step, the way the sunlight glints off his hair.

As we leave the clearing behind, the forest comes alive around us. Birds call to each other; squirrels jump through the trees. Fallen branches and crusts of snow crack under our feet as Galin leads me forward with a steady hand at my back, fingers brushing against mine now and then—deliberate, lingering. Each contact sends heat rippling through me, a quiet reassurance I can't deny.

The air is fresh as a breeze rustles through the trees, blowing away the dank reminders of the dark tunnel.

"It is not much farther now," he breathes, close enough that I can feel it against my hair. "You will be home soon."

I open my mouth to object, to say that the school isn't my home, but I realize I don't have anything to replace it with. Where is my home? Not with my absent father, not at the school, or Under the Hill. Did I ever have one? Did my mom give me a home to feel at peace in? Was there ever a time that I had a place to feel safe?

We reach the edge of the forest, only a long yard of thick white snow separating us from the almost black stone of the school.

"Everyone will see you," I tell Galin with a sigh, completely lost as to how to get him across the lawn, let alone into my dorm.

He laughs softly, a low, almost intimate sound. A finger lifts to his lips in a teasing gesture, and then he disappears before I can respond.

My chest tightens, not with fear, not entirely, but with the strange, dangerous pull of him.

Stumbling through the snow, I'm alone for the first time in a long time.

Really alone. No velvet-draped throne room, no murmured threats wrapped in charm, no glassy-eyed girls watching each other to wonder who'll be next. Just the soft hush of snow underfoot and the whistle of wind through naked trees.

It's almost unbearable.

How long has it been since I was allowed to just *think*? To feel what I'm feeling without worrying who's watching, what mask I should wear, who I might offend, or tempt, or betray?

Too long. Long enough that the silence now feels like it might crack me open. Like all the things I've been burying under clever words and fake smiles might finally come tumbling out.

The shadows cast by the school are long and cold against my skin. As I round the last hill and the familiar stone walls rise ahead of me, I stop, leaning a hand against the outer wall and closing my eyes.

This is it. My last chance to pull myself together before I have to start pretending again. Before someone asks where I've been or why I look like I've been dragged through a blizzard and a ballroom in the same night.

Straightening, my legs are steadier now—still sore, but not shaking. The panic is still there, but it's caged, manageable. I can do this. I have to.

I slip around to the side door near the science wing. It's always unlocked on weekends, and luck is on my side—it swings open without protest. Inside, the air is warmer but carries the same hush as the forest behind me. No buzzing voices. No echo of footsteps.

The soles of my fairy shoes glide silently over the polished floors. I barely recognize myself in the faint reflections in the glass—mud-smeared calves, tangled hair, skin too pale beneath all the leftover glamour.

The high windows let in shafts of thin sunlight, painting dust motes in gold. It should feel safe. Familiar. But it's like walking through a dream of a life I used to have.

Each step brings a new fear: what if someone sees me? What if they ask questions I can't answer? What if this entire fragile return to normalcy shatters the moment someone says my name?

I flinch at the sound of laughter echoing from a nearby classroom. It's not until then that I realize how tense I've been, how every muscle has been pulled tight since I left the court. The laughter is human. Familiar. And for a breath or two, I almost feel like I'm a part of it. Like I could walk in, sit down, and everything would be the way it was.

But it isn't. And I can't.

I pass the door without looking inside.

My hand shakes a little as I reach for the handle to my dorm room. Galin said Joan wouldn't be here—but part of me still expects to see her sitting on her bed, glaring at me, phone in hand, demanding to know what kind of mess I've dragged into her life.

My fingers brush the cold metal. I brace myself, close my eyes, and push the door open.

Nothing. No scolding. No glare. Just silence.

I open my eyes.

Empty.

Of course it is.

I step inside and let the door click shut behind me. The air feels hollow, like someone pulled the soul out of the room while I was gone. Her side of the room is too neat, too untouched. And for some ridiculous reason, my stomach sinks.

I don't know why I expected her to still be here. Galin doesn't lie, not exactly. Not the way others do. He tells truths wrapped in riddles and half-meanings, sure—but when he said she wouldn't be back, I think he meant it.

But it still feels wrong.

I drop onto my bed, not bothering to kick off my shoes, and stare at the ceiling. Pale winter light filters through the curtains. My limbs ache in a way I didn't think was possible. I feel both overused and completely hollowed out.

What am I even doing here? Hiding? Waiting for orders that haven't come?

Galin said Tabitha wants my blood. That it matters. But not *why*.

No one's told me that part. Not even him.

I groan and sit up, rifling through my desk drawer until

I find a crushed granola bar. It's stale and probably expired, but my stomach growls so violently that I don't care. I unwrap it with shaking hands and chew slowly, grateful for something solid. Something real.

The food helps. A little.

If I'd been paying closer attention—if I hadn't gotten distracted, hadn't been so desperate to belong somewhere, to matter—maybe I would've seen this coming. Maybe I could've stopped it before I started.

But what would I have done? Really?

I wanted to be chosen. I just didn't understand what I was being chosen *for*.

I glance toward the window. Snow is still falling, soft and unhurried. Somewhere out there, Galin is…what? Waiting for nightfall? Sneaking back into the mortal world in some dramatic flourish of magic and shadows?

Or maybe he's already watching. He does that sometimes. Appears right when I think of him, like he can hear my thoughts. Like he knows exactly where my attention lingers.

He said he'd stay with me. Protect me. But I can't shake the feeling that he's hiding just as much as I am—that whatever trouble Tabitha is stirring up, he's just as tangled in it as I am.

Still… he didn't have to bring me back. He didn't have to care at all.

And yet—he looked at me like I *mattered*. Like I was something worth shielding. That look—the sharp warmth in his gaze, the way it lingered long enough to catch my breath—has stayed with me longer than I want to admit.

I wrap my arms around my knees and rest my chin on them, staring at the door as if it might swing open and reveal him. The thought makes my chest tighten and my pulse skip.

The problem is... I think I do wish it would open.

I wish it would open and let him inside, close enough that I could feel the warmth radiating off him, close enough that I could let myself lean into it. Close enough to finally admit that I'm tethered to him in ways I don't yet understand, and maybe don't want to.

The snow falls on, silent and endless, and I imagine his shadow at the threshold, watching, waiting...and my heart lifts in a way that scares me more than the darkness ever could.

Chapter Seventeen

Galin appears out of nowhere, leaning against the wall by my bed just as I crumple the granola bar wrapper in my hand. I suck in a breath and nearly choke on my own heartbeat as I lurch to my feet.

"Do you always materialize like that?" I snap, trying to disguise how much my pulse has already betrayed me.

He lifts one shoulder in an infuriatingly casual shrug. "Was it not *you* who expressed concern that someone would see me come in?"

There's a wicked little curve to his mouth, a grin that feels like it could melt snow. It slides down my spine like flame.

"And you're not going to tell me what you were up to?" I ask, forcing myself to step around the warmth gathering in my cheeks.

"I had to ensure no one is tempted to come looking. Disappearing abruptly invites suspicion. A quiet absence is far safer—for both of us."

I narrow my eyes. As frustrating as his evasions are, I

can't argue with his logic. If Tabitha knew where he was, I'd already be cornered. The image of her stepping into my school, flanked by her eerie entourage, sends a chill through me.

"Right," I mutter, arms folded. "Because nothing screams subtle like harboring a fairy fugitive in a boarding school dorm."

Galin moves closer, his steps soundless, and perches beside me on the edge of the bed. He brushes a strand of his dark hair behind one pointed ear. I inch slightly away, the heat of him sudden and electric.

"What is your usual routine, when not entangled in court drama?"

"It's probably the weekend," I say, glancing at the thin shaft of light across the floor. "No classes. Normally, I'd be doing homework, wasting time with Joan, maybe waiting for a father who never shows up."

He turns to face me, cross-legged like a schoolboy, albeit with more grace. "You are not close with him?"

"My father? Not since my mom died." I tried to keep my voice light, but the words land heavier than I expect.

"I did not know your mother had passed."

"You never asked," I say, sharper than I mean to.

His eyebrows rise, but he lets the silence stretch until I look away.

"What happened to her?" he asks, voice is soft.

"I was four. Too young to understand. I just remember her telling my father not to take her to the doctor. He cried. That's...the only time I've ever seen him cry."

I pause, picking at a loose thread in my blanket. "Something was wrong. They both knew. But she wouldn't go."

As soon as I turned five just a few months later, I was shipped off to school. School after school followed until I ended up here, in the middle of nowhere with no father to even pretend to care what happened to me.

Galin watches me like the words are puzzle pieces. Like if he just fits them together right, he'll see something I don't.

"That is intriguing," he murmurs. "You remember how she died?"

I shake my head. "Not really. It was like...she faded. Drifted away."

Something in him stills and I notice the small catch in his chest. He licks his lips and sits straighter. "Drifted away. That phrase—it sounds like one of my people."

His dark eyes are clear, guileless, as he stares at me, waiting for me to process his words. I can't begin to understand what he's saying. It doesn't make any sense.

"What?" My whole body sits tense, waiting.

He meets my eyes, solemn. "It sounds like your mother may have been a fairy. That would explain the nature of your blood."

I shove myself up from the bed and pace across the room. No. No, that's not possible. That's not even *logical*.

"My mother wasn't a-a fairy. She was a woman. A woman my father met while sailing. They fell in love right away and he's never really been able to love another woman since."

I'm not so sure about the last part, but that's the explanation I've given myself for why he jumps from tramp to tramp. Why he can't seem to love me. We'll always be in her shadow.

Galin leans back slightly, his dark eyes flicking to mine with something unspoken—a tenderness I've never dared to imagine from him.

"On the water..." his voice trails off as he thinks, eyes

growing darker as he spreads out over my bed. The scent of earth just after rain washes off him, filling the room and softening the hard line of my shoulders.

"She could have been a selkie or a water nymph if he met her on the water. Although if she were a selkie then I doubt you will find much comfort in this discovery."

"What do you mean?" I ask, my voice betraying a flicker of vulnerability.

His dark gaze holds mine like a tether I don't want to escape. "If your mother were a selkie then she has not passed. She has just returned to the sea. It is what they do. They cannot keep themselves from the water for long, no matter how much they may love their human kin."

It's like a barb through my heart and I must toss away what he's saying. I must reject this information before it can lodge inside me and spread like poison. I can't believe that the last parent I had left with any memories of real love would have tossed me aside because it was her nature. It can't be true.

"Well, it doesn't matter what you say because she was just a woman. A woman who died, like humans do."

She wouldn't have chosen to leave me. Not in the way he's saying. I remember her holding me, caring for me, brushing out my hair and smiling at the gold strands shining in the lamplight before bed.

He shrugs, maddeningly calm, but there's a subtle softness now, a near imperceptible brush of longing in the curve of his mouth and the depth of his gaze. "It is only a theory. But an important one. It may be why Tabitha wants your blood. Why she values you. Why you are not just another girl."

I hate how much that appeals to me. The idea that all this strangeness—my blood, my instincts, the way the world tilts around me—isn't a flaw. That I'm not broken or forgettable or some strange mistake. Just...different. And maybe, for once, that could mean something good.

"If I'm not human," I whisper, "does that mean she can't claim me?"

Galin's grin is all sharp edges and dangerous promise. "Exactly. If your blood carries fairy lineage, Tabitha's claim on you violates her own laws. You would be protected."

Safe.

The word hits something deep inside me. A buried ache I didn't know still had a name.

"But how would we *prove* it?" My voice barely carries. The weight of what he's saying presses down on me, and yet a small thread of hope coils inside it.

"We can find a way," he says softly. "If that's what you want. If you are ready to know the truth. We can start with your mother."

I open my mouth to respond, but another voice—colder and more defensive—cuts in instead. "And what does any of it matter with what's going on right now? How does knowing who my mother was help me survive Tabitha?"

He doesn't bristle. He leans forward, resting his arms on his knees, calm and sure. "Because the identity of your mother might explain *why* Tabitha wants you. Why your blood matters. And if we can understand that, we may find a way to stop her."

I stare at him. "But you already know something. Don't you?"

His eyes glint, reflecting the thin band of afternoon light slipping through the window. "I know enough to say your blood is rare. Gold in your veins is not simply pretty. It means something powerful. Do you want to know what?"

I want to tell him no. I want to say it doesn't matter,

that I don't care. But that's a lie. I do care. I care more than I want to admit. And the truth is, no one's ever looked at me the way he is now—not with pity, not with doubt—but like I might actually matter. Like I could be *something*.

"The fact of your blood alone tells us you are less human than you think," he says quietly.

"I'm not sure if that's supposed to be comforting."

He shrugs, almost playful. "It is not meant to comfort. It is meant to prepare."

Galin leans back and stretches across the bed like a cat, his long limbs spilling over the sides, his head tilted to one side as he watches the ceiling. He looks infuriatingly relaxed, like nothing he just said upended my entire sense of self.

"You can't just drop something like that and go back to lounging around," I say, my eyes narrowing. "Is that the plan? Sit here and hide forever?"

"As I said before," he replies without looking at me, "I am not hiding. I am here to protect you."

"I don't need your protection."

Even I don't believe my lie.

He quirks a brow. "Just like you did not need it when you were with the goblins?"

The words sting because he's right. "If you gave me back my knife, I'd be fine."

He glances at me, his eyes saying more than his words could. I know the knife was no help to me before and is not likely to help now. Of course, I know that. But I refuse to acknowledge that I need a fairy around to keep me alive. I could handle myself...if I needed to.

He pulls it from a slim pocket with a smirk and offers it to me, hilt first. I snatch it back, trying not look as desperate as I feel. I want the blade not just because it might help me, because it's *mine*. A piece of myself I still control.

I flick it open and closed, the motion clumsy at first. Turning away from him, I repeat the movement until the muscles in my wrist remember the rhythm. The knife slides smoother each time, and by the time the sun dips through the trees, it almost feels natural again. Almost.

With a sidelong glance, I catch Galin watching me. His gaze is unreadable. I want to glare at him. I want to blame him for all of this—Tabitha, my mother, the lies—but the truth catches in my throat.

It's not his fault.

Whatever role he played, he didn't create this. He didn't choose it anymore than I did. And if he'd wanted to, he could have turned me over to Tabitha the moment we met. Instead, he risked everything to keep me hidden. That matters, doesn't it?

Still, it doesn't make him innocent.

I rub my temples, trying to shove the beginning of a headache back into hiding. I don't have time to spiral. If Tabitha finds us this, all of this—my confusion, my questions, my feelings—it won't matter.

I need a plan.

But making a plan means I have to talk to him. I have to admit I don't know what I'm doing.

Am I really ready for that?

Asking for help will mean admitting we're on the same side. That I might trust him that I don't want him to leave. And I'm not sure which of these scares me most.

"What now?" he asks suddenly, his grin curling at the corners of his mouth. "What do humans do for fun when they are not busy stabbing each other or brooding in windows?"

I snort despite myself. "I don't know if that's an accurate look at what humans do, but the school doesn't exactly make room for fun. What you see is what you get."

He cocks his head. "I do not believe that." In one fluid motion, he crosses the floor, his hand slipping around my waist. Heat blooms where his fingers graze me. "There is more to you than anyone sees."

I flush, wrenching slightly out of his grip. "Your charms won't work on me."

"I'm not trying to charm you."

I've bled enough that I should be immune to the fairy dust his little app pumped me full of. I'm free. Free to be lost in him because of my own weakness.

"It is not a trick." His eyes flick between my eyes and my lips, his hand still outstretched for me. "You are entrancing."

A strange heat floods my chest. No one's ever looked at me the way he does—not like I'm fragile or broken, but like I'm powerful. Like I could break *him* if I wanted to. I step back, needing space.

"It doesn't count," I say, more to myself than him. "I'm not falling for you just because of whatever magic's in my blood."

"No. You have not given in to anything, not even with the magic. That is what makes you different."

He reaches out, fingers brushing the golden stains along my arm. I should pull away.

But I don't.

"I wanted to come with you." He hesitates, fingers curling. "And not only to protect you."

I freeze. Those words hang in the air between us, taut and dangerous.

"I never asked for your protection," I whisper, though my body wants to betray me and lean toward him.

Galin reaches for me again, but I stay out of his range, my pulse hammering. I don't know what I would do if he were to embrace me again. I'm not ready to face what weaknesses a moment like that would reveal.

A slight frown mars his face. "It is my responsibility to keep you safe," he says, his voice quiet but fierce, "after I brought you into this world."

"That's not how your people usually see it. No one else cares what happens to humans once they're dragged Under the Hill."

"I am not like the others," he says, his eyes darkening. "I only care for you. Everyone else can fend for themselves."

His voice is quiet but fierce, and somehow, in all this, he's gotten close again. Too close. His breath brushes the shell of my ear, and my entire body locks up.

His fingers tilt my chin. My eyes meet his.

This is the edge.

One more step and there's no going back.

I pull away, retreating until my back nearly hits the door. "Why don't you get some rest?" My voice shakes only slightly. "We can figure out the next steps after that."

He studies me for a beat too long, then I have to hide my surprise as he simply nods and climbs onto the bed. No flirtation, no teasing—just silence, and then stillness, as his eyes flutter closed.

I let out a slow breath, but it doesn't bring relief. The tension is still there, stretched taut like a string inside me. Something between us shifted, something I don't know how to name yet.

But I feel it in my bones.

Being with him has changed me.

And I don't think I'll ever be the same.

After a long time, I glance over at his still form. Galin lies sprawled on top of the blanket, one hand resting loosely across his chest, the other curled beside his head. His dark lashes fan across his cheeks, and his unruly curls halo around his face in soft, lazy spirals. He doesn't look like a threat now. Not a seducer or a trickster or the fairy I was warned about. Just a boy, maybe only a few years older than me, worn out from everything we've both been through.

The sight of him disarms me more than I'd like to admit. He looks peaceful. Vulnerable, even. I have to turn away before that thought lands too heavily—before I start to wonder how much of that softness is real, how much of it I'm allowed to want.

I've never seen him sleep before. Honestly, I wasn't even sure if fairies *did* sleep. They always seemed so untouchable, like their energy came from something endless and otherworldly. But of course, he has to sleep. He's flesh and blood just like me—well, almost like me. Maybe it makes sense that he would rest during the day. Every time I've been dragged Under the Hill, it's been at night, and the revels have been loud and glittering, full of light and movement like they never stopped.

But here he is. In my room. On my bed. Sleeping.

It's too much.

I shift my weight quietly, careful not to wake him. His breathing is slow and even, the slow rise and fall of his chest hypnotic in the late afternoon light. For the first time, he looks like someone I could trust. Maybe even someone I could care for, if the world were different.

I pull my gaze away before the feelings sink their teeth in too deep.

Still wearing the fairy dress, I check the pocket for my knife. My fingers close around the handle, and I exhale, steadying myself. I glance at him once more. He doesn't stir.

And then I slip from the room.

The hallway outside is empty. Not quiet—*empty*. That buzzing tension that always lurks around the school during regular days is gone. The walls seem wider, the air cooler. It hits me all at once: this must be Family Weekend. Most of the students are probably home, whisked away to warm houses and smiling parents who make bad pancakes and ask too many questions and care enough to pretend they're not mad when grades slip.

Which means Joan might not be locked away in some underground fairy prison like I assumed.

Maybe Galin is wrong. Maybe Joan isn't suffering the consequences for helping the wrong people or knowing too much. Maybe she's just...*home*. Sitting at her kitchen table. Laughing with her mom. Completely unaware of how deeply I've been dragged into this mess.

It should be a relief, but it just leaves more questions.

Because even if Joan is fine...what about the *others*?

The girls Cillian showed me—some of them are probably gone already, used up and discarded by Tabitha and her court. But what if some of them are still there? Waiting. Terrified. Alone. Their time running out with every moment I spend hiding in my room, spinning in circles with Galin.

I stop in the middle of the hallway and press a hand to

my chest. My heartbeat kicks up like a warning bell. I made a promise. Maybe not out loud, maybe not even to Cillian. But to *myself*.

I promised I wouldn't let it happen again.

I *can't* leave them there. Not one more second. Even if they're not the same girls I saw before, even if I can't save everyone—I can try to save *someone*.

Chapter Eighteen

Snow crunches under my feet, brittle and sharp against my skin, the hard crust digging into my exposed ankles as I run—too fast to be careful, too determined to slow down. The cold cuts at me, but I don't let it stop me. I don't have time to be cold. I don't have time to be afraid.

Behind me, the school disappears into the trees, the last traces of its gray stone walls swallowed by branches heavy with snow. I don't look back.

I'm grateful for the one time Galin didn't use magic to spirit me away. Without his one moment of thoughtfulness, I never would've been able to find my way Under the Hill. That single moment is the only reason I'm able to find my way now.

When he wakes up and finds me gone, when he realizes I slipped past him while he slept—I hope he remembers that. I hope he remembers this was partly his mistake. If he wanted to keep me safe, he should've trusted me with the truth. If he wanted me to stay, he shouldn't have fallen asleep like he wasn't worried.

Because *I* am. I'm terrified. And still, I'm here.

The forest closes in around me like a warning, the air colder here, quieter. But I keep going. I know where I'm going. I retrace every step in my mind, mapping the memory of it like a lifeline. Past the crooked tree with its twisted trunk. Past the stones that looked like they might've once been a boundary marker—or maybe a grave.

And then I see it. The entrance to the tunnel, hidden in the side of the tree.

I skid to a stop.

This is it.

And only now do I realize I've forgotten one thing.

The light.

Galin was our only source of light the last time. A soft glow in the palm of his hand, flickering like candlelight but somehow steadier, brighter, more alive. It had pushed back the dark and made the journey manageable.

I don't have that now.

I stare into the black throat of the tunnel, my breath catching in my throat. The dark isn't just dark here—it's *absolute*. A solid wall of nothingness. No reflections, no shapes. No sound.

For a second, my hands go clammy. My fingers twitch at my sides.

I'm not afraid of the dark. I'm *not*. I've slept in the blackout curtains. I've walked city streets at night. I've spent years keeping secrets in my own shadowed corners. The dark itself doesn't scare me.

But what could be *in* the dark? What might be waiting for me just beyond the edge of my sight?

That's what tightens my throat. That's what makes my spine go stiff and cold.

Now I know the kind of monsters who live there. I've

seen what Tabitha does to girls she catches. I've felt the sharp edge of fairy magic when it's turned cruel. I've walked through rooms full of illusions and seen things that weren't supposed to be real, things that *shouldn't* be real—and yet they were.

I know what she's capable of. And if she finds me wandering the dark alone... I'll wish she had just killed me.

But if I walk away now—if I run back to safety while there's still time—I'll have to live with what I *didn't* do.

Grinding my jaw, I step forward. The snow gives way beneath my boot with a soft crack, the tunnel yawning wide like it's waiting to swallow me whole. The shadows breathe cold against my face.

Another step. Then another.

My hand brushes the wall, fingers trailing along the stone, using it to anchor myself as I descend. Each footstep echoes louder than it should, like the dark is trying to remind me how alone I am.

But I'm not turning back.

I made a promise to myself, and I'm going to keep it.

If no one else will fight for the girls trapped Under the Hill—if everyone else is too afraid, or too blind, or too busy pretending they can't hear the screaming in the cracks of this place—then I'll be the one who does something.

I might not be the strongest, or the fastest, or the one with magic. But I'm the only one who *cares*. I'm the one who *remembers*. And maybe that's enough.

No. It *has* to be enough.

I take a deep breath, let it fill my lungs until they ache, and then let it out slow.

I reach back and shut the heavy door behind me. the sound echoes like a thunderclap. Final. Absolute.

I close myself in with the darkness.

And I keep going.

After the first hundred steps, I finally manage to get my breathing under control. My chest no longer heaves like I've just escaped a fire. It's steadier now, even if my legs still feel like jelly beneath me—shaky, uncertain, already beginning to ache. But I keep going. One foot in front of the other, hand trailing the damp, uneven wall of the tunnel to keep myself grounded.

When my fingers brush against loose stone, a clump of earth rains down onto my boots, soft and wet and smelling of rot. I flinch but don't stop. Better dirt than bones. Better mud than blood.

I try to use the dark time wisely. I can't afford to let fear take up all the space in my head. I need a plan—an actual one—not just a burst of emotion and bravery. It's the only way this will count for anything. Otherwise, I'll just be one more girl who tried and failed. Or worse—one more girl who vanished without a trace.

First, I'll find Cillian. He's the only person I've met Under the Hill who seems to care about more than just his own power or survival. He showed me those girls, and I trust that wasn't an accident. He wanted me to see them. He wanted *someone* to care. And I do.

I have to believe that means something.

If I'm lucky, he'll help me. Maybe he'll even help me smuggle the girls out through the tunnel and back into the human world. But I know better than to count on that. Fairies don't usually risk their necks for humans—especially not when it would mean going directly against someone as powerful as Tabitha.

Even asking Cillian to help might be too much. This might be something I have to do alone.

And that's okay. If I have to be the one to do it, I will be.

Once I know where the girls are, I'll wait until the creature guarding them—whatever he is—leaves. Then I'll get them out. Quietly. Carefully. There's no way I'm going to fight him with my tiny pocketknife. That blade's strictly for emergencies. Or panic. Preferably both. I'm trying to avoid panic this time around.

The door back into the palace is hard and cold against my outstretched hand. This is it. This is where it stops being a plan and starts being real.

I press the latch. It swings open with no sound, just a whisper of breath against the tunnel's still air. A puff of condensation clouds before my lips as I exhale into the chill.

Everything looks exactly the way we left it. The abandoned wing of the palace is silent, cloaked in dust and frost, forgotten by time. The space is huge, and beneath the cobwebs and grime, I can see something exquisite: gold-leaf trim curling along the ceiling, faded velvet drapes, plaster molding that must have taken weeks to create.

Why would they leave this entire part of the palace to rot? With all the important fairies coming for Tabitha's gathering, surely someone would've thought to use this wing. Fill it with guests. Or guards. Or something. Instead, it's like no one remembers it's here.

Which is good for me. It might be the only reason I have any chance of pulling this off.

I slip out from the tunnel's shadow and press my back

against the nearest wall, freezing as movement flickers in the corner of my eye. My heart slams into my ribs so hard it might bruise. My fingers twitch toward my knife. I don't draw it—yet. Instead, I clench my fists and force myself to breathe.

Slow in. Slow out.

Panicking won't help me. Jumping at shadows won't save anyone.

Besides, thanks to Galin's stupidly beautiful dress, I *look* like one of them. If whoever's moving out there only glances, they might not realize I'm human. At least not right away. If I walk with confidence, if I look like I belong—maybe they won't even stop to ask.

I straighten my shoulders, lift my chin, and step forward like I've been summoned here. Like I have every right to walk this hall.

The room is vast and quiet. My boots crunch softly on the floor, the only sound. I scan the shadows, my eyes narrowing. The figure I thought I saw is gone.

My gaze drops to the floor. The layer of dust still bears the tracks Galin and I left earlier. No new footprints.

My blood runs cold.

No one else has been in here—or at least not by foot. Which means...what did I see?

I pivot slowly in a circle, looking for some explanation. Signs that someone might be watching me, hiding, tracking. But there's nothing. Just empty space and cold air. Nothing behind the furniture. No obvious hiding spots.

Except...

There. A slow, almost imperceptible movement behind the long tapestry hanging against the far wall.

My breath catches and my knife nearly slides free from my pocket.

Careful now.

Chewing my bottom lip. I cross the room on light feet, toes hanging softly, every step measured. I press my back to the wall and study the hanging tapestry. No sound. No shadows beneath it. But the movement continues—gentle, rhythmic. Like someone's breathing just behind it.

Or...

Something else.

My hand twitches. I grab the edge of the fabric and yank it from the wall.

It falls in a heavy, graceful heap at my feet, the velvet pooling like spilled wine.

And behind it—

Not a doorway.

Not a monster.

A mirror.

A tarnished, floor-length mirror framed in silver, its surface warped like rippling water. I exhale, the breath tumbling out of me in a startled laugh.

The movement I saw was me. My own reflection. Of course it was.

Apparently, all it takes is one tunnel and a little sleep deprivation for me to lose my grip on reality.

I step closer. My reflection watches me with wide, unsure eyes.

But...it's not *quite* mine.

I trail a hand along the side of the mirror, fingers following the hills and valleys of the silver leaves and flowers covering the gilt edges. It looks expensive, like everything else in the palace. But there's something different.

The girl in the mirror looks different. Elongated. Ethereal. Her curls shine like spun gold. Her gown glitters. Her lips are red and full, her shoulders held back with a kind of regal grace I've never managed in real life.

She's beautiful. Impossibly so.

She looks like she belongs here.

I don't.

Still, I stare.

I'm not this self-assured woman who looks like she can take on the world. I'm just an abandoned girl fighting to save other abandoned girls.

And yet...

For one wild second, I let myself pretend. Pretend I'm the kind of girl who wins. Who gets chosen. Who doesn't run in ruined shoes in the snow and scrape her hands raw in the dark. Who *saves* people without breaking along the way.

I twist back and forth in front of the mirror, letting my long skirt swirl around my legs. My hair falls in long blonde curls along my waist, my lips as red as roses in the reflection of the mirror.

I hate how badly I want to be her.

That thought breaks the spell.

With a sharp inhale, I tear my gaze away. I bend down, grab the tapestry from the floor and heave it back over the mirror, covering it completely.

For the first time I pay attention to the carefully placed image on the fabric I so carelessly pulled down. A skeleton wearing a crown kneeling in front of a mirror. That mirror.

I don't need to be able to read the writing trailing around the figure to know that mirror is bad news.

That mirror is dangerous. That reflection was a lie.

Vanity dressed up as a dream.

I shiver and back away. And this time I don't hesitate.

I turn and run—leaving the mirror, the tapestry, and the version of myself I saw in it far behind.

I start running through lies in my head, trying to come up with something—anything—that sounds convincing if someone spots me out in the open. Maybe I could say I'm on an errand for Galin. That could buy me a few minutes at least. He outranks most of the others here, and he's always been so calm, so commanding. People listen to him. Maybe they'd listen to me if I pretend I'm part of whatever mysterious work he's always doing.

But even as I think it, I know the truth: I'm a terrible liar. I feel like anyone with half a brain would see right through me. They'd take one look at my too-stiff posture, my too-fast breathing, and know I didn't belong.

Still, there's no time for second-guessing. No one's going to hand me a better plan wrapped in ribbons. So instead of lingering in fear, I move—quick and quiet, feet disturbing the dust that blankets the floor like a warning.

I head toward the main hall, but my thoughts tug me elsewhere. Galin.

Why does he live in that cramped little room when this palace has entire wings that sit empty? It doesn't make any sense. Then again, not much about Under the Hill does. Everything here seems deliberately designed to be disorienting—beautiful and eerie and cold. Still, I can't help wondering what his choice means. Maybe it's not about space. Maybe it's about privacy. Control. Maybe, like me, he's more comfortable with walls close around him. Or maybe he doesn't want people to know who he is when he's not playing the part.

My feet take me towards Galin's room without even thinking. The muscle memory is too strong after so many trips. My hand closes around the familiar doorknob. I know the way the metal will feel, cool and solid. This place has always felt like a kind of safety net—even before I admitted to myself how much I like him, how much I *wanted* to be around him.

But I'm not here to feel safe.

My hand drops away, and I lean back against the door instead. The hallway stretches out before me, silent and surreal. Frost spirals across the floor like veins of light. Ivy clings to the walls, dark green and shimmering with cold. It's beautiful—unnaturally so. Like everything else in this place, it's beautiful enough to be dangerous.

So. Decision time.

Cillian or the girls?

If I can find the girls first, maybe Cillian will come looking for me. But that's risky. I've come this far because I finally stopped pretending I could do everything alone. The truth is, I can't. I need help. I need him. He knows this place. He knows how to sneak and disappear and slip through cracks I don't even see.

I exhale slowly, my eyes drifting toward the throne room doors.

That's the most consistent place I've found him—or he's found me. It's risky, sure. Tabitha could be inside. But she doesn't know me. Not yet. And what would she see, anyway? A girl in a borrowed gown with red lips and golden hair, looking a little too confident to be harmless and a little too plain to be important.

Still, I hesitate. This is a world where being seen at the

wrong time can get you killed. Or worse. Would anyone even miss me if I vanished?

My hand curls into a fist. *That* thought lights something in me. Because even if no one else would miss me, those girls in the cells—they don't get a choice. They don't even get to *hope*. If I walk away now, who's left for them?

So yeah, it's worth the risk. Even if my legs feel like rubber. Even if the idea of seeing Tabitha again makes me want to run and hide. I can't live with myself if I let fear decide for me.

My steps speed up. I move quietly, but there's new resolve in me now. A quiet fire. Galin lit the match when he trusted me with the truth. And Cillian fanned the flames by being on my side even when I didn't deserve it.

The hallway is quieter than it should be. I pass old paintings, empty candle holders, echoes of music that isn't playing. Surely not *everyone* followed Tabitha on her little errand. She strikes me as the kind of queen who needs an audience. Someone to watch her reign. Someone to fear her.

Finally, I reach the throne room doors. My fingers hover just above the handle, then fall away. I can't open it.

Something's off.

It's too quiet. The wrong kind of quiet. The kind that presses against the skin and makes hair stand on end.

If I open that door and find her alone, waiting for me like some spider at the center of her web—what then? Could I lie? Could I say Galin sent me to ask her something?

Maybe. But I'm not willing to bet my life on maybe.

My hand drifts to my side, brushing the place where my knife is hidden beneath the folds of my dress. I feel foolish, standing here paralyzed by a door. But isn't it smarter to admit when a plan's not going to work? Isn't it better to shift course than to march straight into danger for the sake of pride?

I turn away, spine stiff with the weight of my own decisions. I'm not going in there—not without a better reason. I told myself I'd save those girls and I meant it. But I never promised to do it stupidly.

The hallway yawns ahead of me. Empty and echoing.

This is the path I've chose. Not just because it's safe, but because it's mine.

I walk faster, toward the place I think the girls are being held. No more second-guessing. No more half-formed plans.

And if I see Galin again—if I make it out of this and find my way back to him—I want to be able to look him in the eye and know I've earned it. That I didn't run from the hard thing. That I tried to do something right, even when I was scared out of my mind.

Because for all his power, Galin never made me feel small.

And I want to be someone who deserves that.

I descend deeper into the heart of the hill, the marbled elegance of the throne room vanishing behind me like a forgotten dream. The polished glamour gives way to damp stone and stale air, the sweetness of magic traded for the sour smell of earth and rot. Light grows scarce, shadows stretching and thickening with each level I pass, until they seem to press in on all sides. I flick my fingers, hoping for a glimmer of illumination—but I have no magic. Only the dim, borrowed glow of the stairwell torches and a very human sense of dread.

I keep moving.

Now and then, I hear something—a footfall, a scuffle, the brush of movement in stairwells I can't see—but each time I turn, there's no one there. It's like the palace is haunted, and maybe it is. Maybe I'm not the only one wandering through these tunnels, guided by guilt and desperation.

The air grows colder the further I go. My limbs tremble —not just from fear, but fatigue. My knees buckle slightly on the stairs. I grit my teeth and force them to hold me. I have no idea how long I've been walking, but I know I can't stop now.

I glance upward into the dim shaft of light above me, wondering—not for the first time—if any of the girls trapped down here could even survive the climb back up. Would I free them only to leave them stranded in this cursed labyrinth? No. I won't let that happen. I'll find a way. I have to.

Straightening my spine, I stop at a promising level and step off the stairs.

At first glance, it's like every other hallway I've passed: earthen walls, uneven floors, and a long row of doors. Each is heavy and wooden and utterly unmarked. I don't even know what I'm looking for. Some sign. A sound. A feeling.

Maybe a bright red banner shouting "STOLEN HUMAN GIRLS THIS WAY!"

The thought makes me huff a laugh. Morbid humor is all I've got left.

The air here carries a different weight—a metallic sharpness that clings to the back of my throat and thickens with each step I take. Fog gathers at my feet, or maybe it's just the cold, but walking feels like pushing through invisible resistance.

This isn't like the first time I was shown the girls. Cillian and I never descended this far, and back then, I could still feel the thrum of music pounding from the throne room. Here, there's only silence and shadow.

Still—I feel drawn. Not by logic, exactly, but something deeper. The choices that led me here haven't felt like choices at all. More like…pulls. Echoes. The memory of pain that isn't mine, but is lodged in my bones all the same. The girls' trauma, probably. As though it's reaching for someone to witness it.

I press my forehead against the first door and close my eyes.

I force my breathing to slow, to soften, until it's quiet enough that I might here something beyond myself. I listen for life.

Nothing.

Just before I pull away, I whisper, "I'm coming for you."

I should've said that a long time ago. When I first learned what was happening. When I still had a choice to act. How many of them bled out in silence, never knowing someone was coming for them? Never believing anyone would?

That's on me. My silence, my hesitation—it cost them hope.

I shift back, palm still resting against the door, and that's when I hear it: the softest shuffle.

My breath catches.

"H-hello?" I drop to my knees, peering through the gap under the door. "Is someone there?"

A shadow flickers on the other side, then pulls away.

"Wait! I'm here to help you!" I try to sound calm, safe,

real. But my heart thunders so loudly it's a wonder anything else can be heard.

"Are you trapped in there?" I ask, quieter now. "I'm here to get you out."

I lean in again, heart hammering, breath shallow.

"Open the door," a voice whispers—low raspy, and entirely too close.

I flinch back with a cry, scrambling across the floor. Laughter trails me as shadows ooze beneath the door like smoke.

"Come and save me little girl. Come and free me," the voice taunts. "Let me out and let me show you what I am."

Panic claws at my chest, but I don't run. Not yet. I force myself upright, heart pounding, and stare down the corridor.

"Come and save me little human," the low voice calls and laughs, the sound driving right into my bones.

I shouldn't be surprised. Galin's warned me—there are creatures in his court far worse than him. But where Galin is dangerous with edges of restraint, this voice is pure hunger it doesn't want to rule. It wants to consume.

Still—I don't run. Something tells me I'm close. That I have to push forward, because if I go back now, I'll never make it upstairs again. If the girls are still in that throne room with the executioner, I'll be powerless to save them. My little knife won't stand a chance against the monster's axe.

But if there's even a *chance* they're down here...

This has to count for something. Right?

The corridor stretches before me, endless and quiet. I don't know if it's a trick of the light or some kind of magic illusion—but the walls feel like they go on forever. Honestly, I've stopped ruling out magic for anything. If

Galin can conjure blue flames from his bare hands, then maybe an infinite hallway isn't out of the question.

Even if I'm getting used to the rules of this strange new world, it doesn't make anything easier.

Glancing back to the beginning of the corridor, the shadows under the first door shift again. A shudder trails down my spine, and I continue with greater determination. If I'm moving forward, then I won't have to go back by that creature any time soon. If I find those girls, then I won't have to go back alone. That probably gives me more comfort than it should.

My feet shuffle along the floor, the only sound in this empty place. The sounds could draw creatures towards me, but I need it right now. The sounds of my own feet are the only thing stopping the ringing in my ears created by being in the silence too long.

I move past several doors until something makes me stop. Backpedaling, I stand in front of the last door I passed. It looks just like every other door in this hallway, but something seems different. Feels different. There's a heaviness in the air that I can't explain.

There's no movement from the other side, no sounds to announce a lingering presence. My hand drifts towards the doorknob, fingers itching to throw the door open. After what happened with the last one, I know I should be more cautious.

But I can't stop. It's a need that's moved into a compulsion.

My hand turns the cold knob, swinging the door open on silent hinges. There is only darkness in the room and the lingering coppery scent of blood. Flinching back, I move to close the door, the compulsion broken and the fear of a darkness that could destroy me becoming too great.

"Wait!"

A small voice. Human. Hopeful. So *normal* it startles me.

From the back of the room a small figure moves into the shadowy light. She wears a gauzy white dress, torn in spots and covered in dirt. Her brown hair hangs in greasy clumps and her feet are bare as she comes closer.

She looks heartbreakingly human.

But my hand drifts to my pocket anyway. I know better now.

"Who are you?" I ask softly.

She doesn't answer. Just stares at the open doorway behind me.

"I came to bring you home."

Her gaze shifts toward me, eyes narrowing. "How do you know where my home is?"

"I don't," I admit, raising my hands in a small shrug. "But I'm guessing it isn't here."

She tilts her head to the side, and I hold my arms up helplessly. This isn't going how I thought it would at all. I'm just glad I've found at least one. That at least one of the stolen girls won't be left to languish here before being bled by greedy fairies. This action alone should make me feel amazing right now, but I can't get rid of the tightness in my chest.

"It is generous of you," she says, "to come all this way, to save me from the dark."

"Leaving anyone down here wouldn't be right."

But my thumb brushes the edge of my pocketknife.

"You are the only one to feel that way," she says, coming closer on silent feet. "Many have put me down here with nary a thought of the effects it would have."

"No one should be stolen from their home." My voice cracks slightly. I'm still not sure why.

She meets my gaze, the light from the hallway sliding over her yellow eyes. Her mouth twists into a grin.

"I *am* sorry for what I have to do now."

"W-what you have to do?"

In the second it takes for her to fling herself at me from across the floor, I barely process her words. Her hands grab my shoulders, nails lengthening until they spear into my flesh. Her mouth opens past the point it should be able to, past what any human can. She launches her fanged mouth at me, and I finally get a grip on my knife and thrust it forward. It meets surprisingly little resistance as I shove it into her chest, halting her forward momentum toward my neck. Her dark eyes widen, glancing down towards the slim knife.

With a hiss, she grabs the knife and pulls it from her chest. The movement is just enough that I'm able to shimmy out from under her and backpedal away from the door. She charges towards me again, her small hand holding my own knife against me as it drips crimson blood onto the floor. It's exactly what Galin said would happen. I'm about to be impaled on my own knife.

As she gets close, I kick out. My foot collides with her chest, shoving her backward and sending my knife skittering across the floor. In the split second of distraction, I grab the door and slam it closed.

Leaning against the comfort of solid wood, my head tips towards my chest and I spy my knife abandoned on the floor. The relief has a slight chuckle pushing its way out of my throat.

"I thought you were here to save me," she says through the crack, her voice small and tender.

"That was before you were interested in killing me."

She hiccups a sob. "Will you not let me out? It is not my fault. It has just been so long. Too long since I was fed."

I climb to my feet, shoving away from the door. I can't listen to her anymore. There's no way I'm going to let her out, but I can't take listening to someone who sounds so... human. It's too much.

This corridor is a dead end. Nothing but monsters behind every door. Maybe I should've stayed upstairs. Maybe I should've brought Galin. Maybe I'm in over my head.

I rest my forehead against the wall, breath catching.

This is too much. I'm just a girl. I shouldn't be down here. What made me think I could do this?

My knees wobble. A sob threatens. But I don't let myself fall.

If I wanted to surrender, I could've stayed in Galin's room, curled up in his bed while he played protector. But I didn't. I chose this. I chose to fight.

I push off the wall and start walking again, folding my bloody knife and slipping it back into my pocket. I'll probably need it again.

This is too much. I never should have come here. Why did I ever think a human girl who knew nothing about any of this a few months ago could have done anything to save anyone?

I can't even save myself.

My knees shake, tempting me to slide to the floor again. To sit on the ground and let myself fall into wallowing, hot tears splashing against my cheeks. It would be so easy to believe there's nothing I can do. That I'm not good enough. It's probably not far off from the truth.

But I can't.

As I move, my thoughts drift back to the fairy prince sleeping on my bed. Has he woken up and realized I'm gone yet? What will he do when he realizes I've abandoned him and moved forward on my own? I wonder if he'll be happy to be rid of me. He's done everything he could to protect me, and I've done nothing but constantly reject his efforts. It will have to be a relief to be done. I know that's how I would feel.

But maybe I'm not as weak as I thought. I faced two monsters and lived. I *survived*.

Maybe I'm stronger than he ever expected.

So why does it feel so hollow without Galin here?

Focus, Grace.

This isn't the time.

This isn't about Galin. This is about the girls. I've been drawn here for a reason. I need to focus on that, and hope that it wasn't one of the beasts waiting behind these doors using their magic to let them out.

Closing my eyes, I allow my arms to extend the tiniest bit from either side of my body. Taking several long deep breaths, I wait for another pull. For something that will tell me I'm headed in the right direction.

A subtle tug blooms in my chest, leading me towards the dark end of the tunnel.

I open my eyes, my heart beating steady.

This is where I'm supposed to be, and I need to trust in that. There's a reason and I'll find it.

Because I'm not done. Not yet.

Chapter Nineteen

My new confidence only carries me so far.

No matter how hard I try to focus, my thoughts keep circling back to Galin. I don't want to think about whether running off hurt him. I don't want to imagine the look on his face when he realized I was gone. But that's the thing about thoughts—they don't ask for permission.

This would have been easier with him. He's quick, clever, and terrifyingly good at navigating this place. I think he would've helped me. I should've trusted him.

But I didn't. I can't take that back now.

The guilt burns, low and steady in my chest, until it's nearly indistinguishable from the fear. I tell myself over and over again that I shouldn't care about him—that I'm here for the girls, not for him—but it's like trying to put out fire with smoke. Haven't I lost enough blood to get him out of my system?

Apparently not.

And I'm not about to volunteer for another round of

magical bleeding just to try again. That would be desperate. Or pathetic. Or both.

I force myself forward, thoughts of Galin scratching at the edges of my focus. It's not real, I tell myself. The warmth when he touched, the way he looked at me like I mattered—none of it was real.

...Right?

Before I can untangle that, light blooms at the end of the hallway. A door creaks open, spilling golden glow onto the earthen wall. I press myself flat against the wall, heart jackhammering in my chest. There's nowhere to hide. If whoever opened that door comes over, or even looks this way, it's over. I haven't even had a chance to do anything yet.

My hands are sweaty as I press them against the side of the wall, loose earth pressing into the creases of my palms. Light steps come out of the open door, the brightness fading as the door closes behind a backlit figure. My heart beats so loud in my ears as I try not to look at who's about to catch me. I can't do it and I turn to see it anyway.

Quick clopping steps come down the hallway towards me, the figure too dark to see who it is.

"Hello?"

The voice slices through the tension in my spine. I nearly collapse with relief.

"Cillian?"

As he steps closer, I catch the telltale bounce of his cloven feet and the tousled curls framing his faun-like face. The adrenaline that had been holding me upright drains all at once, leaving me unsteady and light-headed.

"Grace?" he says, brow furrowing. "What are you doing down here?"

"I'm looking for them." Cillian gives me a blank look

and I rub my dirty hands off on my dress before continuing. "The girls. I've come to rescue them. I want to take them home."

Cillian frowns. "I have told you there is nothing you can do for them."

"I remember," I say, standing straighter. "But that doesn't mean I accepted it."

He sighs heavily. "Come with me."

I hesitate. Something about this feels...off. Not in the obvious way—he's not threatening, not angry, but he's not meeting my eyes either. The tension in his shoulders is a little too tight.

Still, this is Cillian. My friend. The one person in this entire twisted world who's never lied to me. the one who warned me, who helped me.

I follow him.

We walk in silence, the hallway narrowing before opening toward a wooden door at the far end. Warm light glows faintly beneath it, but instead of making me feel better, it tightens the knot in my throat.

Cillian pauses in front of it, gaze still fixed on the floor.

"They are in here," he says quietly. "Would you like to see?"

I try to laugh—something light to break the tension— but it comes out brittle. "That's why I'm here, remember?"

He swings the door open on silent hinges. The pressure in my chest eases as the opening reveals fifteen girls huddled in a corner. Their shoulders press close, backs curled inward as if they're bracing for impact. None of them look up at us.

I step inside slowly. "Are they okay?"

I turn to ask Cillian, he's still in the doorway, jaw tight. With one sharp motion, he slams the door shut between us.

I rush back and grab the handle but it's locked.

"Cillian?" I pound my hand against the wood. "What are you doing?"

The tightness in my chest pushes hysteria to the forefront and I have to swallow it down before I can say anything again.

"Open the door Cillian."

His voice is muffled but firm. "I am sorry, Grace. I cannot let you out."

"What do you *mean* you can't let me out?" Panic rises, and I push it down with a forced breath before my voice gets hysterical.

"It is time, Grace."

"That's not an answer!" My voice cracks as I laugh, high and anxious.

He's silent for a moment. "When this door opens again, you will receive the answers you seek."

"That's so cryptic, it's practically a riddle," I mutter.

I turn. The girls are still pressed together, silent and unmoving. They haven't even looked at me. I suddenly realize how little sound they make. No whispering. No breathing. I can hear. It's like they're afraid I'm not real—or worse, that I am.

"Let me out, Cillian!" I shout again. "You've never tried to hurt me before, why start now? Did I do something to you? Can we talk about it?"

"It is unfortunate," he says, "that you have perceived my actions as acts of kindness. I do not have time to explain. I am needed elsewhere."

"You can't just leave me here," I scream, slamming my hand against the locked door. "Let me out!"

Silence rains down on me. He's really gone.

He locked me in. Left me here with the very girls I wanted to save.

I let out a laugh to hide a sob. "Well. That's poetic."

My legs are tight as I turn to face the other girls. There has to be something here. There has to be some way out, some way that we can work together that the other girls haven't thought of. With Cillian gone, the girls disentangle from themselves. The single light against the far wall illuminates their hunched bodies as they stand with stooped backs and stare at me. My gaze roves over the room, searching for something, but all I see are earth walls and shaking girls.

Turning my attention to them, I take in their skeletal bodies and sunken eyes. They truly look like monstrous cave dwellers.

"How long have you been here?"

There's a long pause. Then one of them, a girl with tangled hair and dirt-streaked cheeks, replies without looking up. "A long time. I think."

"What do they do to you?"

"Nothing," says another girl.

"They don't even feed us," someone adds from the shadows.

The words hit me like a punch. I've known about them for *weeks*. I've been to revels. I've bled. I've chased half-truths in gilded rooms. But I didn't *do* anything for them.

I thought I was keeping them safe by staying close to Galin. By not drawing attention.

But they're starving.

I study their bodies again. Emaciated, yes—but not on the brink of death. Not yet.

They *can't* be the same girls I saw before.

How long can a person live without food? One week?

Two? My opportunity to save them is long gone and a hole burns its way through my heart as I try to push that thought aside.

"Who comes to give you things?" Surely, they must have contact with the fairies occasionally.

"They only come here when they're dropping off a new girl."

"Or taking samples."

My focus snaps to the girl leaning in the corner, her jeans covered in long tears.

"What kind of samples?"

"That..." She waves a hand at the door behind me. "Goat man comes in and takes our blood. He's always there when a new girl comes in. They take a sample from us right away."

"Have they said what they're using it for?"

She shakes her head, the strands coming out of her ponytail pasted to the sides of her face and neck. "That thing has mentioned what blood type the girls are a few times, but not always, and they never say anything more than that. The creature that brings them in has never said any words at all."

"What's your name?"

"Sarah."

She says it calmly, like her name doesn't matter anymore.

"Were you here when the others arrived?"

"No. I was alone."

"You've been here longer than them?"

She nods.

I study her more closely. She seems more alert than the others. Sharper. Like her mind hasn't entirely dulled from the isolation.

It's strange, but somehow, in this awful place where everything feels rigged against me, Sarah is the only one who might actually help. Not because she wants to, necessarily—but because she's the only one still looking at me like I'm not already lost.

"Okay, Sarah," I say, taking a careful step toward her. My voice is steadier than I expected it to be. "If we're going to get out of here, we're going to have to work together. We need each other."

She doesn't respond immediately. Just crosses her arms over her thin chest and watches me through narrowed, wary eyes, like she's waiting for me to fall apart or say something stupid. I don't blame her. I probably would've looked at someone the same way after being trapped like this.

But I didn't come here to be reasonable. I didn't come here to give up.

I square my shoulders, draw in a breath that tastes like dry earth, and cross to the far wall. If there's any weakness here, any gap in the packed dirt or hairline crack in the stone, I need to find it. Slowly, methodically, I start pressing my palms along the surface, dragging them across the cool, uneven wall. One side, then the next, feeling for anything the eye might miss.

Behind me, Sarah's voice is flat. "What exactly do you think you're doing?"

"Looking for options," I reply, keeping my voice level. "There's always something. A pressure point. A pattern. A seam."

"And what happens if you find it?" she asks. "You just punch your way out?"

"If that's what it takes."

She lets out a dry, hollow laugh that sounds far too old for her age. "You really believe that?"

I don't answer. Belief has nothing to do with it. I have to try. I can't just curl up and wait for someone else to come save me—or wait for my hope to rot into whatever's made the rest of these girls stop fighting.

Dirt clumps under my fingernails, separating my nail from the nail bed with its tiny shims. But I don't care. The pain will only be fleeting if I discover a way out of this.

But I was so stupid. I *trusted* Cillian. I believed he was on my side. I told myself we were friends. I let that idea blind me, and now I'm locked in a cell with the girls I came to save, and I let it happen like it was nothing. No fight. No plan. Just blind, hopeful trust.

My fist slams into the wall. A small shower of dirt and dust rains down, clinging to my hair and lashes.

"There's no way out of here," Sarah says again, her voice a notch softer now. "I've tried every inch of it. You're wasting your time."

"Maybe," I say as I move to the next corner. "But I need to see for myself."

She exhales slowly and moves to lean against the wall closest to me. "The only way in or out is that door. And it's locked. Solid. Just like everything else here."

She points at the door Cillian locked. It's thick and heavy, made with the same unnatural craftmanship I've come to associate with the high fairies—beautiful, cold, and impenetrable. But even they have flaws. That's what no one ever talks about. That's what I've seen. For all their elegance and power, they are still creatures of habit. Creatures that make mistakes. If I look close enough, there's always a fracture line somewhere.

I finish the full circle around the room and find nothing.

No seams. No weak spots. No magic pulse I can twist. Rage boils up in me and I slam my fists into the dirt-packed wall again and again until my skin splits and the first trickles of red blood slicks my fingers. The wall doesn't budge, but I keep hitting it.

Behind me, the girls are silent. Watching. Waiting for me to break the same way they have.

I thought I was different. That someone would see something in me and protect me. That Galin might...and that Cillian—no, especially Cillian, would help. But maybe this place strips everyone down until there's nothing left but survival.

Tears sting the backs of my eyes, but I refuse to let them fall. Not now. Not while they're watching me. not while I still have any strength left to give.

Turning my back to the silent girls, I move toward the door. My fingers trail over the carved wood. Dirt and blood mix and sink into the grooves of the grain.

"There's no way out," Sarah says again, bony arms crossed over her chest. "You really think you're going to find something the rest of us missed?"

"I think I won't be able to live with myself if I don't try."

That shuts her up. She huffs but stays by the wall, arms crossed and eyes sharp.

I press my palm against the center of the door. The blood trickling from my fingers oozes, the first hints of gold coming out as I move my fingers in small arcs against the wood. A strange heat prickles against my skin. The surface of the door grows warm under my touch. I press against it, hoping for any weaknesses. Shoving against the wood, blood smearing across it, the sensation under my skin grows.

All at once, a flash of blue light explodes from the door.

I stumble back, covering my face as heat and sound roar through the tiny room. The girls cry out behind me. My vision is full of dark splotches—blue and white starbursts dancing across the dark. I blink hard, trying to clear them.

With a deep, cracking groan, the door splinters.

Not just cracks. *Shatters*. Like something had been waiting—watching—for a key it recognized. And my blood...it was the key.

Chapter Twenty

No one moves.

The silence is thick, like the air has turned to syrup around us. Together, we stare at the jagged hole where the heavy door once stood, its splintered remains hang from twisted hinges like broken teeth. Beyond the threshold, the hallway stretches into darkness —quiet, still, and waiting.

I wipe my hands off on the sides of my dress, ignoring the sharp sting of torn skin and the raw blood coating my cracked knuckles. Faint sparks of blue light flicker along the edges of the wounds, like tiny lightning bugs caught in my veins. I try not to flinch. I try not to look too long. Magic like that should feel comforting—Galin's magic had shimmered the same way—but this feels too close, too familiar, and too much like something I shouldn't be able to do.

But I did.

I step through the ruined doorway, shoes crunching on fragments of wood. Behind me, there's a hesitant rustle, then a surge of movement. The spell of stillness breaks, and the girls shove past one another, hungry for the space outside the walls that have trapped them for days—weeks, maybe longer.

Sarah comes last.

She carries the torch she must have pulled from the wall behind us. The flickering flame throws long shadows across her face, making her expression hard to read. But her eyes —her eyes are locked on me, sharp and knowing.

A chill slides down my spine. She knows something. I don't know what, not exactly, but I can feel it in the way she's watching me. She saw what happened when my blood touched the door. She felt the magic. And unlike the others, she's not pretending it was luck.

I don't let myself hesitate. We don't have time.

"Come on," I say, my voice quiet but firm. "We have to keep moving."

I start down the corridor, the stone floor rough beneath my aching feet. The girls follow close behind, clinging to each other like refugees from a dream turned nightmare. But their heads are higher now, their backs a little straighter. Even a sliver of hope is powerful here. The possibility of escape—real escape—is already working its own quiet magic on them.

I lead them with steady steps, but my mind spins as fast as my heart.

There was a way out of this place. Galin showed me one up these stairs. Do I dare bring the girls that way now— when we don't know who might be patrolling, who might be watching—might get us all caught. There's nowhere to hide in that stairwell. If anyone else is using it, or if Cillian returns, we'll be exposed. I'd be leading them into a trap, not away from one.

Still, what other choice do we have? I could try and find a different route, but we're deep inside a palace designed to confuse and control. If I hesitate, if I wander without a plan, I might get them lost forever.

And I can't afford any more mistakes.

I press a hand to the wall to steady myself, and again I feel that faint warmth—barely perceptible, like a breath beneath stone. Magic. Not mine. Not quite. But connected to whatever just happened at the door. *What is happening to me?*

My thoughts circle back to Galin—how he looked at me that day in the throne room, how he touched my hand like he *knew* something I didn't. He never explained, never demanded. He could've told someone. He didn't.

If he wanted to use me, he's had every opportunity. Instead, he helped me. He got me out.

Galin didn't betray me.

That, at least, I know now.

But Cillian...

My heart clenches.

I trusted him. I trusted him more than anyone. He pulled me from that cursed dance when no one else even noticed me disappearing. He made me believe I was safe, that I had someone on my side in a place where allies are illusions.

But maybe that was the whole point.

The vial he took—was it the same one Tabitha held up earlier? Did he hand me over piece by piece, smiling all the while, just waiting for the right moment to deliver me into her hands?

The thought burns like acid in my chest. It makes me feel stupid and furious all at once. I thought I could tell the difference between a friend and a monster.

Apparently not.

I glance back to make sure the girls are still with me,

then turn down the passage that leads to the stairwell. Even if it's risky, it's the best chance we've got. The palace is enormous and alive in ways I don't fully understand—but I know this path. I know it leads out.

And right now that has to be enough.

I draw a breath and steel my voice. "Stay close. Don't stop unless I do. If we get separated, head for the light and don't look back."

My leg shakes as I take the first step up the stairwell and the girls follow me, one by one, climbing toward whatever waits above.

Freedom. Danger. Truth.

Whatever it is, I'll face it.

But this time I won't do it alone.

We move on swift, albeit stiff, feet towards the stairwell. I guide the girls along the wall, far from the doors where I'd made my earlier mistakes. Even those risky places seem strangely quiet now. Too quiet. The whole floor feels like it's holding its breath, like the palace itself is watching us, waiting to see if we'll make it.

The stairwell yawns open before us, spiraling both up and down into a seemingly endless void. Everything is still. This is it—the point of no return. If anyone else is on these stairs, there won't be time to hide or backtrack. We'll be seen, chased, dragged back. And looking at the girls around me—skinny, shaky, scraped raw from stone floors—I know some of them might not make it.

But this is our only way out.

I clench my hands into fists. A pulse of heat blooms in

my chest and sparks of blue light shiver around my fingers. It's like trying to hold a bird in my palm while praying it won't fly away. I focus, try to direct it—to shape it. If I can use this magic, I might be able to give us a fighting chance. It was enough to take down a door, it should be enough for a few fairies.

Nothing happens.

Just a faint buzz of energy and dull ache in my chest. Not enough.

I exhale sharply. At least it worked once. Maybe that luck will hold again, if it comes down to it.

"We're going up," I whisper, waving the girls forward and taking up the rear.

Sarah glances back and gives me a tight nod before stepping onto the staircase and leading the way. Her spine is straight despite everything—one of the only girls who hasn't started trembling. We might have a chance. We might actually make it.

We climb. The stairs go on forever, curling upward in tight, dizzying turns. My legs start to shake, my breath going shallow with every step. When was the last time I ate something? Slept for more than a moment? Showered? I feel like I've been running on panic and adrenaline for so long, I've forgotten how to exist like a real person.

When this is over, the first thing I'm going to do is take a long, hot shower. Then maybe eat something so greasy and ridiculous that it makes me sick. Then maybe sleep for three days straight.

Assuming we make it.

Assuming I don't get institutionalized for dragging a group of kidnapped girls back to school with a story about fairy prisons.

A sharp clang against the stair rail echoes from somewhere above us. One of the girls screams, the sound bouncing off the stone like a fire alarm. I flinch. That sound could've traveled all the way to the main floor. Or farther.

"What happened?" I hiss through the gaps in the railing, heart hammering against my ribs.

"Rose fell," Sarah whispers back. She's hunched beside one of the girls who's collapsed on a step, her ankle bent at a wrong and terrible angle.

"Can she walk?"

Sarah doesn't answer immediately, and that tells me enough. Every second we stay here is another second someone might find us. I haven't seen anyone on these stairs in the few times I've used them, but if Cillian was here...if Tabitha suspected...they could be closing in already.

"Can she keep walking?"

"Her ankle might be broken," Saray says finally, her voice grim.

My thoughts whirl, fast and useless, until they lock onto a single solution. "We'll carry her."

I force myself forward, weaving between girls, and crouch beside Rose. My knees pop. Her ankle is already swelling. I don't need to be a doctor to know it's bad. I meet Sarah's eyes. "Do you think you're strong enough?"

Sarah's jaw sets. "Yes."

We move at the same time. She slips under one of Rose's arms; I take the other side, ignoring the screaming protest of my legs. I've had more sleep and food than these girls. I should be stronger. I have to be.

We haul her up between us, and I nearly buckle under the weight. I've lost too much blood. I can feel it in the slow, stuttering drag of my heartbeat. But I don't stop. I won't stop.

A smear of blood glistens on the stairs behind us, the metallic smell mingling with dust and sweat.

"She scraped her leg," Sarah explains, breathless.

The fairies aren't bloodhounds—but still, the sight of that glistening trail sends panic straight down my spine. It's a beacon. An invitation. Bending, I mop it up with the edge of my already filthy dress. A deep red stain soaks into the dark silk like an accusation.

Galin would be furious if he saw what I'd done to his clothes. Or maybe not. Maybe he'd give me something more useful next time. Pants, for starters. What I wouldn't give for pants right now.

I push myself upright. We move again, slow and steady. I stagger under the weight of everything—the girl at my side, the exhaustion pressing on my bones, the fear I won't be enough to get through this.

We reach the main landing, and I let go of the last bit of tension I've been holding. The door to the abandoned wing looms before us like a dream. We're almost there. I can feel it. I can taste freedom.

A sound like scattering rocks cascades down the stairwell behind us. My heart slams into my ribs. The hair on my arm prickles. Something is coming.

"Go!" I shout, my voice raw. "Run! Don't look back!"

Transferring Rose to another girl, I shove the group through the door, into the darkness. One by one, they vanish into the tunnel.

I slam the door shut behind them, pressing my weight against it. I scan the stairwell. No one in sight—but I know I heard something.

I've done all I can. The girls are running now, deep into the tunnels. Even if someone follows, they'll be hard to catch.

I've done what I promised.

But the shadows shift in front of me. a puddle of darkness unfurls at my feet, and from it rises a figure draped in black silk and cruelty.

Tabitha.

Her crimson smile splits her face like a wound. "Did you think you could escape so easily?"

My pulse beats faster, my chest constricting until I can barely breathe.

"Like I would not know the source of what I needed was not housed under the same roof as me?"

Several large males in dark uniforms step out behind her, the fabric tight against bulging muscles. The last person to step through Tabitha's portal is Cillian, his hands wringing together as he stands behind the wall of brute force.

That betrayal sears like fire across my chest.

I don't let myself look at him. Not for more than a heartbeat.

Tabitha raises her fingers, arching them like spider legs and tilts her head. "I have a very special use for you," she says, pointed canines gleaming in the weak light. She runs a finger down my jaw. "You should be grateful for the sacrifice I am allowing you to make."

I jerk my head out of her grasp, and she laughs.

"This is truly a great honor, even if you cannot see it yet. Or ever really, but that is just as well. It does not matter if you are unwilling."

The guards advance. I press back against the door, then raise my hands. I *focus*. I find the thread of the heat I felt earlier and *pull*.

Nothing.

Come on, come on, come on—

A flicker. A shimmer. A spark that dances between my fingers.

Tabitha narrows her eyes. "Now."

Her men move—and this time, I *feel* it. Like a crack of thunder behind my eyes. Blue light explodes from my fingertips, twisting around me like a protective shell. My hair lifts with static and a shield grows around me, thicker as I pour every last scrap of strength into it.

One of her guards lunges—and hits the web I've created. A blue strand crosses his hand, and he screams, body held in place as the blue threads wrap around his hand, tighter and tighter as it flashes a bright white light. His screams get louder, piercing my eardrums until a flash of light burns bright enough that it temporarily blinds me.

Blinking away dark splotches, I look for the guard. He's not standing in front of me anymore. Instead, he's collapsed in a curled-up ball on the floor.

Tabitha hesitates.

Another guard steps forward and the web around me dims. My strength falters and my breath stutters.

He hesitates in front of my crackling blue webs. To his left, the first guard still lies in a heap, twitching every so often. The new guard and I make eye contact as he presses towards my ball of protection. His jaw is tight, the lines of the muscles in his neck standing out as he braces himself.

He touches the shield—and nothing happens.

My breath catches, as my confidence wavers. I wait for the screams that came before. Instead, the blue strands coming from my hands flicker in and out, fading as he comes closer. Unharmed.

His hands close tightly around my biceps and all the remaining light leaves me. He tightens his grip, shoving my arms behind my back as he maneuvers me towards Tabitha.

"Now that we have that out of the way," Tabitha says in a cool voice. Triumphant. "Bring her upstairs. We have work to do."

As the guard drags me forward, I glance one last time at Cillian. His mouth is tight. His eyes avoid mine.

I don't scream. I don't cry.

But I do burn. Inside.

I'll survive this.

And then I'll make them regret ever thinking I wouldn't.

Chapter Twenty-One

The guard's hands on me are anything but gentle as they lead me upstairs, fingers digging into my arms with bruising force. They don't even glance at their fallen comrade, leaving him curled on the floor like a discarded puppet. His limbs are bent wrong. He's not getting up again. No one seems to care.

I bite my tongue against the rising bile. I'll be a mess of bruises tomorrow—if I live that long.

They haul me through the halls like I'm nothing, like I'm no one. Tabitha leads the way, her head held high and her midnight dress sweeping the floor like shadows in motion. She doesn't look back once.

The doors open and my feet falter.

Stone walls. No windows. The smell of iron and rot.

Recognition hits me like a brick in the gut. I know this place.

This is where I saw the girls. Where Cillian and I peered through a hidden crack and saw the altar, saw the blood. This is the room I've tried not to think about since. The one I prayed I'd never see again.

But here it is. And now I'm the one they've brought.

I don't know why I expected anything else.

The fair folk wear human faces, but they aren't human. They don't think like we do. I don't think they understand words like *compassion* or *mercy*. In all my time Under the Hill, I've never seen any hint of either.

Except with Galin.

The massive executioner is nowhere to be seen, and some foolish part of me relaxes. Maybe it won't be today. Maybe they're just trying to scare me. Maybe—

A guard beside Tabitha pulls a long, gleaming knife from his belt. My stomach flips, and my palms begin to sweat. So much for hoping.

I guess missing their executioner doesn't mean much. They're perfectly happy to get their hands dirty themselves.

Tabitha gives a slight nod, and I'm shoved forward. My boots skid on the stone floor as I dig my heels in, but it doesn't matter. They're too strong, and I'm still half-weakened from everything—blood loss, fear, magic. The scent of old blood is thick here, coppery and sharp like it's soaked into the very stones.

They press me down against the altar. Cold stone meets the side of my face. I jerk away, only to feel a hard shove between my shoulder blades. My head smacks the altar again and black spots blink in and out of my view. My arms strain as they pull them into position. I know this pose. I saw it once before, when it was someone else about to die.

I try to twist again, a final burst of defiance, but one of the guards slams a heavy hand across my back and pins me there. I'm useless. I'm pinned like an insect.

Tabitha moves into my field of vision. Her crimson lips twist into a smile, sharp and delighted. She looks like a cat preparing to watch a mouse bleed out beneath its claws.

"I am glad you ran," she says, her voice smooth and venomous as she leans over me. "If you had come out and exposed yourself in front of my court, there might have been questions. Questions that would have kept me from doing what I am about to do right now. So really, Galin's foolishness did me a favor."

"You knew?" I rasp, my voice muffled against the altar. "You knew it was me all along."

"I suspected," she says airily. "And then you ran."

"Why not just take me then?"

Tabitha pouts. "We *do* have rules, Grace. You may think we are monsters, but I assure you, we have many rules, and we *always* follow them." She smiles again, wicked and too white. "Well. Mostly."

"And those rules include letting people murder girls?" My voice cracks, my shoulders aching under the pressure. "Torture them? Drain them like livestock?"

"Our rules do not apply to humans," Tabitha sniffs.

"And that's why you think it's okay to kill me, too."

Tabitha's grin grows, stretching wide across her face as she stares at me with gleaming eyes. "You still think you are human?"

I freeze. A chill creeps down my spine, spreading outward like frost.

"There's nothing else I could be," I whisper.

But I already know that's not true. There's something wrong, something different about me. I've known it since the first time Cillian helped me bleed out the dust, when he looked at my blood and went quiet. There's something none of them have been willing to talk to me about. None of them have even been willing to look me in the eye after seeing my blood. Maybe I should have known long before. Maybe I should have questioned my mother's warnings.

I just didn't want to admit it.

"You poor thing," Tabitha coos, grabbing my chin. Her fingers are cold and possessive as she forces me to look at her. "You are neither human nor fairy. A rare creature caught between two worlds. You are exactly what I need."

Her words strike like a slap, but I can't process them. I can't even think. I'm too busy trying not to panic. If I panic, I lose.

"Ready her," she calls to the guards.

They pull my arms straight and tight across the stone. My breathing comes fast and shallow.

So that's it. No escape. No clever plan. No last-minute rescue.

I press my forehead to the stone and close my eyes.

"I knew your mother," Tabitha whispers so close to my ear that I can feel her lips move.

I lift my head, stunned. "What did you say?"

Tabitha's grin grows as she twirls the knife between her slender fingers.

"She was beautiful," she says, her voice low and wistful. "Delicate, clever. She tried so hard to hide you. If she'd survived...maybe she could have protected you. Maybe your fate would have been different."

I stare at her, trying to reconcile this woman's lies with the hazy memories I carry—my mother's hand in mine, flower crowns, laughter in a field of wildflowers. And then silence. Her smile gone. Her face dimming like a candle snuffed out.

Could it really be true?

"You're lying," I breathe.

My mother. My mother. My mother. My mother. The words twist around in my head on repeat.

Tabitha's expression shifts as she waves the blade in my face. "You know we cannot lie."

"You can't lie," I snap, "but you *can* twist the truth until it bleeds."

Her smirk returns. "The sad thing for you is that all I have to do *is* tell the truth."

She grins, showing her sharp canines. Her eyes gleam. She wants me afraid. She wants me broken.

But I'm not broken.

Not yet.

My arms tremble, not with fear now, but with fury.

Tabitha reaches for my wrist.

And I snap.

Sparks erupt from my fingers, blue and crackling. The guards stagger back with cries of alarm as my body lifts from the stone. I hover, limbs outstretched, the air charged around me like a storm about to break.

Tabitha backs away, her expression melting from smug to terrified. "Get her!" she shrieks.

No one moves.

They're frozen. Whether in fear or awe, I don't know. I don't care.

"You will never harm another girl again," I say, but my voice is no longer just mine. It's deeper, resonant, laced with something ancient and wild.

The blue light spills across the altar, illuminating the stains of past victims. The truth of this room. All the blood. All the girls.

No more.

Tabitha trembles as I raise my hand toward her. Her façade slips, and for a moment, I see her fear.

"You do not understand," she says, crawling back. "I

had to do it. The blood—it was the only cure. But yours... yours is permanent. I needed it. You must understand."

"I will never understand," I say, lightning arcing from my fingertips.

She screams—and she throws something, a burst of dirt and ash right into my face.

I reel back, coughing, my vision blurring. A sudden, sharp pain explodes in the back of my skull and I crash to the floor. The magic flickers out. Gone.

Hands grab me again. My arms are yanked behind me, rough and unkind. My shoulders protest as they twist them too far.

Tabitha steps forward, her expression once again smooth and cruel. Like none of it ever happened.

"We would not want to waste a drop of your precious blood by rushing," she murmurs, giving me a sickly-sweet smile that rots my insides. "Such a valuable resource must be properly preserved."

Her smile cuts like a blade.

"Lock her up."

My shoulders burn from being suspended too long, muscles trembling from the constant pull. The manacles clink when I shift, the looser chains rink rattling like bones. It's impossible to tell how long I've been here—no windows, no sense of time, just cold air and the dull throb in my arms. After the...display in their so-called sacrifice chamber, Tabitha had me dragged deeper into the palace. Somewhere the walls are thicker, the doors heavier, and escape feels like more of a fairytale than magic ever did.

The stone beneath me is no longer dirt-flecked or cracked. It's smooth. Marble, maybe. Gilded like Galin's rooms, though without the velvet and luxury. Just a single candle glows on a carved wooden table, throwing flickering shadows on white-gold walls. The contrast makes me nauseous—this place, this beautiful prison, pretending to be holy when it's soaked in blood.

I clench my fists around the chains, grit my teeth, and pull myself off the floor. Pain flares as metal digs into the fresh cuts at my wrists. I sag again, breathing hard. If I could just trigger the blue lightning again, I could blast these chains apart. I'm nearly certain of it. That power— wild, terrifying, mine—was strong enough to knock down a fully armored guard. So why can't I summon it now? What's the trick? Where's the switch?

No matter how I breathe, how I concentrate, nothing happens. My hands stay dead and normal. No lightning. No hum of power. No escape.

I'm left alone with my thoughts, and they spiral. I keep circling back to Tabitha's words. My mother, a fairy. It sounds laughable, and yet...I saw the magic. I felt it. How could it be a lie?

And if it wasn't a lie—if I really am half fairy—then what else have I been lied to about? Did my father know? Was he keeping this from me to protect me, or because he didn't think I could handle the truth?

I want to scream. My whole life feels like a house built on quicksand. Nothing stable. Nothing real.

The door creaks.

I jerk my head up. Pain knifes through my shoulders as I try to sit straighter.

Cillian enters the room like a shadow. His brown curls catch the candlelight, a soft halo around a face I used to trust. His gaze meets mine—brief, uncertain—and flinches away.

"What are you doing here?" I ask, my voice raw from disuse.

He doesn't answer. Just holds up a wooden cup. "I thought you might be thirsty."

I eye the cup like it might bite me. "What does that matter now?"

Cillian doesn't flinch at my tone. He crosses the room with careful, quiet steps, his hooves tapping on the tiles. He brings the cup to my lips.

I hate him. I hate that it still hurts to look at him. But I drink. I'm not stupid.

The water is cool and sharp in my parched throat, and it almost makes me cry.

"I am sorry," he whispers.

I let the water dribble down my chin. "Sorry for what? For pretending to be my friend? For bleeding me like a butchered deer? For handing me over like a present?" My voice cracks, but I keep going. "When did the lies start, Cillian? Was anything you told me ever true? The bleeding, the fairy dust, the way out—was that all just bait?"

He shifts, weight uneasy on his hooves. "The thing about the dust—that was true. We cannot lie."

"But you can mislead," I snap. "You can hide the truths. Twist facts."

He hesitates. "Yes."

I turn my face away. "Then leave. I don't want to hear anymore of your half-truths."

"I am truly sorry, Grace," he says again, quieter. "I did not want to betray you."

I let out a bitter laugh. "You think that matters to me? You think it helps to hear that? What you did, Cillian—it wasn't just betrayal. It was personal. You knew me. You knew what I was risking. You knew about the girls."

That lands. I see it in the way he goes still.

"Did they make it?" I whisper, more to myself than him. "Did Galin find them? Are they safe?"

He doesn't answer. I have to believe they got away. If I believe that, then maybe this—all of this—wasn't in vain. If they're safe, then I can stomach the pain. The chains. The betrayal. I can live without.

But I don't think I'll ever forgive him.

"I did not want to do it," he says.

"I know," I say coldly. "You wanted to save yourself. That's different."

"I wanted to help you," he says. "I did. Even now."

"You were helping me. And then you handed me over like I was nothing."

His voice rises slightly. "You do not understand—"

"No, I do understand. You chose yourself. That's what everyone here does."

His jaw tightens. "If we were truly friends...would you not want to understand why?"

My stomach turns. I hate him for asking. But he's right—if it were Joan, I'd listen. I'd ask questions. I'd look for leverage.

So I nod, slowly. "Talk. And make it good."

He lowers the cup and takes a slow step closer. "I had to bring her human blood. Tabitha demands it of all of us, eventually. But she was particularly interested in you. Because of Galin."

He pauses, watching me closely. "She said he refused to offer you as a tithe, even when pressed. That made her curious."

"She saw us together the night of the tithe," I murmur.

"Yes. She assumed I would earn your trust. She told me if I did not get what she wanted, she would take it from someone else. Someone I care about."

"Joan," I say softly. "You mean Joan."

His face crumples, and I know I'm right.

"If I had known you were not fully human," he says, "I would not have told you the dust would leave your system through bleeding. It was a loophole I exploited, and one I regret."

"What is that supposed to mean?"

"The dust would never have worked on you like that. It would have been impossible for the app's dust to invade your own."

The chains clink as I shift again. "Are you saying that I'm *immune* to your app? Because I can tell you for a fact that's not true."

I never would have reached out to Galin if I hadn't felt compelled to. I'm not that kind of girl. Not even when I'm trying to rebel. I know I wanted to be, but that doesn't mean I *could*. The idea that I brought this upon myself is almost too much to bear.

"Your blood is a testament that you have fairy dust of your own."

"Do you mean because it's gold? Because I don't understand why something called *dust* would be found in my *blood*."

Cillian shrugs, rubbing his hands on his pants. "We are not like the fairies in your archaic children's stories. Shaking us will not make dust float through the air. Humans have always had silly ideas about our nature. The dust is our magic, and it has always been in our blood. The gold of your blood is unique, even among our kind. My theory would be that the difference is due to your human half."

"That still doesn't justify what you did."

"No," he says. "It doesn't."

"And that goes against their own laws. I heard them discuss that at one of Galin's meetings."

"The Queen is not above breaking her own laws to get what she wants."

"Why does that not surprise me," I say, voice dry.

He drops his hands, looking up at me with drooping eyes. "I really did not want to die. I did not think taking your blood would be a problem."

"Why didn't you tell me?"

"I was not allowed to."

"Of course."

Cilian shifts towards the door. "I just wanted you to know that I did not want to do it. I genuinely set out to protect you. Humans have never lasted long Under the Hill."

"If you really wanted to help me then will you continue to protect me now?" I lean forward, the chains pulling at my wrists until they break through the skin.

He steps back. "I never wanted you to die, Grace."

"Then help me live."

He stares at the manacles. For a long time, he doesn't speak. "Releasing you could break my agreement with the Queen."

"She already got what she wanted. My blood." My voice trembles. "You owe me this."

He hesitates.

"And besides," I say, "she doesn't have to know."

That does it. He steps forward again, fingers reaching

for the manacles. He nods. "I will try to help you in what areas I can. It is the least I can do for Joan."

The metal groans as he works the lock. I hiss as it grates my raw skin.

"If it is too much—"

"Just do it." I keep swallow down my pain and grab at a distraction. "Did you know about Tabitha?"

He looks down at me, hands stilling on the chains. "What about her?"

"Why she needs the blood."

His attention goes back to the chains. "She needs the blood for the same reason we all do. The pollution of humans has taken the magic from the earth. If we want to continue working magic, we need the blood."

I shake my head. "It's not true."

"You lie," Cillian says matter-of-factly.

"I'm not lying."

"You are part human; you can lie if you want to."

I must close my eyes and take a deep breath before continuing down this path. "Does that mean you believe nothing I say?"

"Not exactly."

"So why not listen to me?"

The first manacle drops. My wrist throbs, the skin red and angry. He moves to the other, and it clicks open with the sound of freedom.

"You have too much of a vested interest in what happens to the humans. I believe you would tell me anything to get me to change my mind about how necessary their blood is."

My skin smarts where the other manacle still holds me bound.

"I'm not lying to you about this. Tabitha said she

needed the blood because she's sick. She's tricked all of you into following along with her because she needed more and more blood to stay alive."

The last manacle clicks open, and I rub my hands together to get the blood pumping to them again. Cillian steps back and eyes me.

"That sounds crazy. You realize the fairies are not vampires, right? We do not need blood to survive."

I move for the door. "You might not, but she does."

"Where are you going?"

Glancing back at him, I rest my hand on the doorknob. "I'm not letting her get away with this."

Chapter Twenty-Two

Cillian rushes after me down the hall, his hooves clacking against the marble floor as we round another hallway corner. "Have you lost your mind? She is the Queen, Grace. The Queen. And you—you are nothing compared to her in the eyes of this palace. You cannot change this."

I don't even pause. "If there's one thing I've learned Under the Hill, it's that not trying is a good way to die."

My legs burn from exhaustion and barely healed wounds, but I keep moving, breath tight in my chest. The palace twists and warps around me with every step, but I've memorized the path now—Galin's room is close. I can feel it in my bones like it's been calling me back since I left.

Cillian's still on my heels. Maybe that means he's with me. Maybe he just doesn't want to be alone. I can relate to that.

I push open Galin's door without knocking, the handle cold in my palm. The fire is already lit, flames cracking in the hearth.

I freeze.

It should still be dark. No one should be here.

"Surprised?"

My heart leaps into my throat and I whip around. Galin is sprawled across the bed, arms behind his head, a lazy smile playing on his lips like he's been waiting for me all night.

"What are you doing here?" I ask, my voice sharper than I intended.

He arches a brow. "I could ask you the same."

Cillian steps in behind me, shutting the door with a soft but final-sounding click. Galin's smile curls cruelly at the edges.

"You left me for Tabitha's pet?" He sneers, gaze flicking to Cillian with open disdain.

Cillian bristles but doesn't refute him. I step between them.

"I thought you were busy hiding out in my room?" I ask, folding my arms across my chest to stop them from shaking.

"I might still be," Galin says, pushing himself up to sit. "If it weren't for the chaos you stirred up. Did you think freeing twenty girls was something I wouldn't notice?"

The knot in my stomach loosens just a little. "You saw them?"

"Saw them, heard them—was practically tramped by them." He chuckles. "Screaming, throwing shoes, accusing me of kidnapping. It was...spirited."

Despite everything, I smile. "Did they make it back? Are they safe?"

"They are fine." He chuckles, his gaze not leaving me as he brushes imaginary lint from his sleeve. "I pointed them toward the nearest passage to the surface. That was enough. They did not want my help after that."

I wince. "I probably should've warned them about you."

"There was no time," he says, studying me. "There never is. Which brings me to the obvious question—what have you been doing, Grace?"

I hesitate, weighing the risks of honesty. "You already know, don't you? You saw the girls."

"If that was all, you would have stayed with them."

"I got...delayed."

I don't tell him about the chains. Or the bloodletting. Or the whispers of who I truly am.

Galin stands, eyes narrowing as they rake over the state of the dress he gave me—now torn, bloodstained, and stiff with dried mud. I rub unconsciously at the raw skin on my wrists, and his gaze follows the movement like a hunting cat noticing weakness.

"What happened to you?"

It's such a simple question. But answering would mean letting someone else carry the weight I've been dragging behind me for so long. And I'm so, so tired.

We're close enough to touch. Galin stands over me, his hand hesitating at my side. It's easy to forget Cillian is here with us as Galin's warm breath caresses my face.

He reaches up, cupping my face in his warm, steady hands. "Let me help you."

"Why would you want to help me?" I whisper, searching his night-dark eyes.

Galin's gaze flickers away, a secret hiding behind the storm in his expression. I open my mouth to ask him, but before the words leave, he moves. His large hand slides to the back of my head, tilting me toward him with possessive gentleness.

When his lips meet mine, they're warm and insistent, pressing against me with a tension that makes my chest ache. His heartbeat thunders against mine, steady and alive, and I let myself fall into the pull of him, surrendering to the whirlwind of dark, molten warmth.

He nips at my lower lip with his long canine, and the sharp coppery taste of blood blooms on my tongue, pulling me from the trance his nearness spun around me.

I shove him away, hand pressed to his chest. My breath comes in gasps. His does too. There's a smear of gold on his lip, and his eyes burn black as coal.

"We are linked," he says roughly, his voice scraping through the silence. "I feel it, Grace. Whatever this is between us—it's real. And I will do everything I can to help you."

"You can help me by never doing that again." I keep my hand outstretched between us, keeping him at a careful distance.

He smirks, but there's a softness in it. "I do not know that I can make that promise."

"Then promise not to do it unless I ask you to."

That slows him. He studies me for a long moment, then dips his head in a slow nod, his dark eyes glinting. "I will wait until *you* kiss me."

I lower my hand but keep my distance. My lips still sting from our brief kiss, but the ache in my chest is strangely sweet. "Good."

"So," he says, leaning back against the bedpost, trying for casual again. "What now?"

"I'm going after Tabitha."

The smile vanishes. "That is suicide."

"She's gone too far." I glance at Cillian for the strength to continue. He gives me a small nod, his gaze glued to the rug. "If she continues at this pace, I won't survive. I'd rather not wait around for that."

"What did she do to you?" Galin asks, his voice sharp. His body is a tight coil, no longer pretending to be calm.

"She found me," I say quietly.

Galin's hands go white as they form fists. "And?"

"She told me who I am."

His eyes close briefly like the words physically hurt him. When he opens them, he looks older than I've ever seen him. "I suspected. From the moment I met. It is in your face."

"Then why didn't you say anything?"

Galin's jaw tightens, and for a moment I see the raw edge where his pride and fear collide. "Would you have believed me?"

I falter.

Cillian scoffs. "You would not want to ruin a good thing."

Galin shoots across the room, hand around Cillian's neck before I can even blink. Cillian's face turns purple, his eyes bugging out from his face as his little goat legs kick against the wall.

"Stop!" I shove between them, my heart hammering. "This isn't helping!"

I try to press myself between the two of them.

"He will learn to treat me with respect," Galin grounds out between clenched teeth.

Galin finally relents, letting Cillian slump to the floor, coughing. My gaze finds Galin's again, and something in the air changes. He's not just furious—he's raw, protective, and utterly focused on me.

"He kept it from you because it suited him," Cillian wheezes. "He is like all the others. He saw what you could be—and he wanted to use you before you were able to figure it out yourself."

"Enough," I snap. "We don't have time for this. Galin, if there's more I need to know, just say it."

Galin hesitates.

Cillian doesn't. "He knew your mother."

I blow out an exasperated breath. "So do a lot of people apparently. Why should that matter?"

"It's *who* she was," Cillian says, triumphant. "That is the part he chose to conceal."

I turn to Galin. "Is that true?"

He flexes his hands, not looking at me. "I did not know at first. As soon as Tabitha began taking an interest in you, I started to wonder."

"What are you not saying?"

He exhales through his nose. "Your mother was one of the High Court. Not just any noble. Royal. A princess in her own right."

The air leaves my lungs.

Galin glances at me, his eyes dark. "And you, by blood, by your gold blood, are her heir."

"That means," Cillian says with a grin.. "What the Queen is doing to you—draining your blood, using your magic—goes against the very laws she swore to uphold. You should have been protected."

"What is Tabitha doing to her?" Galin says with a frown.

"She needs my blood."

There's silence in the room, interrupted only by the popping flames in the fireplace as he absorbs my words.

"That is against her own laws."

"Well," I lean against the door frame. "That hasn't stopped her. And now I'm going after her."

For a long moment, no one speaks.

"You cannot let her," Cillian says, small hands wringing

together. "You know that to go after the Queen would kill her."

Galin's gaze finds mine. I see the shift in him—the decision, the resolve.

Galin smiles, revealing his pointed canines. "I am coming with you."

The hallway around us is deathly still, the silence so complete it seems to press against my ears. No music, no laughter, no revelry—none of the twisted glamour I've grown used to.

Cillian's cloven hooves click behind us, an anxious counterpoint to our march. Stealth was never the plan—not now. If anything, I want her to hear us coming.

The throne room door stands slightly ajar. No guards. No magic wards. Just a hollow stillness leaking through the crack. I glance at my hands. Will they answer me again? Will the magic rise?

Maybe. Maybe not. But I'm done waiting.

I take a breath that burns in my lungs and push the doors open.

Tabitha sits alone in the vast echoing chamber, perched on the throne like a spider in the center of its web. A single shaft of light gleams down on her, catching the gold goblet in her hand and crimson streaks at the corner of her lips. Blood. She raises the cup in a mocking salute.

"I wondered how long it would take you," she says, sipping delicately. "And I wondered if you would be joining us, Prince."

Galin's voice is like steel drawn from its sheath. "You have broken the laws."

Tabitha tilts her head to the side, bored and amused. "Of course that is your complaint. Not the girls. Not the disappearances. Just the rules. You never cared until we touched your precious little human."

"She is not simply a human, and you know it."

Tabitha's smile is strained. "So that is what this comes down to. Galin, you know as well as I that the rules were never used to protect her kind. You can understand why I might be willing to bend rules for the greater good. This has never bothered you before."

"We're not here to argue semantics," I cut in, stepping forward. Her words are bait, each one calculated. I won't bite.

Tabitha turns red-tinted eyes towards me. "What is it you think you are going to do, little human?"

"You're going to stop stealing girls," I say, proud of how steady my voice sounds. "You're going to tell the truth. The pollution story is a lie, and I can prove it."

Her laugh is light and cruel. "And what, exactly, would compel me to obey a child?"

I hesitate. Just for a heartbeat.

"I'll make you."

She laughs again, her voice a cascade of bells. "Adorable."

"You have to stop," Galin says, stepping beside me. The heat of him steadies my nerves. His nearness is grounding —real. I catch a glimpse of him, the fire in his eyes, the tension in his jaw. No matter what happens, I'm not alone.

I move swiftly towards the throne, the footsteps of my companions trailing behind me. I keep my gaze locked on her. She doesn't flinch, not even when I stop just ten feet away.

"You were afraid of me before," I say softly. "You should be again."

Tabitha rises from her throne, tall and regal in night-dark silks. "I am not afraid of parlor tricks. I have wielded power for centuries."

Fire blooms from her fingers. Red and hungry.

"I refuse to die because you will not hand over one human girl," Tabitha sneers, taking another drink from her goblet. The flames in her hand rise higher and the ground around us shakes.

I reach inward, past the noise in my head, past the fear. I find it—my magic—deep and humming. Blue light crackles around my hand as the pressure builds. A sound like thunder rings through the room as the power responds to my call.

Galin takes a half-step back. "How is this happening?"

"You tell me," I say, my voice electric.

My dress flutters in the rising energy, torn and ragged now. My hair floats around my head, charged with static. I don't feel human anymore—I'm more like a wraith than a princess.

Tabitha smiles thinly, rising from the throne, her form tall and elegant, and lifts her hands. Fire arches toward us, rising from the tips of her fingers.

I thrust my palm forward. A wave of blue energy crashes against the fire. The air explodes in a burst of sparks and ash. I stumble back, but Galin steadies me, his hand gripping my waist.

Cillian flanks our side, wide-eyed but brave.

"I've got you," Galin whispers.

Together, we move.

The floor trembles. Tabitha lifts into the air, spinning her fire in sharp, dancing, rings. She hurls one directly at Cillian, but I twist, catching the flame with my magic. It stings, sears my skin, but I force it to break apart, scattering in harmless light.

"Your tricks will not save you," she screams.

"Neither will yours!" I hurl the energy back—wilder this time. It surges toward her in jagged bolts.

She dives to the side, shrieking, singed along one shoulder.

Galin fires again—clean and controlled. His flames arch with surgical precision. She snarls and deflects with a spin of her wrist, but not fast enough. Fire licks up the hem of her gown. She stamps it out, lips peeled back in a snarl.

Tabitha laughs. "You are going to back this human child, Galin? It would not matter how much power she had; she will never learn to use it."

"I have to do this," Galin says between gritted teeth.

Blue sparks shoot from my fingers, catching Tabitha unaware and sending her to her knees. She coughs, blood bubbling up her throat.

"You are turning your back on your own kind."

"You did that long ago; I am just stopping you from hurting any more of us."

Galin towers over her, ready to take the final shot at her exposed neck. Tabitha's dark eyes flicker between Galin and I, a smile growing across her bloodstained mouth.

"You are connected to this girl."

The flames in Galin's hands sputter. "You know nothing," he growls.

"You will kill me to give her place. How pathetically sweet. I did not realize you were that enraptured with the human to want to make her your princess."

Galin's gaze flicks to me and for a heartbeat, the world narrows—just the two of us. That moment is all she needs. Tabitha reaches into the folds of her dress and pulls out a slender dagger. A cry of warning catches in my throat as she stabs Galin in the upper thigh. The silver hilt of the handle winks in the firelight as Galin's flames extinguish into embers.

He sinks to his knees, hands pressed against the wound as bright gold blood stains his black tunic, and my scream rips free. My throat goes raw, my power blazing unchecked around me.

Tabitha laughs, stalking towards me as blood drips from her outstretched knife.

"No!" I scream. My magic detonates in all directions, uncontrolled, wild. Sparks burst through the chamber like a storm. Light blinds me. I can't see him. I can't see her.

She emerges from the smoke like a nightmare, blood on her knife, power radiating from her like a black sun. I'm shaking. I slip my knife into my hand, but it feels so small.

Dark tendrils snake out from her. I slash wildly. One wraps around my leg. Another cuts across my shoulder. Pain flares hot and bright.

I lash out blindly. One lucky strike lands—barely missing her neck. She reels back, eyes alight with fury.

"You were entertaining," she says coldly. "But all games end."

I scream again, but it's wordless and primal. My power pulses in jagged rhythms, colliding with hers. She raises her blade.

"You should have died with your mother."

Rage seizes me. something inside me splits wide open.

Power roars through my chest—a wave of blinding,

crackling blue. It lifts me from the floor and throws her back.

She tries to shield herself—but it's too late.

The magic spears through her heart. Her body convulses, then falls.

Smoke rises from the hole in her chest.

Spent, I collapse. The air smells of blood and ozone. I can't move. I can barely breathe.

A shadow limps toward me. Galin.

He drops to his knees, one arm wrapping around me. Blood smears his tunic, but he's alive.

"You did it," he breathes. His eyes search mine, wide with awe and something deeper—something that makes my heart stutter.

He cups my face, his thumb grazing my cheekbone.

"I take it you forgive me."

I exhale shakily. "I wouldn't say that."

But I don't move away. I let him hold me. His blood-stained presence is the only anchor I need right now.

Cillian approaches slowly, his expression unreadable.

"Do you have any idea what you have just done?" he says quietly.

"I killed her," I say numbly. "I stopped her."

"No," he whispers. "You made yourself queen."

Galin turns my face back to his. I see the truth in his eyes. It's not over. Not really. But it's a beginning.

"All hail Queen Grace," he says, his voice low and reverent. He presses a kiss to one cheek, then the other.

"She has no idea what she's doing," Cillian mutters.

"All hail the Queen," Galin says again, and this time, it echoes.

And I don't care what comes next. Not yet. I did it.

I saved them.

Chapter Twenty-Three

The throne room is quieter than I've ever known it to be. Not just silent—*held-breath*—quiet. The kind of stillness that comes before a storm, or after a reckoning. The air is thick, heavy with expectation and something else—fear, maybe. Or awe.

It wasn't even this quiet when I came for Tabitha two days ago. Then, the room had buzzed with something sharp and furious, like the air itself was angry. Now it's packed to capacity with courtiers and officials, guards and nobles, all watching me. But no one makes a sound.

Not even a whisper.

I twirl a card between my fingers, its edges soft from handling. Galin brought it to me from my old room at school, like it might be something I'd want. Apparently, my father is getting married. Again.

Congratulations, Tiffany. You're the first girl to convince him into marriage since my mother. Gold star.

A pity I won't be attending. A bigger pity he never noticed my absences, or my plummeting grades, or that I haven't been to class in a week. He never asked why I missed Family Weekend. Never asked if I was okay.

And honestly? It doesn't matter anymore. Not when I've stood on a fairy battleground and survived.

Still, part of me wonders: if I'd know what downloading that app would lead to—kidnapping, magic, murder, power—would I have done it?

Probably not.

And yet...I've come so far now. Too far to turn back.

The rustle of my gown fills the space as I rise, cutting through the silence like a blade. I feel everyone watching, tracking every breath, every shift of weight. But I don't falter. This time, I stand because I *choose* to.

Galin steps to my side. He doesn't speak. Just offers his arm.

For a moment, I think about taking it. His steadiness is tempting. His presence calms the sharp edges in my chest.

But I shake my head once, gently. Not because I need to prove something—not to him, or to anyone else—but because this is something I want to do alone.

His lips twitch, the ghost of a smile, and he steps half a pace behind. Support without smothering. It's the kind of respect I never knew I needed.

The last few days have been a blur. A kaleidoscope of color and sound and blood. The memory of Tabitha's body hitting the floor replays behind my eyelids when I try to sleep. The smell of scorched magic still clings to my skin some mornings. Killing a queen, it turns out, is a *very* big deal.

Luckily, being a princess—and half-fairy—comes with a few unexpected perks. Turns out my mother's legacy was more powerful than I realized. It's the only reason I'm standing here now, instead of in a cell or buried six feet under.

That, and Galin.

He's been the only reason I've made it through the chaos intact. He used his power, his title, his reputation, to protect me. When I couldn't even step outside my room without flinching, he was the one who stood between me and the court's knives. Sometimes literally.

While I was hiding, he made sure the other girls—the humans who were still trapped in this place—got safely home. One by one, he used favors, threats, and brute force to clear them out of the palace. He kept that promise, even when I couldn't watch it happen.

I asked him why he bothered.

He just said. "Because you would have. And I could not let you be the only one who cared."

He's infuriating. And complicated. And impossible to read.

But I trust him. I *chose* to trust him.

That might be the scariest thing of all.

My coronation is today, and with it, everything changes. Once I'm crowned, the app that started this nightmare will be mine to dismantle. I plan to delete it personally. It's the first order of business. No more missing girls. No more games.

There will be people—powerful ones—who hate the idea of a half-human queen. I know that. Some of them are in this very room, pretending to smile while they hope I trip on my gown and shatter my neck.

Let them hope.

Because I'm ready now.

I've spent my whole life being underestimated, dismissed, shoved aside. Not anymore. This crown won't be a mask. It will be a *mirror*. And I'll use it to see everything that's been hidden.

Knowledge. Truth. Power.

No more closed doors. No more secrets whispered behind my back.

I glance at Galin. He's dressed in his version of finery: all black, sharp lines, silver buttons. Regal and dangerous. His face is carved from shadow and marble, unreadable to everyone else.

But I can see the tightness in his jaw. The flicker of worry behind his eyes.

He cares.

This might be the most dangerous thing either of us have ever done.

His fingers crush my arm. Just a whisper of contact.

"Are you ready?" he asks, his voice low.

I look out over the court. At the people who would kill me if they could. At the ones who don't yet know what kind of queen I'll be.

I let the silence stretch, then nod. "As ready as I'll ever be."

He smiles—not the cold courtly smile he wears in public, but the one he reserves just for me.

I take my first step forward, white skirts shimmering as they whisper across the stone like waves against the shore. The dress was made just for me—the first fairy garment that was truly mine. Pale white and iridescent, it catches the light like frost, like moonlight caught in water.

I don't know what kind of queen I'll become. I don't even know what kind of girl I am yet.

But I survived.

And now the world has to survive *me*.

"All hail the Queen," Galin says beside me as the court rises and bows.

His voice is clear. Sure. Like a vow.

Somewhere deep in my chest, something old and aching finally settles.

This is just the beginning.

Acknowledgments

I am endlessly grateful to my husband, whose unwavering support, patience, and encouragement have carried me through every step of this journey. David, Erik, and James, you fill my life with laughter, joy, and perspective, and you are my greatest inspiration.

Megan, thank you for all the times you helped me with ideas, even when you didn't realize it—you've shaped this story in ways you may never know. Mom, Dad, Kristina, and Jake, your love, belief, and constant encouragement mean more to me than words can express.

Roz, I am so thankful for the books you lent me, the ideas you shared, and the ways you nurtured my creativity when I needed it most. Alan, Steve, and Bonnie, your insights, advice, and camaraderie have been invaluable, and your support has made this journey richer and more joyful.

Laura, thank you for believing in this story when no one else would take a chance on it; your faith in this book made it possible for it to exist.

To my readers, thank you for taking this journey with me, for welcoming these words into your hearts, and for breathing life into this story simply by reading it.

And finally, Heavenly Father, thank You for guiding me through this journey, inspiring me to tell this story, and surrounding me with the people who have made it possible.

Dust of Bargains Duology:

Dust of Bargains

Crown of Chaos (coming 2026)

Burden of the Banished Duology:

The Exile's Promise

Fight of the Fallen

The Lost Trident Duology:

Seeking Neopolis

Losing Neopolis

Standalone Novels:

Out of Time

Curse of the Forgotten

Veins of Darkness